TURN AND DIE

Stella Whitelaw titles available from
Severn House Large Print

Mirror, Mirror
Ring and Die
Hide and Die
Jest and Die
Veil of Death

TURN AND DIE

Stella Whitelaw

Severn House Large Print
London & New York

This first large print edition published in Great Britain 2008 by
SEVERN HOUSE LARGE PRINT BOOKS LTD of
9-15 High Street, Sutton, Surrey, SM1 1DF.
First world regular print edition published 2007 by
Severn House Publishers, London and New York.
This first large print edition published in the USA 2008 by
SEVERN HOUSE PUBLISHERS INC., of
595 Madison Avenue, New York, NY 10022.

British Library Cataloguing in Publication Data

Whitelaw, Stella
  Turn and die. - Large print ed. - (The Jordan Lacey
  mysteries ; 7)
  1. Lacey, Jordan (Fictitious character) - Fiction 2. Women
  private investigators - Fiction 3. Detective and mystery
  stories 4. Large type books
  I. Title
  823.9'14[F]

  ISBN-13: 978-0-7278-7660-7

Printed and bound in Great Britain by
MPG Books Ltd, Bodmin, Cornwall.

This book is dedicated to the many, many fans of the Jordan Lacey series who wrote, phoned and emailed from all over the world to know more

Grateful thanks to my exellent editor, Anna Telfer, and the staff of both Oxted and Worthing Libraries who are so supportive and helpful.

Also many thanks, again, to the retired Chief Superintendent Detective for his unfailing patience and who gives me such useful advice. My gratitude also to the incendiary expert who told me how these things work.

One

I was target number one. My lashes were no protection. Little sharp points were attacking me, silvered with splinters.

It was an Arctic wind, north-easterly, carrying flurries of snow. Somewhere a medieval Russian warlord, clad in furs, was hurling bad weather at West Sussex. Latching had not seen snow for decades. But it was seeing some now – scurries of tiny flakes that settled on my nose and shoulders, but nowhere else.

The promenade became wet and glistening. The palm fronds were still curled up inside their winter hairnets, no one able to decide if we'd had the last frost of a cold spring. The decking on the pier was too dangerous to walk on. Somehow the sea swallowed the flakes with indifference, pounding the beach, shifting pebbles and thumping to the beat of a Cossack bottle dance.

I took extra care when walking these days – not exactly convalescent mode but a small module of my brain was always alert. Watch out. Hold on. Don't move too fast. I had moved, an aeon ago, very fast, speed of light, and the consequences were imprinted on my memory in indelible ink.

James had been telling me about the reward. We had been celebrating in a normal law-abiding way, laced with a bubble of excitement. Just a few drinks. Then it had happened. One very nasty accident.

It took some time getting used to having the reward money. It was not mega-bucks but enough to have my shop, First Class Junk, redecorated in alabaster white with tints of waffle, and give my spotted ladybird car a makeover. She was looking ten years younger. The office behind the shop had been brought into this century with a computer, printer and new answerphone. I'd been spending hours on Google at the library, looking up things I didn't need to know. Now I could waste time in the office. It's a drier hook than fishing off the pier.

And I like emailing people. It saves that awkward questioning – 'And how are you these days, Jordan?' All that sympathy stuff. I didn't want to answer those questions.

Several charities came in for windfalls: the Police Benevolent Fund, Cats Protection League, PDSA and the retirement home for elderly jazz musicians sited along the coast. My stalwart pals, Doris and Mavis, got cheques which they blew on a riotous weekend in Blackpool. Don't ask me what they did, but they came back wearing broad smiles. I paid for Bruno to have his fishing boat repaired. Not a word of thanks from that source.

The rest of the reward money went on a self-employed person's pension. Call me cautious, but I don't have any marriage prospects and my professional career was equally slow-moving. Of course, I might not live to draw a penny, but that would be the last of my worries.

Miguel, spectacular chef and owner of the Mexican restaurant near my shop, came to see me regularly in hospital with jungle-sized bunches of red roses. There was nothing I could give him, only reassurance. Not enough when he only wanted me.

Jack, owner of the amusement arcade on the pier also came to see me in hospital, though he'd had enough of hospitals since the fire in the nightclub on the pier. No roses, not even a clean T-shirt. He'd looked morose enough as he came into the side room, but one look at me and his face fell a further foot.

'Bloody hell,' he said.

They'd done a thorough job of bandaging my face after resetting my nose and various other aspects of my head. I'd asked them for the Audrey Hepburn model but I don't think they took me seriously. They'd shaved off my eyebrows and some of my hair, which gave me a weirdly Virgin Queen look.

'Can you speak?' he asked.

'Yes, but it hurts.'

'What were you doing in this pub?'

'Having a drink.'

'With your mate, the DI?'

'Yes.'

'And you got attacked by a suit of armour?'

I nodded, but that hurt even more and I kept seeing DI James moving towards me, in slow-motion replay.

'It was lethal,' I said, remembering the pain.

It was still trying to snow when I got back to my shop. First Class Junk had been my salvation. There was no way I could go back to my private-eye work until I stopped feeling as fragile as a wet moth. But a little genteel retail trading did no one any harm. I could sit and read a book all day if the customers were slow in coming forward. I'd found some interesting books on old Sussex among a job lot waiting to be sorted. Photos of old trams and horse-drawn buses, even a horse-drawn lifeboat on its way to the slipway on Latching beach. Therapeutic photos.

I put on some coffee, my special Fairtrade brew. I lived on coffee these days and the addiction was getting out of hand, but any thought of cutting down was beyond me.

Tomorrow, perhaps. I couldn't eat. Mavis tried to force-feed me my favourite food in her café.

'Come on, Jordan, try a couple of chips and a lovely bit of fresh fish. Just as you like them,' she said. She made the best chips in West Sussex. Her reputation was county-wide.

Even a chip choked me.

Someone was coming into the shop, but I didn't hurry. 'No hurrying' was my current speed. Doctor's orders. Something to do with my head. My head felt all right. It still sat in the same place.

'Hello? Anyone there?'

It was a female voice, pleasant and young-ish. But there was a tension about it that made me curious. I remembered to turn off the coffee before I went through into the shop.

She was good-looking too. Very good-looking. No scars and funny-growing hair. She was wearing expensive boot-cut blue jeans from Ralph Lauren, highly polished suede-and-leather boots with rivets round the top from Russell & Bromley, a silk scarf from Asprey and a grey sheepskin gilet. It was a killer winter look. Her leather gloves were from Mulberry and the suede-and-leather tote bag (more rivets) by Luella. No change from a thousand pounds for that little lot.

I knew these fashion names from the

magazines they'd fed me in hospital. My normal fashion haunts were M & S and charity shops.

Her hair was streaky blonde, but salon streaking, not a home kit. The haircut was expensive too, no scissors cutting sideways in the bathroom job.

'Hello,' I said. 'Can I help you?'

She looked at me curiously. She was older than the voice, about thirty-eight. Any year now and she would be going for the Botox injection and a touch of Restylane filling.

'Are you Jordan Lacey, the private detective?'

'I *was* Jordan Lacey, the private detective,' I said, somewhat sardonically. 'On hold for a while.'

She smiled and it was a sympathetic smile. 'Leroy told me about your accident. I'm sorry. I hope you're feeling better.'

'You know Leroy Anderson?' Leroy was a friend of mine who worked with a team of estate agents along the coast, selling classy houses. I didn't see much of her now, but once she had lent me a floaty blue dress for a special occasion. A very special occasion. Me and DI James, together for once, at a party.

'I met her when we bought our present home, Faunstone Hall. Perhaps you know it?'

I didn't know it, but I knew of it. It lay un-

12

seen behind a high stone wall and a canopy of trees. It was a Grade I listed house, mainly fifteenth-century, set in idyllic gardens, so they said – 'they' being the glossy magazines that wrote and photographed Faunstone Hall from every angle. I should have taken more notice.

I nodded, forgetting that it hurt. 'And you are...?'

'I'm Holly Broughton. My husband is Richard Broughton, the banker. He owns Broughton Bank. I'd very much like to talk to you, Miss Lacey. I won't take up much of your time.'

I'd heard of the bank. It was somewhere in the city, a shaped skyscraper of tinted glass with a constant stream of foreign visitors, mostly Japanese financiers. I was impressed. But Mrs Broughton impressed me even more. There were no airs or graces in her manner even though my reward cheque would have been like pocket money to her.

'Would you like to come through? I was just making some real coffee.'

'I can smell it.'

She followed me to my back office and immediately made herself at home on my Victorian button-back chair, unbuttoning her sheepskin. The sweater was pale-pink cashmere, the pearls real. I got out the bone-china mugs and put milk in a jug. Mrs Broughton did not look the biscuit type.

'Lovely coffee,' she said, taking it black, of course. She sat back, looking round my office. It had a desk and filing cabinet, the Victorian button-back, a faded red-and-blue Persian rug and the new computer. 'I used to have a little office like this once,' she added. 'Very compact.'

'Compact,' I agreed.

'I was doing temping work round the city, but I worked for myself. No agency creaming off ten per cent of my pay. I kept what I earned. That's how I met Richard. Quite a bonus, don't you think?' She smiled again, almost grinning, but I could still sense the tension. Something was not right.

'So why did you want to see me, Mrs Broughton?'

A change came over her face and her hand began to shake so much that I had to take the coffee from her before she spilt it all over herself. She was sweating now and searching for a handkerchief in her pockets. I gave her a tissue.

'Thank you,' she said unevenly. 'You've probably seen it in the newspapers. It made the headlines in all the tabloids: CALL GIRL CLEARED OF MURDER HIT, and some were even worse. It was so awful being in court, being accused of something I didn't do and knew nothing about. Yet people jeered and shouted at me and outside they threw things at me as if I was guilty. It was terrible.'

It all came out in a rush. The distress was obvious. Holly Broughton had experienced mob violence and that was frightening. She mopped her face and smeared her mascara. She looked even more vulnerable.

'Tell me about it,' I said. 'I haven't been reading the newspapers recently. Take your time and start at the beginning.'

She calmed down a bit and took her coffee back, sipping it, perhaps reassured that I knew nothing about the case and she was not already smeared with scandal.

'I met Richard when I was temping at the bank. We liked each other immediately, although I wasn't working for him. We kept meeting in the lift. Then we started going out. That he's much older than me didn't seem to matter. I knew he was rich, so that was a bonus, but it wasn't that important, not then. We fell in love and got married. Roses all the way. Everything was lovely.'

'Sounds idyllic. So what went wrong?'

'That's it,' she cried out, gold bangles jangling on her thin wrists. 'Nothing went wrong. I thought we were happily married, when suddenly the police arrived, accusing me of plotting to murder Richard. Apparently there had been some attempt on his life in the street and it had been traced back to me.'

'That's very strange.'

'Someone gave the police information,

which sparked the police investigation. There were all sorts of bits of evidence that meant nothing to me – phone calls, a meeting in a café caught on CCTV, my drawing out a large sum of money from the bank. Then the attempt on his life, which was some hooded thug trying to knife him in the street.'

'Your husband survived?'

'Oh yes, thank goodness. Richard was wearing a really heavy Burberry overcoat. It was cold. And the knife nicked his throat and slashed the coat. He was shocked, of course, but is fine now. He didn't even need a stitch. I was cleared because there was not enough evidence, but even he thinks I had something to do with it. He's barely speaking to me now.'

'Are you both still living at Faunstone Hall?'

'Yes, but Richard also has a flat in London. He comes to Latching infrequently, mostly at the weekends, flying visits. I really miss him. I ... I want him back and for things to be as they used to be.'

I sat back and looked at Holly Broughton. She appeared genuine and everything about her said innocent, innocent. Jordan Lacey, private eye, was taking a real interest, the first stirring of normality. This could be a proper case.

'What were you hoping I could do?' I

asked.

'I want you to sort this out. Find out who fed malicious information to the police, who planted faked evidence, who is trying to take Richard from me. I want my husband back. I really love him.'

It was persuasive. Even in my fragile-moth state, I could take it at my own pace, no hurrying. Drive around in my newly MOT'd ladybird. Send Mrs Broughton wordy email reports on my new computer. Put my feet up when I thought I was tiring. A sort-of convalescent doddle.

Then I thought of all the travelling to London, tracking thugs in pubs, waiting outside Broughton Bank in the pouring rain, following Richard Broughton at night to his flat. It no longer seemed that easy or attractive.

'My daily rate is a hundred pounds a day,' I said, hardly hearing myself. Was that my voice? Who gave it permission to say that?

'I will pay you that plus all necessary expenses,' said Holly Broughton. 'I want to be cleared at any cost.'

'But the court has cleared you. Not enough evidence, you said.'

'It's not good enough. Someone set me up and I want you to find out who. Then perhaps Richard and I will get back together again. That's what I want. Me and Richard as we used to be.'

I got up. I was tired already. Talking tired

me out. What was I doing, agreeing to sort out the life of some rich woman, who already had a hundred times over what I had? But I liked the look of her. My life had been wrecked. I couldn't do much about that, but I supposed I could help her.

'Let me think about it,' I said, oddly cautious for once. 'I'll let you know.'

She got up. She'd finished the coffee. She looked drained. You can't act drained. It comes from inside.

'Thank you, Miss Lacey. I really appreciate that you have listened to me. You must come round to Faunstone Hall. Let me know when you want to come. You have to talk into the security box at the gates, but I'll make sure you're let in.'

She was buttoning her gilet and starting to go.

'Why did the newspapers label you "call girl"?' I had to ask.

Holly Broughton turned to me. She didn't lie. 'Because I was a call girl, a high-class escort, before I met Richard. Do you think temping pays enough to meet all the bills? But an escort isn't always a prostitute. There is a difference.'

The Internet is a marvel. How did I manage before? I thought of all the hours I had spent in libraries searching books or spinning through microfilm at newspaper offices. The

'Broughton Murder case' was detailed on a dozen sites. OK, so the facts all needed checking, but they gave me the initial background.

Holly Broughton did not sound whiter than white in the newspaper reports. They listed lovers by the dozen. But she was beautiful and she was sweet-natured. What did it matter how many lovers she had had before she'd met Richard? She was trying the water as any sensible woman should. I wished I had her appetite and her sense of adventure. Denzil had been a very bad mistake (the jerk), Josh nothing more than a scrounger of money and meals, but my jazz musician had been a real, enduring love. Even if I could not have him. 'M' for very much married. I didn't see him for months.

Ben had been different. A dedicated detective sergeant who had died in a tragic accident. He had loved me but I had been wavering...

That was the sum of my love life. You could not count DI James. I meant nothing to him. But he meant everything to me.

The sun had disappeared from the lightening sky. Perhaps it was a last fling before spring. I never tired of watching the clouds and their changing shapes, now a witch with a pointy hat, a goblin, a giant, an angel. Show me a cloud and I'll name it.

I put on my anorak and wandered two

doors down to Doris's grocery shop. She was trying to keep going while all her customers were being seduced by the big supermarkets and cut prices. She had two-for-the-price-of-one offers, organic food and now Asian stock.

Doris looked up from painting her nails. Her nails were always blood-red, immaculate. 'Hi, there,' she said. 'Come in for two beans and half a satsuma?'

'I'm not hungry.'

'If you get any thinner you'll be able to come in through the crack in the door.'

'I'll take some cuppa soup. Chicken.'

'Tomato or mushroom.'

'Mushroom.'

I fingered a satsuma, wondering if Doris kept her old newspapers. She might have a stack of them out at the back. I wanted to check on the Broughton story. Read what the local reporter in court thought. I wondered if the operations had given me these rhyming lines. It was weird. Some sort of crossed circuit where none had existed before.

'Have you got any old newspapers?' I asked.

Doris looked bemused. 'You all right, girl? You aren't going to sleep out in one of the beach shelters, are you? Why not go home and make a nice cup of tea, watch some telly?'

'I'm not sleeping rough, Doris; I want to read up on the news that I've missed. Catch up on the world. Something important might have happened while I was in hospital.'

'Like the price of coffee went up or Tony Blair missed a vote. I'll see what I've got. I was going to take them to the recycling bin but never got round to it.'

'I'll read them, then take them to the bins for you.'

'OK.'

I was leaving the shop with a stack of newspapers under my arm when Doris stopped me. 'You'll have to pay for that satsuma,' she said. 'Hygiene regulations. Health and Safety. Can't sell it to anyone else, not after it's been fingered.'

'Good Lord. Things have changed while I've been incarcerated in hospital.'

I paid for the fruit and put it in my pocket. It would probably gather dust and I'd find it shrivelled to billiard-ball size in a month's time.

I walked along the front, clutching the newspapers, not sure yet where I was going, the wind clutching at my unruly hair. Latching is a seaside town full of interesting Georgian buildings and varied, complex people. But the sea is its prime attraction, the vast expanse of strong water that surges and retreats, fathoms deep for trawlers and

21

passing cruise liners then shallow enough for toddlers paddling. Its colour changes by the minute and I love watching its moods, mesmerized by endless waves. I'm a July person, a mood person. I long for the coming summer.

But I knew where I was going now. I was allowed to drive, no longer a danger with risky eyesight. I got the ladybird out, enjoying the feel of the wheel. She was a unique vintage car, small, reliable, fun, with those black spots painted on her red bodywork.

It was quite a long drive and the traffic was horrendous. I'd chosen the wrong time, everyone was coming home from work, and the jams were mega. For a moment I glazed over and then I remembered where I was going and why. The Royal Sussex Hospital, Brighton.

He was the man I had always hungered for, but he saw me as nothing more than a nuisance, someone who needed information, who needed rescuing, who was a pain in the lower regions.

I was going to visit Detective Inspector James.

Two

The Royal Sussex Hospital at Brighton was a huge rambling building, endless corridors and bleak hallways spilling out to adjacent wards. But I knew my way round now. I had been coming for weeks. Some of the nurses recognized my scars.

DI James had a side room, as I'd originally had, because of the complexity of his injuries and his rank. He hated my visiting him. He was helpless and I was the last person he wanted at his bedside. His mother had come to see him and we'd talked outside. She was a sweet woman with a soft Highland accent and we liked each other.

He was lying in bed under yards of white sheet and an insipid-green woven coverlet. He glared at me with those ocean-blue eyes that sent shivers up and down my spine. His hair was growing, so dark but flecked with grey over the ears. His crew cut had lost its crispness.

'Go away,' he said.

'I'm your regulation visitor. Health and Safety. It's a new regulation that says you

23

have to have one visitor a week.'

'I've had my one visitor.' His voice was still deep, gravelly, dominating.

'Bonus week. If you had come to visit me, I would not have been so rude and turned you away.'

'Want to bet?' he groaned.

I knew all about his injuries, having pinned some doctor to the wall. James could not move and could not be moved. He was paralysed but not necessarily for ever. James had broken his back when the suit of armour perched over the bar had crashed down on him. Two compressed fractures in the lower back had caused a sharp fragment of bone to come loose from the vertebrae and lodge itself two millimetres from his spinal cord.

Someone had insisted that he lie still on the floor of the pub until help arrived. That someone had been me. I had known that he must not be moved, not at any cost.

'No, don't move him,' I'd cried, my nose bleeding like a fountain. I was bleeding all over the carpet, face an aching, tender, splodgy mess. I had wanted to hold him in my arms, but knew I must not lift him. If he had been moved, the sliver of bone might have gone straight back and sliced his spinal cord. I had not known that at the time, but instinct told me not to move him. At least the pub carpet was already a Turkish red.

'Have you come to read me a bedtime

story, Jordan?' said James with heavy sarcasm. 'A cyber-fairy story. Something out of space, from that dizzy brain of yours.'

He did not know that I had saved his life. Who was going to tell him? Not me.

'Why don't I tell you the story of a beautiful woman called Holly Broughton, who loves her husband but has been accused of hiring someone to kill him.'

'Different.'

'She and her husband, Richard Broughton, live at Faunstone Hall, one of the best properties on the outskirts of Latching. At least, they did live there together, but now Richard is not around so much. He stays most of the week in London. Holly has been cleared by the courts of having him sliced up, but the accusation has irrevocably damaged their marriage.'

'Faunstone Hall,' said James. 'There was a burglary some weeks back. A minor break-in.' He was remembering, his face occupied, indexing work.

'Did you go there?'

I wanted to stroke his hand but I did not dare touch him. His hands lay immobile on the top of the sheet. The noise of the ward was starting to intrude, clattering, banging, footsteps. He might not feel a touch. I didn't know the state of his skin or nerve ends.

'Yes, I followed it up. A beautiful house – God, so perfect, Jordan. White-walled, big and small windows, low granite roof, small sort of tower at one end, idyllic gardens, grounds with stables, tennis court, pool. It's a dream come true. They are a lucky couple. So some burglars lifted a few things. What did it matter? Probably well insured. The Broughtons live in a rural paradise.'

I had never heard James speak so movingly of a house or home. He had lost his somewhere in the past, when he'd lost his children. He had no real home, rented Marchmont Tower, a local landowner's folly. These were times he would not talk about.

'Check on the burglary again,' said James, his face pale with the effort. He was tiring. 'It may not be what it seems. It could be a set-up connected to this Holly Broughton business.'

'So who is going to tell me anything? Not your mob.'

'Say you are from the insurance company. Phone the station and say I want the name. They'll give it to you.'

He was so long, his feet almost poking out of the end of the NHS bed. Why couldn't we have fallen in love together? I am a clown, skating on the edge, but I can't cast away anything to make life easier. James is the only man I want. But I shall always be on the fringe of his life. Several years on and he still does not want me.

Even though I saved his life. But he didn't

26

know that. I remembered an arm coming up, an arm clad in long-sleeved denim, an arm that took the brunt of the falling armour and turned its projection. It could have killed both of us. The arm was not James's. He was not wearing denim.

My guardian angel? I liked to think so – everyone has one; but I couldn't see for the blood. And when I was at last capable of looking around, nose staunched with blood-ied napkins, he had gone. The denim-clad man was nowhere. I wondered if I would ever see him again, perhaps once. At that last moment, whenever it is, he will come back and take me with him.

'Do you know anything about Holly Broughton or her husband, Richard Brough-ton?' I asked.

'He's a rich banker. She drives a fancy sports car, keeps getting parking tickets. But she pays up.'

James closed his eyes. It was a signal. What could I do but go? Maybe next week he would like a visitor.

I stood up, dizzy for a second. Nothing much. I soon recovered, searched around for my bag.

'I've brought you a satsuma,' I said, searching my pocket. 'Shall I peel it for you?'

His eyes dared me. 'No, thank you. But there is something you can do for me, Jor-dan.'

'Maybe.'

'Go back to the Medieval Hall pub. Get a good look at the canopy over the bar. Check why the suit of armour fell, look for tampering. You might spot something.'

A shudder ran through me. I didn't want to go back to that pub, to relive the scene again. I didn't want to spot anything. It would freak me out. He was asking too much.

'Don't count on it.'

I couldn't drive back to Latching without a cup of coffee. I needed a shot of caffeine. They'd be sending me to dry out in a clinic any day now. I found a trendy cappuccino café where you paid over the top to sit on a lumpy brown-leather sofa. It was a big cup. I could hardly get my hands round it. But the warmth and the aroma were good. I began to calm down. But not even a gallon of good coffee would persuade me to go back to that so-called Medieval Hall pub. Accident or no accident, it was the last place on earth I ever wanted to go to again.

The drive home was uncomplicated. The traffic had thinned. No one cut in on me, no one drove on their horn, gave me a rude-fingers sign. The road-rage thugs were all at home watching football on telly or already in the pubs.

My two adjacent bedsits were my refuge. They were warm and my special things said hello. Not much furniture, one high-backed moral two-seater sofa, one futon and duvet, one television set. Lots of books, pieces of cut glass, old items of bone china. It made housework easy. Flick a fibre brush and the dust retreated to Shoreham. Watering my plants took longer.

The kitchen area was in one corner, dining area in another, leisure area in the third corner. I knew where I was and what I was supposed to be doing all the time. I made a cuppa soup (mushroom) although I did not want it. Nor did I drink it. It grew cold and eventually I threw it down the sink. Seeing James, so helpless, unable to move, nothing like the hard-working, dedicated detective inspector, up all hours, working all night, that I knew and admired. Wanted, adored, needed.

He wanted me to go back to the pub. But I doubted if I could do that, even for him.

I phoned the police station next morning, said that DI James wanted the name of the insurance company in connection with the Faunstone Hall burglary. Some nice WPO gave it to me without a protest. His name opened doors. They were more interested in his progress, his frame of mind. There was nothing much I could say, small talk, mouthing the usual inane clichés. Looking on the bright side, etc.

It was the Avenis Insurance Company. I went into the arcade and printed myself some business cards with their name and a new name, Ruth Grimm, no relation to the brothers. It cost three pounds for twenty-five. A bargain really. No one would make up a name like that.

I phoned Faunstone Hall to make an appointment, running through times when hopefully Holly Broughton would not be there.

'Mrs Broughton will not be here this afternoon,' said the Thai housekeeper in near-perfect English. 'She is at hairdressers, all afternoon.'

'There's no need to bother her,' I said. 'I only want to check some details of the insurance claim. Would three o'clock be a good time for you?'

'Certainly, Miss Grimm.'

It was a good morning for First Class Junk. I sold two Victorian cordial glasses, six inches high, like little lamp posts. It was a shame to see them go. My '£6' label was on the low side, but they were going to a good home, I could see that. A silk fan went without a murmur and a gross toby jug, which I was glad to see the back of.

A nose-ringed girl came in, searching round stuff in a hurry. I distrusted her. She had a big bag slung over her shoulder and big bags are always suspect. Although I was serving another customer, I made sure that I kept her in sight. She was fingering a netsuke – that's Japanese for toggle. It was not a genuine one, as they are made in epoxy resin these days, not ivory or ebony as in their great period.

'Do you know what this was used for?' I said, strolling over to her. 'It's a netski.' Correction pronunciation.

'Nawh.'

'It's a toggle. They were used to secure waist cords, when the Japanese men wore robes. See the little holes where the cord went through. Now they all wear suits.'

'So it's valuable, eh?'

'Not really. It's modern copy. But a signed netski would be very valuable. Let me know if you find one.'

She moved on to thumb through the books. 'Got any Barbara Cartland?'

'There may be a few. People do collect them.'

Wrapping the toby jug took a few moments. He deserved careful transport even though not a favourite of mine, and by the time I'd Sellotaped his stomach, the girl and the netsuke had gone. I wished her luck round the dealers. The signature on the base was mine and scratched on with a pair of scissors.

An insurance agent should look smart, no jeans or anorak. I hunted round my charity box of clothes and found a grey pin-striped suit, double-breasted with very short skirt. I was not averse to wearing a skirt that short, but it meant finding shoes. Shoes are always a problem. I only have two day pairs, trainers and boots. These women who have hundreds of pairs are beyond my understanding. Maybe it's a childhood thing, like having to wear pink bootees with bobbles on till they go to kindergarten.

A pair of black court shoes emerged from the bottom of the box. A previous wearing vaguely rang a warning bell. They might hurt. A wipe round with the inside of a banana skin and they looked almost present-able. No need to put them on till I got to Faunstone Hall. A dark wig covered my growing hair and I pencilled in some eye-brows. Extra make-up added a few years and Ms Grimm was ready for the competitive world of insurance.

The security gate opened to my new name and I drove in.

But Jordan Lacey was not ready for Faun-stone Hall. It was stunning. A long, low, beautiful white-walled house, covered in wisteria and climbing roses. When they were in bloom, it would be a picture. The old windows glinted with fading sunlight and the carved-oak door was already open as I drove round the circular driveway.

The Thai housekeeper was waiting in the

porch, smiling, one of these wafer-thin women in a long, narrow black skirt and embroidered jacket, her black hair pulled back into a tight, high bun. Her face was worn but the cheekbones were still beautiful.

'I am Mrs Malee,' she said. 'Please to come in. Mrs Broughton regrets not to welcome you and sends apologies. Would you like some tea?'

'Yes, please. Thank you.' I gave her one of the three-pound business cards from my clipboard. 'That's very kind of you.'

'I will serve it in the conservatory,' she said, showing me the way. I glimpsed cool and elegantly furnished rooms either side of the panelled hall. 'Please ask if there is anything you wish to be shown.'

I tapped my notes and a pad of blank paper also attached to the clipboard. Clipboards are essential to all undercover work. 'I have all the details I need here,' I said. 'But I may need your help later, thank you.'

'Please to ask,' she said with a slight bow, disappearing silently to brew oriental tea. Or perhaps it would be Earl Grey.

The burglars had apparently forced open French doors which faced the garden, sometime in the late afternoon before the house alarms were switched on for the night. They had stolen the weirdest collection of things: an old ivory letter-knife from the desk and a paperweight made from a World War One bullet case, some ornamental brass horse-shoes, several pewter tankards from behind the bar (ignoring the alcohol), CDs and DVDs from the television room, and a quantity of cash, foreign currency and postage stamps from the top desk drawer in Richard Broughton's study.

'Postage stamps,' I murmured, going down three steps to his study. 'Were they going to send a thank-you letter?' There was every kind of expensive computer and printing equipment in this home office, but they hadn't touched it.

It struck me straight away that everything they'd taken was small, portable and un-breakable. But as I wandered from room to room, I saw Georgian silverware, Dresden porcelain and valuable pictures which had not been touched. The rooms were long and cool and graceful with Holly's good taste in furnishing and curtains, beautiful Chinese carpets on polished floors and vases of flowers everywhere. Here and there were fairy-tale touches, Venetian-style mirrors, tall glass candlesticks, a four-panelled gold-leaf oriental screen.

'I have served the tea,' said Mrs Malee.

The conservatory at the back was delightful, Victorian style, lots of white paint, deep basket chairs with floral cushions and tall plants growing in earthenware pots. Tea was served in a silver teapot on a silver tray, and there was a plate of small sandwiches and cakes. The cup and saucer were gilded Spode bone china. My appetite stirred at the aroma of salmon and cucumber.

'It looks lovely,' I said, sitting down. I wanted to take off the court shoes. They were pinching. And the wig itched. Perhaps I could scratch my scalp with the spoon. 'Thank you.'

Mrs Malee lit incense burners on the sills and soon the air was filled with orange blossom, tiger lily and wild fig. I knew what they were because I could read the names on the Jo Malone pots. Nothing wrong with my eyesight. The housekeeper poured tea into the cup. The pale liquid aroma was very Earl Grey. She left me to add a slice of lemon.

'They didn't steal this silver then,' I said. 'Is it Paul Storr?'

'It is kept in the kitchen,' she said, leaving with a slight bow. 'Mrs Broughton uses it every day.'

The tiny sandwich suited my wrecked taste buds. It tossed my reticence aside and per-suaded me to take a second one. The tea washed them down and they stayed down.

The thinking part of my brain had not been used for some weeks and it was having difficulty in assessing what I had seen. It was an odd burglary. If it had been kids they would have taken the alcohol for sure. If it had been antique thieves, they'd have taken the Georgian silverware and more. If it had been drunken thugs on a bender, they'd have smashed up the place.

None of the stuff had been recovered and the police were no nearer finding the thieves. They never would find them. Long gone, off to play the CDs and open their junk mail with the ivory letter-knife.

Somehow I felt I was missing something.

Afterwards I wandered round the garden, enjoying the peace and solitude. It was far enough away from Latching to escape all the traffic noise. The late spring flowers were in full display, daffodils and tulips and wall-flowers in abundance, even bluebells grow-ing wild in the far reaches of the garden. Their gardener kept everywhere spick and span, not a leaf out of place. I wondered how the burglars had got in past the security gate. The high wall would have needed a ladder. It might even be electrified. I'd checked the French door and it had been recently re-paired.

It was easy to find the kitchen, a big mod-ern room, probably two rooms and butler's pantry and larder knocked into one. It had all the latest gleaming equipment, granite work surfaces, eye-level oven and grill and large mirrorball pendant lights. Mrs Malee was washing up the china with quick, neat movements. No dishwasher for fragile Spode.

'Thank you for the tea,' I said again. 'I'm going now. I'll see myself out.'

'Thank you, Miss Grimm. Please to close the front door. It is not warm yet. Still cold.'

'I will. Goodbye.'

I took those damned shoes off as soon as I got into my car and rubbed my aching feet. Big mistake occurred to me at once: I should not have come in the ladybird. Ladybird car would be remembered. Now, when I came again as myself to see Holly Broughton, I would have to find alternative transport. Perhaps Jack would lend me his flash blue Jaguar. Perhaps he wouldn't.

Mrs Malee came running out of the house, in tiny steps because of the tight skirt. She was carrying a big bunch of wallflowers cut from the garden.

'I have spoken to Mrs Broughton on the telephone and she would like you to have some flowers from the garden. She says as a thank-you for coming.'

'How lovely,' I said, opening the passenger door so she could put them on the seat. 'I love flowers.'

Second big mistake: Mrs Malee saw that I had taken off the shoes, realized maybe that I was not used to wearing heels. Perhaps the significance would escape her, but her eyes glinted for a second with amusement.

Third mega, horrendous mistake: the itchy wig lay on the passenger seat and my own unruly tawny-red hair stuffed in a hairnet. A hairnet with holes.

'Didn't have time to wash it,' I said, hoping she believed that too.

Three

My burglary report for DI James was ready for posting when the shop door opened and a man and a dog came in. I could hear the dog sniffing about. It sounded big. Thank goodness I didn't have that valuable period dress on display any more. It had gone back to the museum. Modest reward and free admission ticket for life.

'Hello,' I said collectively to man and dog. It *was* big. A vast shaggy dog, the size of a small donkey. It grinned at me, tail wagging, sure of a welcome anywhere. The man did not look strong enough to keep the dog under control. He was small and wiry, jerking like a monkey on a stick, a brown cap on his head, tweed jacket and raincoat dating from the sixties. They didn't look at if they had ever been washed.

'You the detective lady who found the lost dogs – them miniature things, all hair?' he asked.

'Word does get around fast,' I said. 'I found one dog and replaced the puppy, to be more accurate. The chihuahuas. Can I help you?'

Even if it was business, I was not asking either of them into the FCI office. The dog would probably sit on my pink-velvet button-back and I wasn't having that.

'There's a thief about,' he said. The dog was pulling on the lead, eager to explore. 'Sit,' he said, and the dog sat, clumsily, legs splayed, but still grinning. Dog went up one degree in my estimation.

'Several,' I said, finding a notebook. 'Tell me about it.' I put the date, time, man and dog with brief descriptions of both. I felt mean about not asking him back into the office, but I wasn't having him sitting on my button-back either. I fetched my desk chair for him. Dog got up, sensing biscuit tin in vicinity. Shopping list: plain wooden chair for shop.

'Sit.' That was man to dog, not me.

'Please sit down,' I said, trying not to make it sound like a command. 'Now may I have your name?'

'Arthur Spiddock and this is my dog, Fruit and Nut Case, Nutty for short. He's got a lot of retriever in him.'

'Hello, Nutty,' I said. Dog sprang up to rush over and say hello back, double-sized grin, tail thudding the floor.

'Sit,' shouted Arthur Spiddock.

'Sorry, my fault. I won't speak to your dog again.'

'I've got an allotment see, out Topham

way, my pride and joy. Spend all my time up there since I lost my job with the railways.'

I nodded. Ouch, I knew the unemployed feeling. 'Yes?'

'I grow cabbages and spuds and beetroots and swedes, then runner beans in the summer. Can't grow carrots, though. Wrong soil. Don't grow that namby-pamby lettuce or salad stuff.'

'Beetroot is for salads,' I murmured.

'I don't eat no salads. I like my beetroot hot.'

'Wow, hot beetroot. Very Russian. So what's the problem, Mr Spiddock? Has someone been swiping your cabbages?'

'I'll have you know I count my cabbages. No, it's worse than that. Someone has stolen my hens and my rabbits. All my hens and all my rabbits, all gone. Two nights back it was. Next morning they were all gone.' His face crumpled. I daren't ask if they were next week's lunch.

'Dear, oh dear,' I said. 'All your hens and all your rabbits. How many would that be?'

'Eleven hens and four rabbits. Six brown hens, three brooding hens and two pedigree bantams. I've got pictures of the rabbits.' He fished out a worn photograph and handed it to me. Surely he wouldn't have been taking photographs if they were meant for the stew pot. 'Them lop-eared rabbits.'

Not exactly on the menu, more like

pampered pets. All four rabbits were large, white, overfed and had long floppy ears and crafty expressions. I began to like Nutty quite a lot. 'And the hens?'

'All good layers. Get my breakfast from them every day. Even Nutty likes a fried egg.'

'Good for Nutty.'

'Sit!'

'You're surely not expecting me to find your hens and your rabbits?' I doubted if they were still alive, but said nothing.

'Course I am. You found them puppies, didn't you? They took feeding stuff and the cages. And a load of straw.'

'Pedigree puppies are more traceable. They have papers and chip numbers.'

'I ain't got no papers for my hens but I want them back and I'm offering a reward.' Mr Spiddock was getting quite worked up now. I hoped my office chair could stand the jerking. Nutty gave a deep bark of encour-agement. 'I'm offering a hundred pounds reward for the return of my hens and my rabbits.'

It was quite a lot of money for Arthur Spiddock. You could see it was, the way the words trembled on his thin lips. Probably his entire savings, give or take a few cabbages.

'Mr Spiddock, I can't promise to find your hens or rabbits, or even find out who stole them. My rate is ten pounds an hour. I also have a daily rate but I don't feel this case needs a full day's commitment.' I didn't tell him I'd already got a daily commitment. 'Did you report this to the police?'

'Yes, they came and trod all over my allotment. Found nothing. No wheel marks, nothing. But it had rained so there weren't nothing to find. I could have told 'em that.'

I had once found a missing tortoise and my fame from that success was not entirely deserved. He'd been found by a police car, wandering down the A27. I'd discovered him in the police canteen, eating left-over lettuce. But hens ... I didn't even know what a pedigree bantam was.

'You must think carefully about this, Mr Spiddock. Surely it would be better to buy some new hens and new rabbits with the reward money. A hundred pounds is a lot of money.'

'You don't understand,' he raged, face contorted. 'These animals were my friends.'

Nutty howled. It was a terrible noise. I retreated to my office. 'I'll get a registration form for you to fill in.'

It was going to be a criminal waste of time and I probably wouldn't even charge him. How could I? He didn't have any money. Call me crackers. I grinned at Nutty. We had something in common.

I made more notes: dates, times, addresses. His allotment was at the foot of Topham Hill where the prefabs used to be during the war.

After the Council pulled them down, the land became allotments for hot-beetroot eaters. I noticed he did not put a home address. Slight problem there with invoicing. Do you invoice an allotment?

By the time he left, I'd missed the post. But I had made a friend. Nutty was obviously crazy about me.

'Read the report to me,' DI James growled. 'You know I can't hold anything.'

I was not into counting his tubes but I had a feeling there was one less today. It might be indelicate to ask. Good news if he was less strung up to medical technology.

'All beautifully printed on my new laser jet,' I said, waving the sheets. 'Single spacing, left aligned, pages numbered.'

'Get on with it.'

'Just letting you know that I know what I'm doing.'

'I doubt it.'

My description of Faunstone Hall was detailed and accurate. The rooms came alive. I was a born estate agent. They ought to employ me. New career move: send sample of work to all local estate agents and suggest freelance employment.

'So this struck you as a very odd burglary?'

'Very odd indeed. Nothing normal about it at all. And I still don't see how they got over that wall.'

'An inside job, perhaps? Someone let them in. What about Mrs Malee?'

'Inscrutable Thai.'

'She might have a motive we know nothing about.'

'What's this – *we* know nothing about? The burglary is your case. Mine is the attempted murder of Holly's husband.'

'Jordan, think. They could be connected. A burglary where they take nothing of importance in a house that is bulging with valuable stuff. They took something that we don't know about or were looking for something else. Mrs Broughton said she had been set up. What did they take of hers that was then planted? Find out how she was set up and you'll find a connection to the burglary.'

'This is making my head ache,' I said. 'Now I've got stolen hens and rabbits to find and three of them are bantams, and I don't even know what a bantam looks like.'

'A bantam is a small species of domestic fowl,' said James wearily.

'Not even the normal size,' I wailed. 'I can't cope with this.' It was clouding over and the room was getting gloomy. Even finding the light switch was beyond me.

James pressed a small buzzer under his hand. A young fresh-faced nurse came in immediately. He smiled at her.

'Nancy, this is my good friend Jordan, who saved my life. Do you think you could find her a cup of coffee? She's in a state of not being able to cope.'

'Of course, James.' Nancy was clearly besotted, almost blushing. Calling me a good friend didn't help. But he knew: he knew I'd saved his life. 'How would you like your coffee, Jordan?'

I nearly said 'in a cup', but James would not have been amused. 'Black, please. Thank you.'

We talked about something else but I don't remember what. I could not bear to see him chained to a bed. James was looking at me closely as I drank the coffee. I felt crushed between the past and the present. The vaulting halls of my head were filled with floating fragments like the other morning's snow. Pieces of information swam in and out like silver minnows.

'I'm phoning for someone to drive you home. You don't look well,' James was saying. He'd got a voice-activated phone. Clever stuff. He was issuing orders down the phone as if he was on duty.

'You can't, I've got the ladybird here.' My voice sounded as if it came from the other side of the room.

'An officer at Brighton owes me a favour. He'll drive you home in your car and get the train back.'

It was still snowing as the detective sergeant drove me home. His name escaped me

– Luke or Duke something – but he was kind and amiable and did not try to make me talk. Then I discovered the snow was not in my head, but outside the car, clogging the windscreen wipers. The ladybird didn't have an interior heater so he couldn't heat the windscreen, but he did drape his coat over my knees. I was still in that short insurance-type-person skirt.

It was enough to send me to sleep and I left him to cope with the weather. He got directions from James on his mobile and I didn't even have to tell him where I lived. He stopped outside my two bedsits.

'Thank you,' I remembered to say. 'Very kind.'

'I'll park the car in a side road. I expect you've got a resident's permit. Goodnight, Miss Lacey.'

I couldn't remember if I had.

Somehow I staggered upstairs and rolled into bed, only stopping to peel off the skirt and jacket. The duvet was warm and I was asleep in seconds. Flaked out.

When I awoke, the snow had all gone and the dark sky was bright with stars. The headache had gone too and for once I felt the stirring of hunger. There was only tinned soup in the flat. I sprinkled on stale garlic croutons and grated hard cheese. Gourmet in lower case and a big soup plate.

It was too late to do any sleuthing but I wrote up my notes. I am a great note-taker. Then I listened to some slow jazz and the plaintive notes of the tenor sax player were healing. I wondered where my famous trumpeter was now. Probably cruising on the *QE2*, selling CDs in the interval between gigs. I had not heard from him for a long time.

The next morning I realized that I had done nothing yet for Holly Broughton's case, nothing to earn a daily fee. I would have to take a taxi. In the good old days I would have cycled. I phoned first to make sure she would be in.

Holly Broughton answered the phone herself. 'Yes, please come over. It's my housekeeper's day off and I hate being in the house on my own. Spooky and all that.'

'Not a real spook, I hope,' I said flippantly, thinking hurrah, can use own car, own hair. 'Any fifteenth-century ghosts?'

'No, I don't think so, not those kind of ghosts; but I don't feel safe any more, not after all this hassle and the court case. I'm quite frightened.'

'I'll be there in half an hour,' I said. 'Don't be afraid. Put the kettle on.'

'Sure, I can still remember how to do that.'

The ladybird had a parking ticket but I didn't have time to get into a fuss about it. Pay up and forget it. The driver detective had left his coat behind on the passenger seat. I hoped he hadn't been cold going back to Brighton on the train. I wrote myself a Post-it note and put it on the windscreen: return detective sergeant's coat.

Faunstone Hall looked lovely in the morning sunlight. There was a touch of spring warmth in the air. It was such a low and mellow old house, nothing grand and stately, immensely appealing and gracious. No wonder Holly loved it. I felt an urge to get this couple back together, to sort it all out for them. The security gates opened for me.

Holly was in the porch, looking like a model on a shoot – tight jeans and a music-clef brooch pinned to a brilliant-white shirt, suede gilet, gold watch and bangles, lovely hair. She made me look shabby and second-hand. I tried a bright smile to make up for unintentional shabbiness.

'Hello, Jordan. I'm so glad to see you. We'll have a cup of tea first and then I'll take you on a tour of the house and gardens.'

'Thank you. I particularly want to know if you have noticed if anything else is missing. Any little odd thing, quite small, something of yours. It could be relevant.'

The service was not quite up to Mrs Malee's standard – no tray – but the tea was hot, the mugs pretty, and there were cranberry muffins on a plate. We sat on stools in the gleaming kitchen and I let Holly talk.

She seemed to want to spill it all out.

'I know I'm lucky. I have this wonderful Thai housekeeper, Mrs Sanasajja Malee. Isn't that a fantastic name? I can hardly pronounce it. She looks after me and the house. But she has a sister who has a Thai restaurant in Brighton and she likes to see her once a week. So this is her day off.'

'Does she do all the work?'

'No, there's a woman from the village who helps with the housework. We have five bedrooms and three bathrooms, rather too much for one person to look after. There's a gardener, Tom, and a boy to help him. Some of the garden has gone wild.'

'And downstairs?'

'Three reception rooms, kitchen, Richard's study, conservatory, and a gym in the tower. Richard uses the gym. I occasionally pump a few weights, very lazy. Some of it is very old. There's bits that date back to a seventeenth-century manor house, even a priest's hole somewhere. We've never found it.'

As she took me on a tour, I was again surprised by the things that the burglars had missed. Lladro china figures, a collection of medals from the Boer War, a set of miniatures of former owners of Faunstone Hall. Then all of Holly's fairy-tale touches. The peacock feathers, the ferns, the glass, loads of delicate pink items. She was a collector of odd pieces.

'We discovered the miniatures in the attic. No idea who they are, but if they lived here once, then I'm happy to have their portraits around.' We peered at the expressionless faces in the tiny oval frames.

'Gives a sense of continuity,' I said, with no idea of what I meant. I didn't know any of my ancestors. Probably barmaids at rural hostelries or farm labourers.

'Exactly.'

We went up the wide, easy-flowing staircase with cast-iron balustrade. It was one of those staircases that cried out for long swishing dresses. Jeans would not make the same impression.

Holly took me to her bedroom. It was spacious with windows on two walls overlooking the garden. Her bed was king-sized with a draped pink-silk canopy and everything was crystal and pink and breathtakingly beautiful. My futon began to look less than functional.

'And I have a dressing room for my clothes,' she said, throwing open another door. We walked in.

It was like a shop, sided with wardrobes and mirrored sliding doors. I had never seen so many clothes, some still with price tags swinging from them. Holly chattered on about where she had bought this and that. There was a whole cupboard full of shoes, ranged on shelves, colour-coded and photographed. Photographed? Who would photo-graph their shoes? I barely had time to clean mine.

'Is there anything missing?' I asked.

'Funny you should ask that. But there is. Look, a pair of Christian Louboutin heels. Here's the photo. Look at them, like the curve of a woman's body. But they are not here any more. I can't even remember when I last wore them.'

'Who would steal shoes?'

'Don't ask me. It's a mystery.'

Holly stopped the tour suddenly. 'There was evidence in court about finding my shoes at some man's flat. I had to identify them at the trial. He wasn't a lover. I didn't know him and I don't leave my shoes around. It was rubbish. And the earrings evidence was pure nonsense.'

'If you were leaving some flat, you'd put your shoes on, at least,' I said, making a statement for the first time in seemingly hours. 'Wouldn't any woman?'

'Of course. It makes sense. No one leaves anywhere without their shoes.'

'You said earrings. What earrings?'

'A pair of my earrings were found in this man's flat, little gold dolphins with dia-monds for eyes. Very pretty. I liked them, one of my favourites. But I hardly ever wore them because they hurt.'

'Are they missing?'

'I don't know. I've never bothered to look. It seemed unimportant.'

'I think you should look for them.'

It was like searching a haystack for a hat pin. Holly didn't know what she had, or what she hadn't any more. The gold earrings, despite the diamonds, were apparently kept in a jumble of jewellery in a mother-of-pearl box. She scrummaged around, tipping it out on the bed.

'No. They're not here.'

'So someone might have taken them?'

She was right with me. 'Those burglars? Those louts who took all my favourite CDs? I see what you are getting at now. Was that a fake burglary, in order to lift things to incriminate me? Perhaps they took the shoes, too. I think you're absolutely right. You know, that makes me feel so much better. There is some chance, then, of finding out who did it. So I can clear my name. So that Richard and I can be together again.'

'It's a long way from that,' I said. 'But there's a chance. You need to go through your home and your possessions very thoroughly and see exactly what is missing, make a list, even the most trivial thing. Most of us don't know exactly what we have.'

'The ironing went missing once.'

'The ironing?'

'Lots of undies and things, waiting to be ironed. Just disappeared. And there were

53

some letters, from long ago, before I even met Richard. It was someone I knew before I went to work at Broughton Bank. I don't think they were dated – probably not. He was a poet sort of person. Out of work. His name was Darrell. He wrote the strangest poems.'

'Why did you keep them?'

'They were sweet and funny letters. But I hadn't looked at them for years. It was all over.'

'And they've gone?'

'I thought they must have been thrown out by accident. They meant nothing. It didn't bother me.'

'And were they used in court as evidence?'

'They produced love letters at the trial. I was asked to identify them as mine, but they were years old, nothing to do with the situation now. They were old love letters, poems too. Jordan, what am I going to do? It's all been rigged against me. Sometimes I wonder if Richard thinks I've gone back to my old life. You know, the glamorous high-class escort.'

'But why should you?' I asked. 'You have all the money you need now.'

'For the excitement, perhaps. It isn't true, of course. But Richard doesn't trust me any more.'

Holly's face broke and she sat on the bed, shoulders drooping, her hands clutching each other in a sort of torment. If it was acting, it was good acting.

'I think I need to read the court evidence,' I said slowly. 'If you'll give me the date at Chichester Crown Court, and the case number, I'll be able get a verbatim copy. It should only take a few days.'

'Thank you, thank you. Do you think I should tell Richard about the missing things? He might believe me then,' she wept.

'I think we should wait,' I said. 'Until we have some solid evidence. It'll be hard for you, but we need to have real proof. Insist on your innocence, by all means, but for the time being don't tell him what we have discovered today.'

She did not seem so sure. 'All right, if that's what you think I should do, Jordan. I'll go along with it for now, but only for a few days.'

A phone rang and Holly picked up a receiver. 'Hello?' Her voice changed tone. 'Adrienne? I don't think you should ring my home. Richard isn't here, you know that. If you have to talk to him, ring him at the office.' There was a long pause. 'I'm sure he'll give you the advice you want. And please don't ring here again.' She put the receiver down but did not explain the call. She went over to a mirror and did things to her hair.

Adrienne? Perhaps I should follow that up.

Holly had not sounded too pleased. Her face had closed up, eyes blanked out. She did not like this woman.

I thanked her for the coffee and left. But as I drove away from Faunstone Hall, I saw that Holly was already on her mobile in the porch, talking animatedly. That seemed a bit strange for someone who was upset. Perhaps she was phoning Richard against my advice or perhaps she felt she needed to book a facial before Richard came home.

Four

Topham Hill was a half-hour cycle ride on my mountain bike, gears and all. There was no point in taking the ladybird as the tracks were too narrow and bumpy for a car. The view from the top of Topham Hill was spectacular: distant sparkling sea, the Seven Sisters, Isle of Wight and acres of sky. But I wasn't there for the view. I free-wheeled down to the allotment site.

It was the usual ramshackle collection of sheds and vegetable-growing. Some grew plants in tidy lines, not a weed in sight, shipshape, ex-merchant navy. Other plots had reverted to the wild with only a line of giant sunflowers nodding to each other.

Arthur Spiddock's plot was easy to spot. There's that rhyming thing again. Empty hen runs and rabbit hutches. His cabbages were countable. I didn't know why I was here, because I wasn't making any money out of this. Arthur and an invoice were total aliens.

It was my conscience. For getting all that reward money for finding the diamonds.

Somehow I felt I didn't deserve it. I'd only followed a hunch.

Snow was now a distant memory. Today was touched with spring. The breeze wandered in and out of the allotments, like a tourist who doesn't quite know where to go. I foraged around the runs and the hutches. It was all as Arthur had said. Everything had gone. Not a wisp of straw left. They would have needed a vehicle.

I found some horse droppings. A horse and cart? Would the West Sussex Police officer have noted horse droppings? Not exactly on their training course. Wheels, yes, but not hooves. Instant camera at the ready, I took a photo of the droppings. What would the young girl at Boots' photography department make of it? I drew a line at taking a sample. The DNA databank had not progressed to horses. Or had it?

There was nothing else to note. You can't fingerprint a cabbage. Cigarette ends littered the plot but Arthur Spiddock was the smoking type. Nutty had left a few clues as well. This case was going nowhere.

But I took a few good breaths of the view before I left.

I cycled back to Latching, enjoying the exercise. For the first time, I began to feel that I was recovering. But not enough to go to the pub and find out how the suit of armour had fallen. Not my remit. DI James might think he was running the force from his bed but I knew differently.

'Jordan?' Jack shouted. His flashy blue Jaguar drew alongside, engine roaring, brakes screeching. 'Whatcha doing out here, girl?'

'Eleven hens and four rabbits stolen from an allotment,' I said. 'New case.'

'Always the big time,' he said. 'Hop in.'

'I'm on my bike.'

'Shove it into the back.'

The amusement arcade on the pier was a steady gold mine for Jack. People love losing their money. Jack spent most of it on his car. He seemed to wear the same clothes day in, day out. Maybe every night as well. I had no idea where he lived, nor did I want to know. If he took me home, he might lock me in an ivory tower with catering-size jars of instant coffee and crisps and throw away the key.

'You're looking better,' he said. 'You gave me a fright in the hospital.'

'Gave myself a fright,' I said, tying my hair back with a scarf. Hint: always carry a scarf. Useful for tying back, tying up, tying to-gether. Almost anything, apart from lassoing a horse.

'Horse,' I said.

'Wotcha say?'

'That's how they got over the wall,' I said. 'Horse and cart. They took a horse-drawn cart up to the wall and climbed over the wall

59

from there. Bet that's how they did it.'

'Right, sleuth at work,' he said. 'What's that about?'

'I'm investigating a burglary and I couldn't work out how they got over a very high wall without a couple of ladders. I thought it was an inside job but now I'm not so sure.'

'The hens and rabbits?'

'No, this is another one. That was a fake burglary.'

'Clear as mud and twice as smelly,' he grinned. 'How about a drink? Wine's your usual tipple, ain't it?'

I had not been into a pub since the suit of armour had crashed into my life. Pubs were sort of no-go areas till I got my nerve back. It might be years. I shook my head. Less of an ouch today.

'Sorry, not keen on pubs any more.'

'Rubbish,' he said, driving into the car park of the Green Man. 'Nobody's not keen on pubs.' The Green Man sign had six legs. There was no logic to that, unless it was one for each day of the week and legless on a Sunday. 'Still got your concussion, you have. Glass of wine'll put the colour back in your cheeks.'

He meant well. He was hardly your proto-type rough diamond, more like a clay-and-mud-encrusted nugget of gold. A flying tackle on a thief in his amusement arcade had brought me instantly to his notice. He'd kept both eyes on me ever since.

I hung back from the entrance to the Green Man. It was nothing like the Medieval Hall but the smell of beer and cigarettes wafted memories though my brain which I wanted to forget. Jack's company was not scintillating enough to banish those thoughts. Nothing was going to drive them away except time. Or a new head. Perhaps I could down-size it.

'Come on, kiddo.'

'No, please.'

'There ain't no green man going to jump on you.'

'Don't joke.'

'I never thought you were a coward,' he said. 'You always had a lot of spunk, a real go-getter.'

'I'm not ready for this.'

'I'm suggesting a single glass of wine in a pub, not an all-night bender.' He was exasperated, kicking the gravel. He was not often thwarted. He thought he was helping me and it irritated him that I wouldn't let him.

I did it for him, really – so Jack wouldn't feel so bad. Here I was, helping him so he could feel good that he was helping me. It was an extraordinary situation. Shopping: buy self-help book to get head back on straight and buy suitable aromatherapy oil.

The pub was full, people eating, drinking,

chatting. I sat hard against a wall and a pumping radiator. I nearly melted into an historic puddle. But the wine was good. Jack always bought the best, no house wine out of a box. It was an Australian Shiraz and the berry taste reminded me of the good times.

He was making me laugh. He told me he'd glued a silver ten-pence piece to the floor near the roll-them-down shunting coin machines. Nearly everyone had tried to pick it up.

'I crease myself sometimes,' he said, gulping his cold beer. 'Even little old ladies try to poke it off the floor with their umbrellas. It's a scream.'

'I shall have to come and see this immovable coin,' I said. 'If it's still there. Who's looking after your place now?'

'It's closed. Having it painted.'

This was a shock. I don't think the amusement arcade had ever been painted since the day it was built. The walls were a cheerless khaki with layers of grime clinging to the original. It could have been cream, or white or yellow underneath.

'What colour are you having it painted?'

'Blue.'

'Blue?'

'Your favourite colour, ain't it?'

I got back to the shop eventually. It had become two glasses of the best Shiraz and I was having an amusement arcade on the pier painted in my favourite colour. Is that devotion or attitude?

Jack drove off in his Jaguar with a satisfied grin. He'd done his bit for my rehabilitation. He'd sleep better tonight. My sleep was different.

Doris was waiting on my doorstep. 'You been boozing again?' she said. 'That's a good sign.'

'I was on a case,' I said haughtily. 'And Jack gave me a lift back.'

'I can smell it on your breath. Are you going to open your shop or not? I'm not waiting here for ever.'

Haughty turned to humble. 'Sorry, opening up right away. Do you want something, Doris?'

Doris was occasionally a customer. I always gave her a special price. No £6 label for her.

She followed me into the shop, sniffing at the dust. She went straight over to the glass cabinet which housed the crested china ornaments. Crested was the description for when a town put its coat of arms on a jug or pot and holiday-makers bought them by the drove. They were going up in value now. A really good Willow Art crested Brighton jug could bring in £12.

'We went there when I was a little girl,' she said, pointing to a tiny Scarborough vase. 'I didn't have any money of course, in those days. My pocket money, if I was lucky, was threepence a week or sixpence on holidays. A bit late, but I'd really like a souvenir of that holiday. There's a castle on the hill, y'know, and the grave of Anne Brontë and beaches that stretch for miles.'

I had no idea how old Doris was. She looked a well-preserved forty but she might be much older. Mavis was in the same age group but frequent sex with virile sun-browned fishermen kept her looking younger.

'Scarborough has got a minute chip,' I said, getting the tiny vase carefully out of the case. No one could see the chip. It was in the furthermost reaches of my imagination. 'So I'm afraid I'll have to let it go for three pounds.'

'Done,' said Doris, beaming. She fished around for some coins. 'It'll go on my mantelpiece. Place of honour.'

'Have you read any of Anne Brontë's books?' I said. 'I've got one here called *Agnes Grey*. Would you like to borrow it? Like a library but no overdue fines.'

'Spot on, Jordan. Glad you're feeling better. I've got some packets of mushroom pasta that only need five minutes to cook. Might suit you.'

'I'll pop in later.'

But there wasn't any later. I was dressing the window with some new pieces, those cheap copies of Arita blue-and-white patterned Japanese porcelain that people collect in vast quantities. Vaguely oriental but not quite the top notch. A man came in and closed the door, and without my really noticing, he put the lock catch down.

'Miss Lacey?' he said.

He had once been quite handsome. Tall and slim, brown and ash-grey hair on the longish side, heavy-lidded blue eyes and a carefully engineered smile. His suit was black mohair with a fifties look, shirt from Harvie and Hudson with red designer-striping, shoes from John Lobb bootmakers. But I had the feeling that the tie was off-the-counter M & S. Not all designer shopping.

I stepped back. 'Yes?'

'Do you have somewhere we could talk?'

'Do you want to buy something?'

He smiled but it wasn't sincere. 'Not exactly. I've come to warn you to get off my back.'

Once I would have immediately phoned James and he would have been on my doorstep, sirens blazing, in a flash five minutes. I wondered whether to dial 999. I'd look foolish if it was nothing.

'Perhaps you'd like to come through to my office,' I said. 'I feel sure there has been some mistake.'

'No mistake. My wife has been to see you here and you have visited my house, Faunstone Hall. No denying that, is there, Miss

65

Lacey? You have been snooping around and I don't like it.'

Ah, so this was the wealthy Richard Broughton of banking fame and court-case ignominy.

'Your wife invited me to her house. There was no intended snooping. When exactly does a look around become a snoop?'

He didn't frighten me. All the posh banker's clothes in the world cut no ice. There was a certain bloating around the eyes that told me he was not fit. 'I think you should leave before it gets dark, Mr Broughton. We've had several muggings around here recently.'

'My chauffeur is outside. Wilkes is a formidable chap, ex-army. I doubt if I shall get mugged stepping into my own Daimler.'

Chauffeur. No one had mentioned a chauffeur before. This was a new character entering the scenario. Casting nebulous. Hero, thug, accomplice, bodyguard? If he had a role, it might be anything.

We went through to my office. Richard Broughton ignored my Victorian button-back and instead perched on the edge of my desk, taking the higher position of authority. I stayed standing, if he was going to play that game.

'No doubt my wife has told you that she tried to have me killed,' he said.

I wanted to say what a pity she didn't

66

succeed, but that was hardly ethical.

'Holly told me that she had been found not guilty of trying to have you killed. Hardly the same thing. It was all circumstantial evidence, which the court threw out.'

'My wife is a consummate actress, Miss Lacey. The fluttering eyelashes, the flick of blonde hair, the tears welling in her eyes. She doesn't have to say a word.' He took out a silver cigarette case and opened it. His fingers were stained with nicotine. 'May I?'

'No, sorry,' I said, shaking my head. 'Asthma smoke-free zone.' A tiny suspicion entered my thoughts. I hadn't seen an ashtray anywhere in Faunstone Hall. Odd. It wouldn't hurt to hear his story. I got myself a glass of water from the tap outside. I was damned if I was going to make coffee.

'Perhaps you'd like to tell me your side of the story,' I added.

He settled himself further back on my desk. I decided to sit down. It didn't matter who held the higher position now. 'Holly and I met when she was working as a temp at my city bank. She was gorgeous as well as being a good secretary and I fell for her straight away. It was love at first sight.'

So far, same story.

'She was already going out with some guy, but she dropped him when she realized I was interested.'

Holly hadn't mentioned another suitor, or

was that the poet? But no doubt she had dozens in the wings.

'We got married after a whirlwind romance and for a time we were very happy. We bought Faunstone Hall and Holly enjoyed changing things and furnishing it to her taste. She has ... an interesting taste.'

Same story. But he didn't like all the pink.

'But living in the country soon become irksome for her. I work long hours and couldn't keep taking her out. I'm too tired and I often bring work home to do.'

I remembered his study and the array of computer equipment, filing cabinets and bookshelves. He probably did bring work home and was too tired to go out. True again.

'So Holly found company and amusement elsewhere. She always got her own way. She said that if I didn't take her out, then she'd find someone who would. And she did. Quite a few, I believe.'

This was new. Holly had not mentioned new escorts or social arrangements. But nor had I asked her.

'She was lonely,' I said.

He exploded, his face colouring. 'Lots of people are lonely. I'm lonely. You're lonely. Half the people in the world are lonely. They knit, they read, they walk the dog. They work in a charity shop. They do something – play bridge, go to flower arranging classes. They don't take dozens of lovers to fill in their time.'

'Are you sure? Dozens seems rather extreme.' I didn't know what to say. 'Have you proof?'

'I don't need proof. I know.'

This was vitriolic anger. He spat the words out, eyes dangerously narrowed. Reconciliation seemed the last thing he wanted. He wanted revenge, retribution, repayment for all the hurt he'd endured. I didn't want to listen to a tirade about Holly's morals.

'So why, if Holly was getting what she wanted – company and outings and plenty of sex – why should she want to have you murdered?'

'Money, as simple as that. Not satisfied with the house, a generous allowance, enough men at her back and call, she wanted my fortune. Every penny of it. Without strings, without an inconvenient husband who kept turning up. She wanted to be a wealthy widow.'

'And how did she organize your murder?' I said, without emotion, very matter-of-fact, as if I was asking about a dinner party.

'She hired one of her lovers, one who has a dicey past, someone she could blackmail into killing me. They planned a break-in at my London flat. I would wake up, hear a disturbance, go to investigate and get killed. But it didn't happen like that.'

'What did happen?'

'I crept out of my bedroom and saw this man's shape in the doorway. I hit him on the head with a brass lamp stand. Knocked him out, kicked the knife out of his hand. Going through his pockets I found Holly's diamond earrings. He knew her. Obviously she had given them to him in part payment. They're worth a lot. The diamond eyes were blue diamonds, very rare. She had planned it, knew it was going to happen. Satisfied now, Miss Lacey?'

Totally different story from Holly's. What were the pair up to? For 'pyjamas', read 'Burberry overcoat'. For 'inside flat', read 'in street outside'. Did he think I was daft? That I was an inexperienced local hack detective whose high spot of the day was serving paternity papers?

'Did you call the police?' I said.

'Of course I did. They came straight away.'

'Then I'm satisfied,' I said. Satisfied that he was a thoroughly unreliable and devious man. 'How lucky that you came in to see me or I might have been forced to waste a lot of my time.'

He was not sure how to take that. He levered himself off my desk, fingering his cigarette case again. The craving was getting to him. I got up, unlocked the shop door and opened it. There was a gleaming maroon Daimler parked outside. I hoped the neighbours were watching. The chauffeur came round and opened the car door. He was immaculate in a navy blazer with gold buttons, dark trousers and chauffeur's peaked cap. I only caught a glimpse of his profile and jutting jaw.

'Good day to you, Mr Broughton.'

He nodded curtly. 'Goodbye, Miss Lacey. I hope we don't have to meet again. Faunstone Hall, please, Wilkes.'

Five

The need for a strong coffee sent me straight to the coffee pot. I drank two cups without letting my thoughts simmer down. I did not like what I had seen or heard, nor Richard Broughton's manner. Handsome, but ruthless. I was not easily scared – at least I never used to be; but I was not sure of my current reaction.

'No way,' I said aloud to my friendly bubbly percolator. 'He doesn't scare me.'

Hopefully DI James's voice-activated mobile was switched on, so I dialled his number and he answered. It was a surprise. I'd thought it wouldn't work. He sounded tired. Well, it was the end of the day and it must have been a tiresomely long day for him.

'DI James,' he said. That faint Scottish accent against a pillow was emotive. There ought to be some kind of protective pill I could take.

'Is that really you?'

'Of course, Jordan. I guessed it was you. That tentative dialling.'

'You can't dial tentatively. I've connected.'

'You sound scared, girl. Spill it out. What's happened?'

'A handsome bully called Richard Broughton came into my office now and tried to warn me off Holly's case. Holly – that's his wife. He almost threatened me. He says she's lying. That she did try to have him bumped off and he can prove it, despite the court deciding she was not guilty. I can understand why she might want to get rid of him because he is a pretty nasty customer even with film-star looks.'

'But you handled the situation?'

'I sat down and drank water.'

'Cool, man.'

'How come you're talking so funny?' The phrase sounded odd coming from the austere DI James. 'Is it a side effect of your medication?'

'Some of the younger nurses are trying to get me to join the twenty-first century. It's their current training project,' said DI James dryly.

I wanted him here, at my side, giving me physical support and assurance. All I got was a voice. But the voice was alive, not some dead recording, and I sent a million thanks for that to my guardian angel. Detective Inspector James was my ideal man, damn him, even if it was a lost cause.

'I don't really want this Broughton case

any more. I'm getting bad vibes,' I said nervously. 'Stolen hens and rabbits are more to my liking. I reckon the thieves used a horse and cart to get past the electronic gates at Faunstone Hall. The evidence is there.'

'Horse and cart? So what? Gardeners need manure to feed their crops,' said James. 'It's normal, could be delivered by horse and cart. Or mushroom compost.'

'I prefer my theory. How else would someone steal eleven hens and four rabbits, plus hutches and straw?'

'Hey, Jordan, I can see this is one complicated scenario. Hutches and straw as well? Straw is difficult to trace. Have you got a sample for matching up?'

I controlled a smart reply. He could take the michael as much as he liked. It was a relief to hear a glimmer of humour in his voice, as if some part of him was coming to life again. That's what I wanted. The mind first, then the back, then the whole body. It could happen, in any order. I was sure. It would take time.

'Jordan? Jordan, are you still there? Before you decide anything, do you want to come and talk about the Broughton case? You could fill me in about Faunstone Hall and what you discovered. I'm interested.'

'OK. Tomorrow morning. I want to know how I find out if the police answered a 999 call to Richard Broughton's flat on the night of the attack.'

'Can you bring me some decent DVDs? I've seen most of these at least twice.'

Shopping: go buy decent DVDs.

First thing next morning I braved the commuting traffic, drove to Brighton and bought the best. Classics, modern, musicals. An armful. But no police procedurals. Not a screeching squad car or screaming chase in sight, hump-bumping the steep hills of San Francisco. I went into Café Nero for a late breakfast, coffee and warmed croissant. It was very busy with local office staff buying large takeaway cappuccinos. Where had the office kettle and jar of instant gone these days? Did it need a new plug or was it banned because of a Health and Safety edict? Hey, you could burn yourself if you put your hand in front of the steam. Watch that hot mug.

I was chasing croissant crumbs with a finger when I saw a flick of blonde hair. She was sitting with her back to me, across the other side of the café, talking earnestly to a man opposite her. It was Holly Broughton. I recognized the hair, the couture grey-suede gilet, the jangling gold bangles. It was impossible to hear what either of them was saying.

The man was arguing with her, his face grim and steely. Holly was shaking her head.

Her shoulders shrugged with exasperation. She got out her mobile and made a call. It seemed to be satisfactory, because then she turned to the man and made several emphatic remarks. He pursed his mouth, looking reluctant.

Holly opened her Gucci handbag and took out a small flat black-leather box and pushed it across the table. The man took the box and put it into his inside pocket without opening it. He got up abruptly and walked out of the café. She sat very still as if exhausted by the encounter.

I saw him clearly as he left and made a quick mental description. He was not someone that I knew, but I'd certainly know him again. He didn't have six legs like the Green Man, but he was pale-faced, fortyish with thin eyebrows and hair, not a pigment in skin or hair. He was wearing a raincoat with shoulder flaps.

I wondered whether to go over to Holly and say hello, Mrs Broughton, surprise, surprise, nice to see you. But it might pay me to stay quiet and follow her. No handy disguise for surveillance, only average scarf and sunglasses. They would have to do, plus slouch and change of walk. I turned in my toes.

With the scarf twisted tightly over hair and tied round my chin, vaguely Islamic, I followed Holly through the famous Lanes and antique shops of Brighton. She did not seem too steady on her feet, though it could have been the uneven pavement and the high-heeled boots. I was worried about her even though it was early for anyone to have been drinking unless they were an alcoholic. My mind was programmed for the worst. The white-skinned man might have spiked her coffee.

She was at a bank cash machine, trying to draw out money, but it would not accept her PIN number. She was having trouble getting it right. You only get three tries (I know) and then it swallows your card. Gotcha, dreaded PIN-number criminal.

In the moment that she staggered and seemed to grab the machine in a kind of faint my attention was diverted. A gang of goths and chavs, current teenage tribes, stampeded the pavement, pushing and shoving, shouting abuse, and I was thrust aside in the melee, stepping back into the gutter. Why do they do this? Why aren't they at home glued to their play stations?

The girls were as rough as the boys. Unbelievably wielding bags and phones and water bottles like the best of Boadicea's legions. They were all school age. It was some kind of school vendetta, very personal. Where was Holly? They must be trampling her into the pavement.

It was all over in sixty frantic seconds. But

when I re-established my feet, Holly had gone. I couldn't believe it. Had she gone with them, through them, or had she been kidnapped by some other gang? All in broad daylight.

I picked up my bag of DVDs and rushed into the bank. No Holly inside being pampered by bank manager. She wasn't inside or outside. Had Scottie beamed her up? My head was starting to ache and I had to give up. She'd disappeared. I made for the hospital, hoping for a bed right next to DI James. That would suit me fine, even if he was unaware of a companion.

But the sea at Brighton is as mermerizing as at Latching and I was lured first to the wide stretch of promenade. The beach was all pebbles. You might think this sea would be rougher or more vulgar, but it isn't. The waves were as blue as indigo and as deep as any secret. They washed the pebbles with gentle waves, topped with froth, beckoning the brave. But it was too early for the paddlers and too cold for the nudist bathers.

The two piers – so different, one a brash, gaudy crowded funfair and vibrant with life, the other a gaunt Edwardian ruin, the rusty ironwork being swallowed and wrecked by the sea. It was there to be painted and photographed, memorabilia for coffee-table books, for future exhibitions. No one remembered walking on it. No one alive, that is. There were plenty of ghosts.

And the light was so pure, so pellucid. It was if it had been washed overnight. The clarity was almost painful. Shopping: sunglasses, SPF15 sun lotion.

It was a long trudge to the hospital. I was beginning to forget where I had left my car. Brighton is hemmed with grim, Colditz-style multi-storey car parks ruining the town. Planners have a lot to answer for. Perhaps there's a special cloud for planners, halfway between heaven and hell, where they can spend eternity trying to find where they have parked their cars.

DI James had been shaved, bathed, and left watching mindless morning TV. I would have bathed him tenderly.

'Turn that bloody thing off, Jordan,' he said, eyes glazed. 'I need some conversation. Even yours will do, though some of it is not of this planet.'

'Any more insults and I'll turn right round and go, carrying home my cache of entertaining, up-to-date DVDs.'

'You're wonderful, you're brilliant. You even have nice eyes.'

This was decidedly new. I didn't know if he had ever noticed my eyes. I'm sure he hadn't, although an observant detective should take in such details. I decided to test him.

'OK, big shot,' I said, closing my eyes, and

peering at him through my lids, 'what colour are they?'

The pause was not too long. He was going through his memory bank. Perhaps minutes are longer than they used to be.

'Jordan Lacey. Five foot eight inches. Nine stone maybe after a proper meal. Hazel with shots of gold. Funny red hair.'

I had to give him an A-plus. I forgave him the funny. My heart soared with ridiculous possibilities. It was a mean start. So I was not exactly invisible to James.

'You can have these for passing the test.' I showered the DVDs on his bed, forgetting that he could not move. His fingers twitched. I scooped them up and read out the titles and racy blurbs.

'You done good,' he said. More of the nurses' vocabulary training. It was a step forward into this century. I didn't care if he spoke Anglo-Saxon or Gaelic. He was looking better. There was colour in his skin. Somewhere, lurking, his life blood was returning. Any month now he would be on his feet, telling me off, striding back into his patrol car, leaving me on the pavement in the pouring rain.

He pressed his hand buzzer. The nurse came in as if she had been hovering outside the door. He was obviously a favourite patient, and why not?

'We'd like some coffee, please,' he said.

I liked the plural. We ... It might go to my head, start of dizzy apron-and-duvet fantasy. But I made myself return to earth – polished-floorboard, hospital-type-room earth. James had to be fed the coffee.

'I'll do that,' I said, taking the feeder from the nurse.

'Jordon, no...' It was his protest. His eyes blazed.

'Shut up. Who saved your life?'

'Call this a life?'

'Brother, listen to me: you are going to get back on your feet. Then you can say what you like to me, boss me about, send me back to my bedsits. Meanwhile, I have the upper hand, once in a while. So drink your coffee, James.'

Those eyes, icy ocean-blue eyes, locked on to mine and for once we connected. It was an electric feeling. James and me. He was unable to move. I was beside him, holding this weird baby-feeding mug, loving him with every shred of my being. It held coffee. It could have held a love potion from ancient Greece. Maybe it would work.

'Faunstone Hall,' he prompted, forever the DI. 'Tell me about it.'

'I went as an insurance agent, Ruth Grimm. Perfect name, don't you think? The break-in was a fake. They took nothing of any value, when the house is loaded with silver, porcelain, paintings, let alone the

81

loose jewellery upstairs, kept in a box. And there was a bar loaded with alcohol. Untouched. I don't know if there's a safe.'

'They weren't disturbed, so they had plenty of time to search the place. Holly Broughton? What did you make of her?'

This was difficult. My feelings were mixed. I liked her. I was rooting for her. But this morning had shown something else was going on and I did not know what. Where was she now?

I tried to tell DI James everything. He listened, taking in all my ramblings. I talked and talked, trying to remember every little detail that James could latch on to. He was the brains in a body that wasn't working for the moment.

'This morning, she was obviously upset, trying to make some deal with some man. There was a jewellery box passed to him. One of those flat things that contain a necklace or a bracelet. Very posh.'

'How would I know?' James said. 'I've never given anyone a necklace.'

'And I have never been given one.'

He grinned. 'That makes two of us.'

I did not know what to do or say. Again this was a moment when we were in tune. We were sharing the same feeling. In that moment it came to me. I knew where Holly had gone. She had not gone upwards or sideways. She had gone downwards.

'There could be one of those traps in the pavement and she went downwards,' I said. 'Like outside old pubs for delivering barrels of beer. A sort of chute. I hope she didn't get hurt.'

'You said this was a bank.'

'It could have been a pub in the past. Brighton is teeming with new pubs and old ones from smuggling days. There's practically a pub per person. And how do I find out if Richard Broughton made a 999 call?'

'I'll check if you give me the date. And go into Latching police station and look at some mug shots. That man's face – shouldn't be too difficult. It could be a lead.'

'Anything else you want me to do?'

'Get some sleep. You look worn out. You've been doing too much. It's early days yet and you are not fighting fit.'

He actually sounded as if he cared. My imagination was rioting. Was my luck about to change? I didn't know what to say.

'I've no one to sleep with,' I said, getting up to go. Usual idiotic, brainless comment. He closed his eyes, retreated. I'd blown it again. I need to go on one of those personality courses: How to Captivate Your Man By Not Saying the Wrong Thing.

'Buy a teddy bear,' he said, closing his eyes.

Other thoughts swam around as I went on a tour of the multi-storey car parks to find the ladybird.

1. Had Richard Broughton set up his wife?
2. Was Holly setting me up?
3. Had she set him up?
4. Or were they in this together, setting up some as yet unknown third party?

The permutations were endless. I passed by the bank. Yes, there was a two-door trap-door in the pavement right outside. It could have been opened. Holly could have opened the flaps. The latch was loose. I opened the trapdoor gingerly. It was ringed with dust and cobwebs. There was a chute, but no one was lying helpless at the bottom. And it looked as if it hadn't been opened for years.

I went inside and queued along the rope. 'Excuse me,' I said. 'But did you used to be a pub? Perhaps a smugglers' pub?'

The cashier looked at me in alarm. 'Excuse me, madam; if you'll kindly wait, I'll fetch the manager,' she said, disappearing fast. This brief encounter with a maniac aged her. She would talk about it for weeks, keep buying the Retinox.

The manager was out in an instant, his hand clasped round a mobile in case he needed to call for help. No, this had been a bank for twenty years. He knew nothing about a pub. Mrs Broughton had not come down the chute and entered the bank from the basement.

'Why don't you go home and have a nice cup of tea?' he suggested.

'Great idea,' I said, backing out with dignity. I still had to find my car.

A gang of skateboard kids were swarming round the ladybird, inspecting her. I smartened my step. She was vulnerable, crimson-red with nine black spots, and I loved her to pieces.

'Hi there,' I said, striding forward, voice full of authority. 'Do you like my car? Do you know what she's called?'

The kids stopped swarming, not used to friendly overtures, baseball caps back to front, baggy pants, loads of piercing.

'Herbie?' one said.

'Ladybird,' I said. 'She's like that spotted insect that flies around in the summer. Although they are being killed off by insecticides. Come and have a look at her.'

'Did you do the spots, miss?'

'No, I was lucky. Someone else had painted them on. Isn't she fun? Cars should be fun.' They mixed around, temporarily interested.

'Is she a proper car or a toy car?'

'Of course she's a proper car. Petrol, brakes, gears and everything. Now, will you show me the way to get her out of this concrete concentration camp? She has to breathe. Which is the best way to go? Round there, or down that ramp? You should know.'

The gang of truant school kids saw me out of the multi-prison. They waved goodbye, then went back to skateboarding up and down the ramps. It was their playground.

James had said sleep, but I knew I had a lot to do. It was hard without him. He was still in charge but I needed his physical presence. He was fastened to a bloody hard bed, fed by nurses, his every need accommodated. Well, I hoped not every need.

There was a woman customer waiting outside my shop. I waved to her and parked the ladybird in the yard at the back. It only took a few minutes to unlock the shop and rush to the front door and open it for her.

'Hi,' I said. 'I'm sorry I'm late. Urgent business.'

'I've come twice,' she said.

'Then you deserve a bargain,' I said.

She was after the Chinese blue-and-white chinaware. They were copies, not the valuable and sought-after Chinese ware. Plates, jugs, vases and sauce boats, all with the distinctive blue rural pictures on a white background. She was starting a bed-and-breakfast place along East Latching and wanted a theme in the breakfast room. Apparently it had a good shelf under the cornice and it could show off a lot of ornaments.

She liked them all. There were about twenty pieces. She wanted the lot. Twenty times £6 was a lot of money. She was hesitant and so was I. I didn't want to lose the business.

'How about all twenty pieces for a hundred pounds? And I'll throw in a couple extra. Well, not exactly throw in ... but if at some time in the future – and please understand it may never happen – could you give me a bed for nothing and no questions asked? And never mind the breakfast.'

'Done,' she said, smiling. 'The Anchorage, Welborne Road. My name's Mrs Holborn. I'll give you the phone number. Come, any time. How about a password, so I'll know it's you?' She'd been reading too many spy books.

'Great idea. How about "ladybird"? You can remember that.'

'Ladybird. Sure. But if we are full, it might be pretty basic accommodation.'

'I understand.'

I wrapped every item carefully and packed them in a big box. I wished her well with her new venture. It all depended on the weather. Latching has wonderful summers but cool springs. It was a hazardous profession, dealing with holiday-makers who came and went.

'Tell your guests about the theatres and the cinemas,' I said, as she left. 'A show on practically every night.'

'I didn't know there were any theatres,' she said. Where had she done her research before buying the place? I gave her a town map and marked the best venues for shows and films, and Maeve's Café and Miguel's restaurant.

I sat down and wrote up my notes. Time was passing and I was losing track. James was right. I was tired. I wanted to sleep, somewhere, somehow, with anyone, anyhow. It was in these moments that I thought of Ben, felt him near. Dear lost man, anywhere, somewhere. It had not been fair. A stupid accident. It had never been meant to be for us and I had not loved him. He'd deserved better.

It was pouring with rain as I went home and climbed upstairs to my bedsits, the old-fashioned sash windows rattling. As I closed the curtains, I caught sight of a man standing on the corner under a big golf umbrella. He was getting drenched. I hope she turned up soon.

Six

DI James had been right. I did need sleep, and the pattering rain was my lullaby and I slept deep as a well, despite the usual upside-down and turbulent dreams, none of which I could remember when I woke up.

My appetite was returning slowly, if you could call the minute amount of food that I was consuming an appetite. Breakfast was a spoonful of muesli with a slice of apple or banana chopped on top. Lunch was two leaves of lettuce. Supper was a mouthful of home-made broth. Where are the calories in all that? Floating in the washing-up water?

Go back to the Medieval Hall pub, James had said, have a look at the plinth on which the suit of armour sat. He was suspicious but had not told me why. It was some kind of police instinct, beyond me. I couldn't go by myself. The circumstances were too harrowing, the memories too vivid.

But he had said again that he wanted me to go with the kind of authority that was difficult to ignore. If I phoned them, perhaps he would consider that I had made some attempt.

I dialled the number after checking it in the phone book. I don't carry pub numbers around. A male cleaner answered, coughing passive smoke fumes.

'There's no one here at the moment, miss,' he said. 'The manager won't be in till about eleven.'

Funny how I knew that. 'How silly of me,' I said. 'Of course, their hours are different from everyone else's hours. But you are in, working.'

'I've been here since six o'clock, clearing up. You should see the mess. This is a big place, restaurant and all. There's only me. I do the lot. But not for long now. Half of it's going.'

Half of it's going? Now, that's odd, for a pub. 'What do you mean, half of it is going?' I asked.

'Well, they've sold it – the Medieval Hall bit.' The cleaner was pleased to have a chatty break. 'It's going to be moved quite soon. All the talk, that is. Going to lift it up on a hydraulic whatsit and put it on trolleys or trailers or something. Tricky job. Costing a bomb, I expect. The police are going to close off all the roads.'

'But where is it going?'

'I dunno, miss. Some Russian millionaire has bought it and wants a Medieval Hall to put next to his mansion. I know the boss is pretty pleased – lining his pockets no doubt.'

'Do you know when this is happening?'

'No idea. Going to make a lot of dust, I reckon, which I'll have to clean up.'

'And who is the buyer?'

'Dunno. Rockafellar.'

'I don't think so. He lives in America.'

Would James have known about this? Had he been approached to close off the roads, provide a police escort, waste public money? More than likely. And he would not have been too pleased.

'What about the suit of armour? Is that going as well?'

'That bloody suit of armour. It's here now, on the floor, looking like a stuffed dummy. I had to clear up the mess, you know – blood everywhere. I never seen so much blood. Had to wear me wellies. And rubber gloves. Infection, y'know.'

'You mean, you know where it is?'

'Yes, it's in the boiler room. Nobody wanted to put it back over the bar, being all bloody and bad luck to boot. And off its perch, as you might say. So we left it in the boiler room.'

'Is it still there, now?'

'Unless it can walk about by itself. Part and parcel of the Hall, so to speak. I hope the ghost is going, too. Both been in the wars, again. Well, miss...'

The cleaner was starting to tire. It was easy

to tell when someone was not used to talking. This conversation had probably been a week's worth of verbal exchange.

'You've been very kind,' I said slowly, giving him a breathing space. 'I do appreciate it. I won't keep you from your work any longer.'

'Righto, miss.'

''Bye.'

I rocked backwards and forwards, reliving the moment when I had flung myself towards DI James, seeing him standing there, our drinks in his hands. A therapist would say that you should relive bad times to purge them from your memory. But this wasn't helping. The muesli sat untouched. I could not eat or drink anything. This was purgatory, like those tortured medieval pictures of horned devils prodding bodies with forks.

I went and showered, but blood seemed to run down the walls instead of water. I soaked my hair, but it still smelled of blood. His blood, my blood. No amount of herbal shampoo could rid me of the smell. Even now, weeks after, I could still smell it.

It was a blustery east wind along the front, whipping my anorak, the unguarded sea a frothy coffee colour, stirring the sand as the tide went out. The tide would go out for a quarter of a mile. It crashed on to the pebbles, taking its pennyworth of payment in rage. Why didn't the sea fall off? No one had really answered that one.

Maeve's Café was open. She didn't do breakfasts, preferring a bit of a lie-in. But Mavis came out of the kitchen in a new pinny and immediately pushed me into my favourite window seat with a sea view.

'I can see you've had nothing to eat, so no arguing. I'm making you a mug of milky coffee with honey, scrambled eggs on toast and a chocolate muffin. And I shall sit here until you have eaten every crumb.'

'I couldn't eat a thing. Especially not a muffin.'

'I said no arguing. Here's today's papers. Read about other people's heartbreaks and feel lucky you're still alive.'

Mavis knew how to ram it home. Her hair today was a russet red, frizzed in all directions, different from her usual plum. Perhaps Superdrug had run out of her preferred shade. I dared not ask about Bruno, her current bit of rough.

He and I were not on speaking terms, even though he had rescued me from the pier and I had paid for the damage to his fishing boat. He distrusted female detectives.

She put a mug of coffee in front of me and a jar of honey. Honey was my absolute cure for everything. The monks used it. The Romans used it. Jesus used it. No one wrote down if cavewomen used it. Who had time to write in those days? Bring me an axe-head, mate, I want to chip a recipe on a rock.

'Bruno sends his thanks, but not verbally, if you understand. He's never said thanks to anyone in his entire life. But I know he was stunned when you paid for the damage to the keel of his boat. He's been able to keep fishing and that's his livelihood.'

'Good,' I said. 'I'm glad he's pleased. So I don't owe him anything now for getting me off the girders. We're quits.'

'You could say that,' said Mavis, serving her perfect scrambled eggs. She placed tomato sauce, salt and pepper in front of me. 'Now I'm not feeding this lot to the seagulls. So eat it up.'

Many times I had eaten here at this window table with DI James. He liked cod in batter and chips with lashings of tomato sauce. He rarely ate anything else. It was an odd diet, apart from the occasional station-canteen menu. What sort of mush did they give him in hospital? I felt an urge to take him a cod-and-chips takeaway in a box and feed it to him with my fingers.

Mavis made her scrambled eggs in a microwave but I didn't know the secret of its fluffiness and perfect taste. A dollop of cream, perhaps? Yoghurt? Skimmed milk? Sea salt? She wasn't going to tell anyone.

She brought me the local paper. 'Have a read,' she said. 'Seen the dead guillemots on the beach yet? It's a crying shame. Everyone's talking about it.'

I shook my head. I hadn't seen any. My head had been elsewhere and I was hardly listening. A prominent news item had grabbed my attention. The Grade II listed Medieval Hall was on the front page. It had never had an ancestral name, was simply known locally as the Medieval Hall. If there had once been a manor house attached, that had long since gone and the stone been recycled. Some time in the seventies the restaurant had been added. There was a photo, too, of the Hall. It was two-storeyed, brick and timber with exposed cross-beams and arches.

MEDIEVAL HALL LIFTED TO NEW HOME

Latching's most prestigious Medieval Hall is to move to a new home. The Hall, built in 1464, is to leave its present site and will be moved two miles to the home of football millionaire Sven Rusinsky.

Costing thousands of pounds, the operation will mean hoisting the Hall off its original foundations and stabilizing it on to giant trailers. A great many spectators are expected to line the route to see the Hall on its record-breaking journey.

'It has taken months of planning,' said the site manager, Rik Henderson. 'The police have been wonderful. The roads en route will be closed and we shall have a police escort all the way. We may even have to remove a small bridge.'

The vacant site will become a new shopping precinct with cafés and a bowling alley.

It stank. The police had probably opposed the move from the start. It would cost the ratepayers thousand of pounds and tie up valuable resources for hours. The 70 ton Hall would move like a giant snail. The traffic confusion would be horrendous, costing time, money and maybe even lives.

And who wanted another shopping precinct? Latching had enough shopping centres and even more huge retail outlets spreadeagled either side of the main Brighton road. How much was the pub owner getting for the Medieval Hall? And for the shopping site? He'd probably already bought his villa and pool in Spain.

Remove a bridge? Even a small one would cause chaos to train services for months. Passengers would be diverted. And who was paying for that?

I felt like marching on the Russian football millionaire and demanding that he leave the Medieval Hall on site. What did he want it for? Parties? A gymnasium? I was sliding into banner-and-protest mode.

If the Hall was moving soon then I only

had a few days to find out what James wanted to know. Jordan Lacey could not go. It would be too cruel. Her mental state was fragile. But how about some bumbling history student, someone who was writing a book, or a ghost buster, digging out Sussex ghost stories? Jordan need never say a word. She could stay at home.

'Where does this Russian live?' I asked Mavis. She was sitting opposite me, checking every forkful.

'I shan't tell you till you've finished that scrambled egg.'

'I can't eat the muffin,' I said. 'I truly can't.'

'It's a big white house, on the South Downs. Used to belong to that rock singer. The group was always throwing things around the stage.'

Mavis's description was accurate. I knew the house. It was so big, it didn't need a medieval hall as well.

'Thanks for the breakfast, Mavis,' I said, getting up, feeling bloated. I put some money on the counter. 'Delicious.'

Mavis put the chocolate muffin in a bag. 'Elevenses,' she said.

Well, students and writers wear jeans, so that wasn't difficult. A baggy camouflage jacket and hair tucked under a baker-boy cap, little gold-rimmed specs with plain glass. I painted on some freckles and bold black eye make-up. A notebook and pen in my pocket and I got on the bus. This student had enough money for the fare. Maybe she would have to walk back. The exercise would do her good.

The bus dropped me near the Medieval Hall pub and restaurant. I waved to the driver, not wanting him to leave me.

I didn't like going in. But there was only the faintest tremble in my voice as I introduced myself to the pub owner and explained the purpose of my visit. I made it all up as I went along, quite the little scriptwriter.

The proprietor was a small, rotund and jovial man, wearing a white apron tied round his middle, putting a shine on pint mugs with a professional flourish.

'I'm writing a book about Sussex ghosts,' I said, getting out my notebook. 'So far I've got some smashing ghosts and spirits and ghouls, lots of cranking and creaking. Someone said your Medieval Hall has a ghost. I wondered if I could have a walk round and see if I can feel its presence?'

'You'll feel a few inebriated spirits all right. My regulars can knock it back.'

'Has anyone ever seen your ghost? Any of your staff? Or customers? How about you?'

'Don't believe in ghosts, miss. Lot of twaddle, if you don't mind my saying so. Would you like a drink? It's a bit early for ghosts so you might as well have a drink.'

'Pineapple juice, please, with ice. Day or night is not a problem. Ghosts are there all the time, you know, they don't just come out at night.'

'Really? You don't say?' He beamed, looking interested. His cheeks shone. He leaned forward. There was no image in the glass wall of the bar behind him. That was spooky. I moved to catch his reflection but there was nothing, only a shift of light. Something wrong with the mirror.

'They can be seen easier at night, that's all. The daylight takes away their aura.'

'They got an aura? Well, you seem to know what you're talking about, miss, so if you'll excuse me I've got things to do.'

He went through a door at the back. He had not poured me the promised drink. Never mind.

I knew the way through to the next-door Medieval Hall. It was strange to see it empty and desolate. The last time it had been crowded with people drinking and talking, listening to great jazz music, everyone having a wonderful time. James and I together for once, on neutral ground, not sparring, at ease and companionable.

The canopy over the bar had not been replaced. That was where the suit of armour had sat and fallen from its plinth. The murals seemed fresh on the walls, the beams now cleared of their laurel branches and military flags, ready for the momentous move.

It was a magnificent old hall. I loved it, every nook and cranny, absorbing vibrations from the past. Yet distress crept out of the walls. I sucked in the distress from the carpet and drapes. The heavy lanterns wept. It was not only for James and me. It had seen many traumatic happenings spread over hundreds of years of tormented history.

I wandered around making obscure notes in my notebook. I couldn't feel anything, only a sense of loss. No presence. I wasn't psychic. James and I were the only people who mattered here.

There was nothing to see on the canopy unless I could find a ladder to climb up and make a survey. It looked normal from a distance, but I needed a closer look. How was I going to get up there?

The boiler room was where I expected it to be, down some damp steps behind the bar. No boiler room merits description, but this one did because it was dominated by a huge galvanized boiler and a suit of armour covered in rusted blood on the floor.

I froze.

That was my blood and his. I relived the moment, the fear and the smell. The sharp-pointed slivers of steel that were the boots of the suited knight severed my face again.

Then I remembered the sleeve that had deflected the armour. No one had come forward and claimed heroic saving.

I made myself go down on one knee and examined the armour. Tap, tap – it was hollow. There was no one inside. Thank goodness for that. I could not have faced a disintegrating skeleton. Pass the smelling salts, the flower rescue remedy.

The suit had been fixed to a plinth on top of the bar. Seemingly safe. I did not want to touch it but I had to turn it over. Hapless suit of armour, dented in places. It had fitted a short man, a long-ago soldier, whom none of us knew. Men had been shorter in those days, except for Henry VIII, who had been tall.

This was a botched-up job on the base of the suit, hardly appropriate for a suit of such immense age. Museum officials would have flinched at such amateurishness. And it had been tampered with. The main shaft had been sawn through, to within a whisper of complete severance. Its weight had been held in place with strong fishing line, line that could take the weight of a shark. It would only have needed a slash of a knife to trigger the moment when the suit fell on DI James, who would be standing below. Perhaps the line had been removed in the chaos that followed. There was no way of telling exactly how the suit had been dislodged.

I got out my disposable camera and checked for best angles. This was a flash camera and as soon as the red light showed I started clicking fast. I got several good close-ups.

'Excuse me, miss, what the hell do you think you are doing down there?' A stocky man was hurling himself down the steps, his face red, sparse grey hair sticking up from a shiny bald skull. I didn't know him. I whisked the camera behind my back. 'Get out of here. You're trespassing.'

'I was given permission,' I said firmly. 'I'm researching Sussex ghosts. The man behind the bar said I could look around the Hall and sense any presence. I'm ... er, sensing a presence here.'

'This is the boiler room, not a bloody presence. This isn't the Hall. Get out, like I said.'

'I don't understand. I'm only looking. I'm not doing any harm, besides I was given permission.'

'Not from me you weren't.' He glared at me, slitty eyes glinting. I didn't like the look of him at all. 'Clear off or I'll call the police.'

'And who are you?' I asked, with serious-student dignity, straightening my spectacles.

'I own this pub, that's who I am. So f— off. And don't come back.'

Oh dear, that unpleasant f-word. I supposed I had to go. At least I had the photos and I had seen what I wanted to see. So this was the man who was selling the Medieval Hall to a Russian football millionaire. He needn't bother to invite me to go swimming in his pool near Malaga.

Seven

It was a quick escape. I didn't have time to say goodbye to the barman, the jovial one who'd offered me a drink. I had an odd feeling about him. I ran out on to the roadway, past parked cars and clipped suburban gardens, and took a short cut between detached houses to the main road. A single-decker bus was trundling along.

'You can throw me off now or set me down early,' I said to the bus driver. 'But I don't have enough change on me to pay the full fare to Latching.'

He took in my student outfit, ingenuous smile and apparent honesty. 'Give us what yer got,' he said. 'And I shan't notice when you get off. But heaven help you if an inspector gets on. Checking up a lot they are these days.'

'Thank you,' I said. 'I'll own up immediately or pretend I fell asleep and went past my stop. It could happen.'

'It often happens.'

My head was spinning. So much information was crowding into my head. But I had done it and I had got some photos. I had gone back to the pub on my own. No prop, no friend, no police escort. DI James would be proud of me, or would he? Maybe he didn't know that a portion of my mind had disappeared on that night, that some part of it was empty. It might be a bit too complicated for an injured officer to take in.

The route passed Topham Hill and I remembered my rabbits-and-hens case. Perhaps I should nip off now and have another look round, but then I would have further to walk home. Total inertia won and I stayed on the bus, watching the old Iron Age hill disappear behind trees. I couldn't imagine myself living on that bleak hill in mid-winter, nothing but a hole to live in, rabbits to catch for food, with some smelly, hairy mate grunting his need for food, warmth and copulation. A long word for him. What was grunt for 'sex'?

Maybe the rabbits hadn't been stolen. Maybe a latch had been left open and they had scuttled off to join their ancestors on the hill. Same with the hens. But that did not explain the feed and the straw. A rabbit would hardly have had the brains to drag a bale of straw along as a 'hello, look who's here' present.

Cases: stolen hens and rabbits, wife unfairly accused of intent to murder husband, attempted assassination at Medieval Hall.

The last one was not exactly mine. And I'd forgotten the threat from Richard Broughton. Not a case for me, but another layer of the same mystery.

I didn't like the way any of them were going. I preferred that disappearing-fishing-tackle case. At least I'd known what I was doing, sitting under the girders of the pier, making notes until I had to be rescued by Bruno.

The bus screeched to a halt, skidded sideways. I had been dreaming, not taking any notice of the other passengers, the 4x4 traffic, the countryside of furrowed fields, houses, garden centres and sprawling shopping malls. A rash of self-sown daffodils sweetened the verges. I was a typical non-paying passenger, peering into other people's gardens. We were going along a derelict stretch of road, nearing the railway crossing. No houses now, nothing, only a sparse canopy of trees. Call it 'deserted Latching'.

A youth was standing beside the driver, black-hooded, jeans, with some sort of baseball cosh in his hand. Oh, God, this was a hold-up. I slid my camera under the seat. That was the only thing I had on me of any importance. The bus had stopped.

He was going along the rows of passengers, demanding money, credit cards, jewellery. They were giving him everything – pensioners, wives, mothers, schoolkids. People were white-faced, shaking, frightened. It was alarming.

He reached me. His face was masked. I saw only drug-bright eyes and a spotted neck. He was on a high. There had been a lot of drug trafficking recently in Latching, reported in the newspapers.

'Hand it over,' he said.

'Hand what over?'

'All you got.'

'Would you like my notebook, my sanitary towel or my lip gloss?' I asked.

'I want your money.'

'A bent ten-pence piece, that's all I've got. Ask the driver.'

'Don't mess with me. Your credit card.'

'Don't have one.'

'Your mobile phone.'

'Ditto.' I didn't have it with me. Left it at home. Good move, apparently.

'Jewellery.'

'You're joking. What jewellery would I have? Do you want my charity rope bracelet? This PDSA brooch? I doubt if it would make tuppence. And, by the way, your boot laces are undone.'

He looked down and I was on him in a fraction of a second. A nanosecond. Instant wham. I nailed him to the floor of the bus with sheer weight and annoyance. Some out-raged schoolchildren, shorn of their essential texting mobiles, threw themselves on top of me with glee. I could smell sweat and take-aways, unwashed clothes, nuts, alcohol and cola. All at the same time.

'Phone the police,' I yelled, gasping. The kids were heavy and they were having too much fun.

'Kill him, kill him,' the kids yelled, thumping me and him.

'Don't thump me. I don't deserve this,' I gasped. 'He's an amateur. Wait till you meet a real killer.'

We got him tied up to the seat legs in the bus with scarves and belts and straps of schoolbags. He couldn't move. I removed the mask. His face was even more spotted. The kids were exhilarated. I let them use their imagination. They could write it up for an assignment. 'What I Did Today' by Damien Bloggs. The passengers crowded round me. Miss Bus Hold-Up Heroine. Someone gave me a biscuit. Another took my photograph. Big deal. My mouth was too dry to eat.

'Thank you so much, miss. That was my pension,' said a frail woman whose bones were about to fall apart.

People patted me on the back, retrieved their belongings although, strictly, I should have stopped them. They were needed as evidence. But I was no longer a WPO, having left the force due to a corrupt rape case where the rapist had walked away free. At least the DS involved had been moved north.

A couple of striped patrol cars screeched to the scene, sirens howling. Some officers got out and strolled over to the stranded bus. It looked like a foundered red whale, still spouting.

'I ought to get on,' said the driver, his colour returning. 'I'm behind schedule.'

'You're going nowhere,' said the officer. 'Anyone hurt?'

'Only that piece of scum. Those school kids certainly carry a punch. And talk to that brave student girl at the back. She threw him. She deserves a medal. Saved us all, she did.'

'She saved my pension. I couldn't manage without it. I've got nothing in the house.'

'Took my wedding ring.'

'And my mobile and my iPod.'

Funny how brave student had got off the bus unnoticed and was already legging it across a field, head down, keeping close to the hedge, out of view. Now I would have to walk home.

The last time I was a heroine, my picture was all over the newspapers. I had made a flying tackle on a robber at the amusement arcade. My brave action had merited life-long devotion from Jack. This was far less elegant, sprawled on the hoodie, a pile of schoolkids on top of me, thumping and pounding. My glasses were broken. Thank goodness they were not prescription. At least, not for this student.

It was a long walk back to Latching, especially when I had to keep weaving and dodging and keeping out of sight. I got torn by brambles, stung by nettles, chased by territorial cows. I'd lost my notebook but not the camera. Brain partially intact. Somewhere along the way I shed the student look, the freckles, pocketed the cap, turned the jacket inside out, shook my hair in all directions. My ten pence would not buy me a drink. I had to cup my hands under a standing water tap for thirsty dogs and gulp. I filled their bowl, hoping St Peter was watching and marking my record.

I was not far from Faunstone Hall, a short detour inland and I'd be there in ten minutes. Would Holly Broughton be pleased to see me? There were a few things to sort out with her. As long as her husband Richard was not around. Fingers were as good as a comb and it was all my hair got. Some women paid Knightsbridge prices for the same tousled look.

I gave my name to the intercom machine at the electronic gates and Mrs Malee answered.

'Please to come in, Miss Lacey. Mrs Broughton has been expecting you. She's waiting in the conservatory.'

The gates opened and I walked up the drive, rubbing the last of the freckles off my face. The grass had been manicured and the flowers counted and found present and correct. Not a weed in sight. The Broughtons had one heck of a gardener. It was the first sunny day of spring, a weak glimmer of warmth, clouds scurrying in disorder not sure if they were allowed to play.

Holly was in the conservatory, stretched out on a lounger, eyes closed. Her white designer jeans were perfect, red silk blouse knotted at the waist, bare feet in gold sandals. It was warm enough for bare feet. Her diamond rings flashed like radar signals. I felt and looked like a scruff beside her. My throat dried up again.

'Hello, Jordan,' she said. 'Mrs Malee is bringing some coffee. You look worn out.'

'It's been a long morning,' I said. 'I made an early start.'

'On this case?'

Ah, tricky. She was paying the daily rate. She was entitled to every hour of my working day. Ghost-busting was not exactly related to her marital problems. Nor could I think of a good lie.

'Sorting out a slight incident on the bus,' I said, not elaborating. And that had taken all morning? I could sense her thinking.

'Ah, so you were the Good Samaritan. It sounded like you. Who did you rescue?'

'A few pensioners, schoolchildren. It was no big deal.'

'I believe you, though Splash Radio just now made it sound as if there was a heroine involved. They are searching for you. The police want to question you and the mayor wants to give you tea in his parlour.' Holly was smiling.

'No way. It wasn't me. I have to protect my clients' anonymity. If the police started to question me, they might get curious about my destination, my client and why she is a client. Now, one would not want that, would one, especially after a spectacular Old Bailey acquittal?'

It was ambiguous enough to satisfy Holly. Mrs Malee brought in a tray of coffee, silver coffee pot, pretty china with a plate of smoked salmon rolls and a dish of fresh grapes.

Two cups of black coffee and I was feeling more up to speed. I even ate some of the refreshments, but Holly did not touch anything. That's how she kept her perfect figure.

'So, Jordan, tell me what you have found out so far,' she drawled. 'I hope it's something interesting.'

I took a deep breath. I was not sure what to tell her. It did not amount to much, but it had to sound a lot in order to justify her generous payment and the smoked salmon.

'I have met your husband and he was rather unpleasant,' I said with feeling. 'I can understand why you might want to get rid of him, but it would be simpler to divorce him through the courts. You might be a few million less wealthy, but surely it would be worth it? You would have your freedom and your dignity.'

'Nice speech, Jordan. Carry on.'

'I understand he has a replacement ready and willing to fill your shoes, so it could be a simple procedure. Get yourself a good lawyer and fill in the forms.' I don't know what made me say that. It was something in the evidence about a good friend.

This was a calculated guess on my part. It was possible. Rich men gather women like honey. And he was handsome in a ruthless way. Holly looked stunned. It was obviously news to her.

'Someone else? Is this true? I never knew,' Holly faltered. 'But then he's always surrounded by beautiful women, throwing themselves at him. And he flies all over the world with perfect freedom. It's not surprising, although I thought we were so happy. Yes, we've always been so happy...'

'Perhaps *you* were happy, but did you ever ask him if he was happy?'

'No, he always acted as if he was happy.'

'And I bet he was. He had the best of both worlds: loving wife in the country, model number two tucked tidily away in London. Who could ask for anything more?'

Line from song. I had been playing Gershwin a lot.

'Are you sure you didn't know?' I went on. 'It makes a very strong motive for murder.'

Holly was shaking her head. 'So do you want me to carry on?' I said, as if I was about to throw in the bath towel and the soap and the loofah.

'Yes,' she said, grimly, but not drinking at all. 'I want you to find out how he set me up. And find out who she is. If there is someone else, it gives him a motive for putting me behind bars. Convicted prisoners wouldn't get alimony, even in an open prison, would they? Do you think I would have got an open prison?'

I invented a smile. 'They'd have fixed an ankle tag on you and put you up at Claridges.'

That made her smile too. She ate a grape. Was that lunch?

'There's one thing I would like to know, Jordan,' she said, taking a second grape. Dessert? 'Why were you following me in Brighton? Why was I under surveillance? That wasn't very nice of you. Rather dented my confidence in your services.'

Ah. No point in lying. She had spotted me.

'It was accidental. I was not following you then, though I was later.' Clear as mud, as

114

usual. 'I went into the café for a coffee. I'd been visiting a friend in hospital.'

'But then you did start following me.'

'Yes, when I saw you handing over a jewellery box to the man you were talking to. It was a flat leather box, the kind they use for necklaces.'

'I know what kind of box it was,' she said tartly. 'It was my box and what I was doing with it is none of your business.'

'Everything you do is my business,' I said with remarkable control. 'That is, if you want me to find out the truth.'

'And you decided to follow me?' So the Islamic scarf hadn't fooled her. Not a competent disguise.

'Yes. Until you disappeared down the pub trapdoor.'

'I beg your pardon?'

'I lost you. We were outside a bank that used to be a pub. Did you go down the chute into the barrel-delivery area?'

'In these clothes? You think I would go down a chute, voluntarily? You're joking.' Holly looked amused. 'I appreciate your diligence, Jordan, but I did go into the bank quite normally. I was withdrawing quite a lot of cash from my account. And the jewellery box was a diamond-and-sapphire necklace, a gift from the devoted Richard, worth a lot of money. I was trying to raise money on it. My companion was a jewellery broker. He asks no questions.'

I drew a long, deep breath. How was I going to talk my way out of this one? Surprisingly, I was feeling quite odd. The room was swaying. I decided to go home. It seemed very desirable to find a cocoon where I could hide.

'You need money?' My voice sounded a long way away.

'I need a substantial amount. It's a business deal.'

'That's very s-strange...'

Holly's face seemed to waver before me as if caught in a broken mirror. She was still saying something but I didn't catch the words. Mrs Malee came to take away the tray and her face turned into a small, bruised moon. I tried to remember her name. I made to lift my mouth into a word but it didn't work. It was an uneasy moment, and as I slid back into the chair, my last thought was what on earth was happening?

Something like an elephant was plodding through my head. It was a jungle and I had been ambushed. Now the mayor would never give me tea in his parlour.

Eight

Pebbles are hard, round objects and several hundred were prodding my soft places. They are even harder on bones. I was too stiff to move. I opened one eye and a small, wrinkled, black creature was about to attack my nose. It was a scorpion. A gust of panic sprayed sand over me.

I was on a deserted shore, miles from any beach hut, café, car park, litter sign. Where was this place? I didn't recognize the stretch and I had once walked all the way from Latching to Littlehampton for a cup of hot chocolate at the swimming pool.

The other eye opened and I focused on the frond of dried seaweed near my face. Not quite so predatory, on second thoughts. For a moment I wondered if I was still me, but the hot-chocolate memory proved that I was.

The sun was warming my face, the sky a washed blue, and clouds drifted like migrating flamingoes. They were flamingoes, flying through the sky. I could have watched them for hours, but some sense told me it was not sensible. Tides come in and tides go out and it occurred to me that my feet were getting wet.

I sat up abruptly without finding my elbow. My left elbow had disappeared in a curtain of skin. A rush of tiny waves were swirling round the crater my heels had made in the pebbles. These were my second-best trainers. A bigger wave chased me further up the slope, slithering on my bottom as the pebbles slid away from under me. How on earth had I got here?

It was coming back to me. What a morning ... my solo trip to the pub, the hold-up on the bus, and my slightly frosty meeting with Holly Broughton. She had not been as friendly as before. Perhaps she hadn't liked being spotted in Brighton. Why had she been trying to raise some money by selling a necklace? Was she paying someone to keep quiet? It had a different kind of smell.

But how had I got here? I climbed up the slope to the top of the beach with knees that did not work, starting to feel sick. It was empty, not a fishing boat in sight, sparse windward bushes along the edge, withered by the salt air. There had to be some way back to civilization.

I stumbled on for some hundreds of yards or metres, according to your taste, peering through tangled scrub for some long-lost smugglers' path. These beaches had seen some smuggling in the past – brandy, cloth, spices, even gold. Heaving boats and lines of men humping the casks ashore at the dead of night.

The lowering sun reminded me of the time, that soon night would fall with a suddenness, but not until the sky had been shot with red and gold and a stream of silver shimmered along the sea.

An unexpected gust of wind separated some branches and I saw the makings of a path. The shrubs were singing, birds swaying. No, I mean the other way round. It had definitely once been a path, trodden earth, nettles growing each side, sweeping down branches of sad bushes. I shot off the beach, taking a chance.

Evening. Where had I been all afternoon – or which day was it? I remembered going to Faunstone Hall but not much else now. It felt as if I had been drugged, because this was not a normal-feeling ill feeling. I wasn't ill. I was getting better. The bulge in my pocket assured me that I had not lost the camera. I had lost something else but I couldn't remember what it was. Pity the camera was not automated to take candid shots every other minute. Then I might have known where I had been and what had happened.

Head down, brambles tearing at my hair, my feet slipping on muddy patches. Rain drifted in drapes and scallops and festoons.

It was a trek to the unknown. I prayed that I was not going round in circles and would find myself back on the beach. I was in a fantod state, word gleaned from *Countdown*, watched while in hospital. What hospital?

My feet squelched, a smell rising like stale eggs. It was unpleasant, as if the ground was contaminated. It might be refuse or something worse. I didn't wait to find out.

Light loomed ahead and I hurried forward, nearly tripping, clutching at branches which scratched my hands. I came out on a narrow road which also seemed deserted. But it was some sort of civilization and I walked quickly in the direction of Latching, taking the setting sun as my west. West was Cornwall, east was Brighton. I hadn't been a Girl Guide for nothing.

The road stopped abruptly. It was a cul-de-sac. Posts stood across the tarmac, chained, with notices warning trespassers. The posts might stop cars or horses, but they weren't intended to prevent pedestrians. And certainly not pedestrians who were becoming desperate to get home, somehow, anyhow. I started to run and walk, on a sward of grass now, hoping to get my legs working again.

This was part of a big private estate with gardens sweeping down to the sea, towering hedges so that no one could peep and spoil privacy. Wind-blown shrubs bore the onslaught of gale force 8 and 9 gusts, the ferocity that the Sussex coast had to endure. The houses were big, sprawling mansions, 1930s era, gabled or thatched, flat-roofed, Georgian. The styles were all different, architects let loose with blank cheques. No sign of people, but I bet there were plenty of very noisy dogs ready to pounce on intruders.

My mind had slipped into neutral. I still couldn't find my elbow. The flamingoes had turned into white witches, broomsticks pointing east to Lapland. Physical cramp was slowing me down but I couldn't remember what to do about it. I was a walking fruit salad.

To the left was a five-barred gate that led to a wide grass avenue between houses. It was left-over land that no one had bought and was not large enough to sell as a plot. My fingers fumbled with the bolt and I opened the gate but forgot to close it.

It wasn't walking now, or running; it was crawling. The grass was damp and smelled of lawn mowers. No one was around. This was no man's land. Perhaps no one lived here any more and all the houses were empty. Everyone had run away to the moon.

Dusk was descending in folds and I could see the crescent edge of a new moon. Luck says turn your money over when you see a new moon. I didn't have any money, not even that ten-pence piece.

I heard footsteps, or was it the pattering of rats? Rats come out at night and it was almost night.

'Hello, is anyone there? Do you need help?'

The voice washed over me like an uneasy buckle of noise. It grated on raw edges. I had not heard a voice for hours and hours. There was a void of voices.

'Hello, this is security. Who's there? Answer me, please. Do you need help?'

I nodded. I needed help.

I heard crunching feet. They were breaking the grass. Splinters of grass spattered across my face. I saw boots stamping in front of me, several of them, toecaps laced with strands of grass, bits bitten off by the rats.

'Is that Miss Lacey, Jordan Lacey?'

The name seemed familiar. Yes, that was someone I knew.

'I don't know. I'm not s-sure,' I said, dredging sound from somewhere within my throat.

I felt myself being lifted up by a pair of arms. There was nothing I could do about it. I was seeing a man, quite ordinary but tall and well built, wearing dark clothes. He wore glasses and light from a lamp some-where reflected off them. There was some-one else in a uniform but I could not see him properly.

'Miss Lacey. We've been looking for you.

Don't be afraid. I'm going to take you home. You are quite safe now.'

'Do you have some water?' I said, mouth very dry. Yes, I wanted water. That was it. I needed water.

'Of course. There's a bottle of water in the car. Come along, I'll help you walk. Your legs are a bit unsteady.'

'I don't have any knees,' I said.

'Yes, you do. Your knees are quite all right. Perhaps you can't feel them but they are there.'

'And I've lost my elbow.'

'Your elbow is OK. Both elbows present. Perfectly OK.'

'Thank goodness,' I said. 'I thought I had lost them.'

It dawned on me that I was talking nonsense. This was complete rubbish. What was making me say it?

'Where is this?'

'It's near Climping. Quite a way from Latching. We've been searching for you.'

'Why?'

'Detective Inspector James was worried. You weren't answering your phone. There had been nothing from you for hours. He knew something must have happened. You are usually pretty good at reporting back.'

'Am I?'

'Can't you remember anything?'

I was being put into a car in the front

passenger seat. The man with glasses fastened the seat belt and gave me a bottle of mineral water, twisting the cap off. I drank and drank. I love water. The taste was cool. It spread through me, trickling along all the little veins and channels.

'Try, Miss Lacey. Try to remember what happened.'

I dredged through my mind. It was like a sponge sodden with slime. If only I could tap the fluid and grab at a few nuggets of information.

'I went somewhere this morning,' I began, struggling. The man was driving the car slowly along a road, the other policeman sitting in the back. I didn't really care. It was warm in the car. 'I was doing something.'

'Good. Well done. Then what happened?'

'Something about a bus.'

'A bus. You were on a bus? What can you tell me about it?'

The bus. It was crowded. 'I was looking into people's gardens. I put my camera under the seat.'

'Excellent. Why did you put your camera under the seat?'

'Because, because...' It escaped me. We were driving along leafy lanes, lined with identical retirement bungalows. Neat front gardens, tidily parked cars. They looked so normal. I had to trust this person. He said he was taking me home.

'Try to think, Miss Lacey. It could be important.'

'Coffee, I remember coffee in a silver pot. Lovely china. And little rolls of bread filled with smoked salmon.'

'They don't serve those on buses. Was it somewhere else?'

'Yes, I was somewhere else.'

'Then you found yourself at Climping?'

'On a beach with scorpions and flamingoes and white witches. It was awful. I couldn't move. My elbow had gone.'

'Miss Lacey, please don't be alarmed. Although I said I would take you home, actually I think I should take you to hospital. I think you have been drugged, probably with the date-rape drug, Rohypnol – or roofies, as they call it. It suppresses the central nervous system and respiratory system. It's tasteless and odourless and ten times stronger than Valium.'

'I don't understand,' I said vaguely. I didn't understand anything, but some sort of world was swimming back. 'I wasn't on a date.'

'I have to get you to hospital. All traces of this drug disappear after twenty-four hours. You need to be tested. Please trust me. I was taking you home but now I'm taking you to hospital.'

A dark velvet curtain seemed to draw apart. I saw a flash of light.

'Are you taking me to the hospital where

125

DI James is? The same one in Brighton?'

'It's the nearest big hospital with the equipment.'

'That's all right then,' I sighed.

I seemed to switch off into sleep as we sped along some fast road, under bridges and through underpasses. The oncoming traffic was all lights, headlights flashing in the dark. I let myself drift into slumber, trusting this man with the pleasant voice and glasses. He wasn't hurting me. His voice was full of concern. He sat beside me, a comforting bulk, knowing what to do with driving a car.

'Do I know you?' I asked, remembering something.

'I drove you home once before.'

'Luke?' The name came out of some abyss.

'It's Duke, actually. Duke Morton. Detective Sergeant Duke Morton. I'm new. I was recently transferred from Newcastle. Perhaps they thought I needed a break.'

'I think I've got your coat.'

I don't exactly remember the tests. I fell asleep on the trolley and was out for what seemed hours. Hospitals are not my favourite places. I have been in more hospitals than most people have had hot takeaways. It's a wonder that I am not banned, forbidden entrance, no more drips, transfusions, X-rays. I'm a drain on the NHS.

DI James was pretending to be asleep

when I was allowed up and went into his room, although the television was flickering in a corner. It was distressing to see him so still and immobile after being such an active man. His toes came almost to the end of the bed. He was a six-footer but it looked as if he had stretched a few more inches.

'Come in,' he said. 'Stop dithering in the doorway. I'm sick of television. Anyone will do.'

'This anyone is also a patient, so speak to me nicely,' I said. I still had my own clothes on, even though they were filthy. I pulled up a chair and sat on it gingerly.

'I heard from Duke Morton. So they found you. What had you been up to? Why didn't you keep in touch?'

'Because I couldn't and I can't remember why I couldn't. That's it – I didn't have my phone with me. It needed recharging.'

'Always charge your phone overnight.'

'Thank you, O Guru of Mobile Wisdom.'

'What's been happening to you? Duke tells me he found you crawling about in Climping looking for a lost elbow.' James hid a smile. But it was not funny.

'I don't really know what happened. I think I was drugged with something, somewhere. Surely not by Holly or Mrs Malee? They are such nice people. It doesn't seem possible. I wish I could remember what happened. There were flamingoes in the sky and then they turned into witches...'

'Confusion, Jordan, one of the side effects of Rohypnol. It suppresses the central nervous system and respiratory system. But all traces disappear after twenty-four hours so Duke did right to bring you straight to hospital. Have you been tested?'

I nodded, thanks to the bottle of water I drank in the car.

'And the result?'

'Don't know yet.'

'I want to know everything. What else have you been doing?'

The drug was still filtering out of my body but I felt I could remember most of what had happened, except afterwards. That bit was a confused blank.

'I went to the pub,' I began. I almost said, 'as ordered'. 'I had a good look round but I would have needed a ladder to get up to the canopy over the bar. The two proprietors were there and the second one was not at all pleased to see me. But I found the suit of armour in the boiler room and there definitely seemed to have been some tampering to the means of securing it to the canopy.'

'What do you mean?'

'I don't know. Sawn bits.'

'That's not good enough.'

'Did you know that they are going to move the Medieval Hall to some other site? The owner has sold it to a Russian football millionaire with a mansion in West Sussex.'

'I know that.'

'Did you oppose it? On the grounds of wasting public money, of course. It's the kind of thing you would do.'

'I did.'

'So maybe someone wants to get rid of you, or at least put you out of action for a few months while the Hall is moved.'

'That is possible. What an astute mind you have, Jordan. Have you recorded the evidence before they decide to remove it?'

'Record the evidence. Why don't you say did you take any photos? You talk like a policeman.' I nearly said, No wonder your wife left you; but then I remembered the horrific circumstances. She must have been unhinged, to take the lives of two little boys. James was still grieving. He would grieve for the rest of his life.

'Well, are there any photos?' His voice softened with half a degree of warmth. Perhaps he was mellowing. I straightened a sheet that didn't need straightening. I wanted to put my hand over his. I wanted to send him strength and healing. He was holding on to his computerized control panel.

'Yes, I took photos, different angles. Flash camera. Not yet developed, but then a lot has happened since.'

James did not seem to mind my hand on his. I did not know now whether to remove it or how to remove it without drawing attention to the fact. It could look like an accidental touch. It was a moment of decision and one I could not make. My hand lingered and absorbed his warmth. He had never held my hand, but I was holding his.

James came to my rescue. 'Could you pour me a glass of water, please, Jordan?'

I flashed him a smile of relief for having been extracted from a tricky situation. He was still drinking from a silly cup with a spout, so that he didn't have to sit up. He couldn't sit up. Of course some spilled, so I dabbed it up with a towel.

'Thank you,' he said. 'Quite the little mother figure.'

'Not long now,' I said.

'No, not long.'

'You'll know soon what the doctors think.'

'Thank you for reminding me. What else has happened?'

He was hopeless. I couldn't have a normal conversation with him when he was so touchy. It wasn't kosher to smart-answer a sick and helpless man. Not fair on either of us.

'Apparently there was a hold-up on a bus, a hoodie wanting money for a fix.'

'So I heard on local radio. He was tackled by some plucky schoolgirl heroine who took off rather than talk to anyone.'

'Very plucky.'

'But you've saved your camera? Well done. Have the shots developed as soon as you can. I want to see them and get a police expert to give me an opinion.'

'As soon as they let me go home.'

'Duke will drive you.'

'Is this a permanent arrangement?' I asked, quite saucy. 'My own police driver? Cool. I'd like that.'

'Don't push your luck,' he scowled. 'And don't say "cool". It isn't professional.'

He was getting better. That was the old DI James.

Nine

They let me go home as soon as I was given the all-clear. I was told, strict instructions, to take it quietly for a few days, write out a few price tags, dust a few books. Nothing strenuous. Maybe I'd take their advice for the first half-hour.

Again and again I went over my visit to Faunstone Hall. It had to have happened then. I remembered that Holly had not had any coffee. And she'd been annoyed with me. For being a good detective? But I could not believe that Holly or Mrs Malee would have spiked my coffee. There was no reason. To scare me? To get me out of the way? I could see no sense to it.

I sat quietly on my button-back Victorian chair the next morning. If it had had the magic words 'Howard & Sons' on its underside, it would have been worth £3,000, the Rolls-Royce of armchairs. Fortunately it had nothing and was worth only a few hundred pounds, so I could sit on it without worrying.

A long time ago, it seemed, I had been

checking through a box of old books, bought as a job lot. There had been a book on Sussex history which might bring in a few pounds. The rest of the box had been rubbish, or had it?

Nothing strenuous, they'd said. Rifling through a few old books was not strenuous. Dust rose politely, but not enough to bring on my asthma. Old orange- and green-covered Penguin issues, Enid Blytons, Agatha Christies, a scrapbook full of postcards.

The tooled-leather cover had a patina of sweat and polish. They were seaside pictures, ladies in flounced swimming costumes bathing from machines, children in sailor suits playing on the beach. Then further on came war pictures, bedraggled soldiers in mud-filled trenches, desolate battlefields with crippled canons and pillboxes, rows of gravestones. World War One, the bloodiest of them all. If I had the energy this should go to an auction in Chichester. It would be worth far more than my usual £6 ticket. I'd hardly get drugged at an auction.

The rest of the Japanese Arita blue-and-white ware had gone quickly, as I'd known it would. The window needed redressing or the customers would be nil. Teddy bears. There was a box of teddy bears out the back, a rumble-tumble of beige and gold mohair plush that I had collected from charity shops. I couldn't resist abandoned teddy bears. Their faces pleaded with me to take them home. But it was time to move on, to rehome them. I doubted if there would be a Steiff or a Chad Valley bear among them, but people would love them all the same.

Some of the oldest bears were in plastic bags with mothballs to kill any infestation. I fished out a black bear, much sought after, and put him in the centre of the window, then surrounded him with bears of all shapes and sizes. Then I arranged a set of doll-sized teacups and saucers in front of them, as if they were having a bear party.

The door flew open and a woman came in, bright-eyed and eager. She was tidily dressed but everything was of the 1950s era, left over from her youth or charity-shop buys.

'I've just spotted that bear,' she said. 'That one in the window. I think he used to be mine. I'm so excited. He vanished when I got married. My mother threw him out. I didn't know where he'd gone and I missed him so much.'

Oh dear, one of those tear-jerking stories. My £6 ticket began rapidly dwindling. How could I possibly charge her £6 for her own bear? This was becoming a charity shop, not First Class Junk, apparently, dispensing charity to all and sundry.

It was an ordinary brown sort of bear, no shoebutton eyes or distinctive button mark in the ear. He looked a bit chewed. The paw pads needed mending, a few stitches. I took him out of the window and removed the price ticket.

'You'd better take him home then,' I said. 'He needs some tender loving care.'

'Oh yes, he does ... How much, miss?'

'Are you sure he's your bear?'

'Oh yes, I'm sure. He's my bear all right. I always chewed that ear.'

'Then you can have him.'

She was genuinely pleased, words getting all mixed up. Her pension didn't stretch to impulse buys. She kept patting my arm, which was a bit embarrassing.

'I can't thank you enough, young lady miss,' she kept saying. 'Don't wrap him up. I want him to see and breathe the air. I'm going to show him the sea. Teddy, I called him.'

'I'm sure he'll like the sea,' I said. 'Good-bye, Teddy.' I waved to him. He had a sort of pleased look too, which was somewhat alarming. He'd looked quite downhearted before. It didn't matter whether he was her childhood bear or not. If she thought he was, then he was home and dry. Honey for tea for ever.

'I've got a box of bits and pieces at home,' she said, as she was going out of the door. 'Shall I bring them to you? I'm down-sizing, as they say. Two rooms to one.'

'Thank you,' I said. 'Any time.'

I needed sight of the sea as much as Teddy. I closed the shop, bought some rosy apples from Doris and made my way to the beach. The tide was on the turn with the sea pounding the shingle. I crunched my way to a groyne and found a length of timber to sit on that was not wet.

The waves thrashed the moving pebbles, coming towards me in great rolls of moss-green water topped with dancing white. They spoke to me in a language that I couldn't understand. They grumbled and rumbled, whisking and whispering, washing the hidden edge of sand with teasing wavelets. Baby crabs struggled to find old hiding places. Seaweed streamed like green threads in a Chinese soup.

The apples were sweet and juicy but I was not sure if they were breakfast or lunch. My mobile rang and I answered the call. It was Holly Broughton.

'Jordan, Jordan. Are you all right?'

'Just about.'

'Thank God, thank God. We were so worried. We didn't know what to do. We thought you were dead. Mrs Malee and me, we were distraught. Who found you?'

'The police and a security officer. They were out looking for me. So it was you who dumped me on Climping beach?'

'Yes, we were at our wits' end. I'm sorry if

it was the wrong thing to do, but you couldn't be found at the Hall. We couldn't have that – not after me being accused of plotting to murder my husband. I couldn't go through all that interrogation again. It would have been the end of me.'

'So you dumped me on Climping beach,' I repeated. 'Rather callous, wasn't it? I find it difficult to believe.'

'But you were found, weren't you? So that's all right. I'm so relieved. I'm sorry if you've had a bad time but we couldn't be involved. Perhaps we should have taken you to a hospital.'

'Exactly. It would have been more sensible to dump me on the doorstep of Latching hospital. A beach in the middle of nowhere is not signposted for the paramedics. Fortunately I have good friends and they were out looking for me or I could have drowned on that beach. The tide was coming in.'

Holly caught her breath. 'I'm so sorry, Jordan. I didn't want this to happen. I had no idea. We weren't thinking straight.'

They weren't thinking at all. She sounded sincere but it was so naive. Surely she'd known I might die on the beach? Perhaps she was a hinge missing on the top shelf. It had been a gross error of judgement. The seagulls cawked a flat note. I swallowed a healthy retort. I thought I heard a movement, a chair scraping.

'Well, I was rescued, so we won't talk about it any more. All I want to know is who put the drug in my coffee? Is that why you didn't have any?'

'No, no. I try to cut down on coffee. It isn't good for you. I don't know anything about a drug or what anyone put in your coffee. All I know is that you suddenly slumped over and passed out and were hardly breathing. We thought it was a stroke.'

'I'm so glad you didn't call 999 for an ambulance,' I said dryly. 'I didn't have my clean undies on.'

'I realize now that we should have done, but at the time we just wanted to get you out of the house. Mrs Malee helped me get you into the car and we drove to the beach,' Holly went on. It sounded like a pack of lies. She was breathing fast as if she wanted to tell me something urgently. 'Where are you now, Jordan?'

I wondered if the call was being recorded or someone was there, listening in. It made me look over my shoulder. The beach was deserted apart from a distant man walking his dog. It was a shaggy sort of collie.

'Holly? Mrs Broughton? Are you still there?' But the phone was dead. She had gone, though her voice lingered. All I could hear was the waves and the gulls in concert. It was a raucous tune and I didn't have to buy a ticket.

It was time to do some work on the hens and rabbits case but I had no idea where to start. There was a big pet shop in Latching that sold puppies and kittens as well as food, baskets, kennels, bird baths and bouncy cushions. The window was full of hand-written adverts looking for good homes for sweet, adorable, frisky little baby animals of all kinds, furred and feathered.

Three adverts were selling lop-eared rabbits. I took the phone numbers and spent an interesting few hours looking at various bunny rabbits. They all looked the same: long-eared, nose-twitching, suspicious. Some almost matched the description of the missing rabbits. I took photos of them all, making sure I included some background details so that later I could identify where I was. The owners were terribly impressed.

'I want to buy them for my niece who is visiting me soon, so if I send her photos, she'll be able to chose which ones she would like.'

'That's very sweet. You must be very fond of her.'

'I am.'

'Let's hope you find the rabbits she likes.'

'I'm sure I shall.'

This finished up the film and I took it to be processed and printed. I paid the top price for the hourly service, which went against the grain, but there were the pub photos on the same film and James wanted to see them. A reason to visit him again, photos hardly dry in my hand.

A whole hour free. It was an oasis of time just for me. Not enough time to solve a case, or open the shop and sell anything, or go to an auction. But I could lie in the bath and let lavender oil soothe away the last traumatic hours. I turned on the tap. A little smooth jazz would help. I wondered where my famous jazz trumpeter was these days. I had not seen him for a long time. When he came to Latching, it was always as if he had never been away. When he played the trumpet, those teasing melodies, and the high notes, melted my bones.

I picked up the developed photos. The ladybird started up without a murmur, a little spurt and she began to move as if glad to see me. I eased her out of the parking lot behind my shop and drove to Brighton. This was becoming autopilot. I wanted to take James a gift but perhaps the photos were enough.

He had not moved an inch since the last time I'd seen him. That was the treatment. Not to move him till the fragment eased away or dissolved.

'Spinal waistcoat next week, Jordan,' he said without looking at me. 'Things are looking up, thanks to you. If you had sat me up after the crash, the sharp slither of bone would have gone straight back and sliced my spinal cord.'

I nodded knowingly, as if I was a qualified neurosurgeon.

'And what about this bit of bone?'

'They reckon it will eventually dissolve. Light physiotherapy and then maybe, after a scan, I'll be allowed back on duty.'

'Does that mean your transfer north?'

'No, that post has been filled.'

Hurrah. I curbed a desire to dance wildly round the room. 'Oh dear, I'm so sorry,' I said with false sincerity.

'No, you're not. Now, show me the photos. I'm hoping you have brought them with you. Hold them where I can see them. Put the light on.'

'Use your remote. I know you can put the light on yourself.'

I fed him the photos. They were pretty good if you knew what you were looking for. Close-ups of hinges and screws and brackets. Very art deco. His eyes glinted.

'These are good,' he said. 'You've done well. I'll get them blown up. I'd like an expert's opinion. Does the owner know you've taken these photos?'

'No, I sort of got ordered out. The owner was quite nasty. He didn't like me looking around. But the other one was nice. He offered me a pineapple juice.'

'The other one – what other one? You're

141

getting confused again.'

'No, I didn't get drugged until long afterwards, remember? Events were in this order: ghost-busting visit to Medieval Hall, bus hold-up then being drugged.'

'My brain is still working, thank you, Jordan.'

'I'm glad about that.'

'And what are these other photos? Ah, dear little bunny rabbits. How delightfully sweet. I didn't know you were into the species. Are you planning to keep rabbits?'

'This is my other case. The stolen property from an allotment on Topham Hill. My client is Arthur Spiddock. He's got a dog called Nutty. I'm trying to find his rabbits and hens. It's not easy. No leads at all. Not a feather in sight.'

'And what's this photo?' He nodded to a blurred one, which I had skipped over, taken halfway between pub and rabbits.

'I don't know. I don't remember taking any other photos. Let me see. Heavens, it's on the bus. Look that's the hoodie that held up the passengers. A bit sideways, but if you turn it round, like this ... It must have taken itself as I took the camera out of my pocket to hide it under the seat. It does happen, you know. The button gets pressed accidentally. Once I took an excellent photo of the pavement outside M & S.'

'You'd better let the station have this one.

Sergeant Rawlings is back on duty, so give it to him. Any kind of evidence is always useful. He's due in court tomorrow morning and will probably plead it wasn't him. Mistaken identity.'

'They all look alike these days.'

'This one doesn't. Look at the tattoo on his hand.'

It was a serpent curled round a dagger. Very fetching. Not easy to forget.

'I'll take it in,' I said, putting the photo back into the folder with the rabbits. 'It'll give me a chance to say hi to Sergeant Rawlings. I'm glad he's better.'

'He was on the point of retirement but got talked out of it. Recruitment is slow these days. We are under-manned.'

'Aren't you suppose to say under-personed these days? You know, political correctness.'

'Go home and have a bath,' he said, closing his eyes as if he was tired of the sight of me.

'I've just had one.'

His phone rang and he activated the voice. 'Yes? What? I'll ask her.' He looked towards me, his face blank. 'When did you last see Holly Broughton?'

'Yesterday, about lunch time, at Faunstone Hall when my coffee was drugged. I was talking to her there then.'

'Yesterday about lunch time at Faunstone Hall,' he repeated down the phone.

'But I also spoke to her earlier this morning on my mobile,' I went on.

'Why didn't you say that?'

'You asked me when did I last see her. Different verb, James. She phoned me this morning when I was sitting on the beach eating an apple.'

James was exasperated. 'Did she sound all right?'

'Well, I don't really know what all right is. She sounded different, stressed. She phoned to apologize for dumping me on Climping beach and leaving me there to die.'

'I don't believe it. You're too heavy for a woman to lift.'

'Then how did I get there?'

'I don't know. Then what?'

'Then nothing. She rang off.'

'Why didn't you tell me all this?'

'You didn't ask me. Look, you are obviously in a very bad mood and I don't blame you for that. I think I'd better go before you leap out of that bed and bite my head off.'

'Don't go.' He said something else, not to me but to his caller, then rang off. His eyes looked very tired. And he wasn't even on duty, up all hours, no time off for a sleep. He'd had more sleep in that bed than he'd had in a lifetime.

'Have you had a look at the new wood garden being built on the far end of Latching beach?' he asked.

'You mean all those trunks of upright wood and rock and the occasional plant that grows without soil? I suppose it'll be all right when it's finished, but a beach is a beach and trees are a forest and never the twain should meet.'

'I've some bad news for you,' said James.

News from James is always bad news. When was there ever good news? If you won the lottery, that was good news. If you forgot to buy your usual ticket, that was bad news.

'Tell me.'

'It's about Holly Broughton. They've found her impaled on one of the stakes in the wood garden on the beach. When she phoned you, it was probably only moments before she was killed. Perhaps she knew they were going to kill her.'

A talon of fear gripped my heart. Her killer had been with her when she'd phoned. I knew that now. The strangeness in her voice had been suffocating, primeval panic.

Ten

Holly Broughton. It was one of those things you could hardly believe. Such a lively, glamorous woman and so pleasant in many ways. Yet my traitor mind produced another thought. I had lost a case. A paying case. And a well-paid case. Shame on you, Jordan. But I could hardly bill her estate for work logged before her death. I'd lost out on this one.

I went home and drove along the marine promenade past the newly built wooden beach garden. It was swarming with police and cordons and flashing lights and vans. A tent had been erected on the beach, among the statuesque pieces of wood, the rocks and palm trees. Kids skateboarded on the opposite pavement, neck-craning. Dogs were being walked on the beach. A police helicopter hovered in the air. It was nearly normal.

Suspects. That was police routine. Husband? Extracting revenge. Maybe one of her contacts wanting more than a diamond necklace. Blackmail? Had Mrs Malee been blackmailing her for a sum she refused to pay? I could think of a half dozen suspects. But not one really sound motive.

But it wasn't my case any more. I could bow out. I'd got the photographs for James. Photographs for Arthur Spiddock. Photograph of bus hoodie. Quite soon I'd be Latching's photographer of the year.

It was accidental that I checked my current account. I asked the wall for a mini statement to be printed out, more out of curiosity than anything. I'd spent so little recently, my frugal habits difficult to shed. The balance of the reward money was untouchable as I'd invested in a pension to be drawn when I was sixty. If I lasted that long. Thirty years ahead. I couldn't imagine being that old, but it would come. I was hoping the capital would have grown in pace with inflation. I'd probably still be living in two bedsits or down-sizing like the teddy-bear woman.

There was quite a tidy balance. An un-accountable cheque for £500 had been paid in. I couldn't think where it had come from. It meant queuing in a slow queue while people with nothing else to do chatted to the cashiers. Trance time. When it was my turn, I had almost forgotten why I was there.

'A cheque for £500 has been paid into my account,' I said. 'Can you tell me where it came from?'

The girl did all sorts of clever things with

her keyboard and screen. She probably even knew my blood type. Then she scribbled something on a notepad and passed a piece of paper under the bullet-proof grill.

'There you are,' she said with a flourish, like completing a magic trick.

'Thank you.' I took the scrap of paper to a quiet corner in case the content was explosive. Holly Broughton. She had paid in £500 to my account, without even being asked. My bank account details were on the contract form that she had signed, down at the bottom, in small print, just in case.

The bank had a leisure area of tan-leather armchairs and a coffee table, but no coffee; so I sat in one for a minute of comfortable thinking. If Holly Broughton had paid me £500 for what I had done so far, it meant that I still owed her considerable time. It was the least I could do. Work off the balance.

How did she die? Hopefully not impaled on a stake. It would take a long time to die like that. Someone would have seen her and called an ambulance. Maybe she was already dead when the gruesome scene was set. A bit like my nun on a butcher's hook. She had taken many months to forget. But some details were still fresh.

I pottered round to the station, the new brick one, all shiny and modern. I couldn't get used to it. The body-heat-activated automatic doors, the glass screen at the desk, the barrage of computers. I'd never get a cup of tea here.

'Sergeant Rawlings, please,' I said.

'Have you got an appointment?' said the WPO, very small and pert. Wasn't there a height measurement for women?

'I don't need an appointment,' I said, using every centimetre of my five foot eight. 'I'm Investigator Lacey.'

That sounded very grand. Vaguely American, FBI, White House, undercover work. The days of thick tea and fluff-coated biscuits were long gone. The old station was being pulled down to build a block of retirement flats.

Sergeant Rawlings came to the desk. I got a shock. He looked a lot older, skin hanging on a crippled structure. I was appalled. His hands were gripping the edge of the counter.

'What on earth has happened to you?' I said, unable to be less blunt. He'd been my friend for years, especially during the time when I was an WPO and had been suspended for defending the truth.

'Bloody arthritis,' he said. 'Everywhere hurts. But I don't want to go. What would I do at home? Watch telly all day, like a moron.'

It came in a flash. 'You could work for me,' I said.

'Perfect,' he said, grinning. 'Any time. Sign me on.'

It was done, just like that. I had staff.

'But first,' I said. 'I need some information. About Holly Broughton. She's my client – was my client, and still is. She paid me in advance, and there's a signed contract. How did she die? Have you any information?'

'We don't have much.'

'What do you know?'

'I'm not supposed to tell anyone.'

'How about a cup of tea instead, hoping the brew has improved. And a biscuit. I'm starving.'

'Come through. I'll activate the doors.'

'It used to be "I'll open the door".'

'Times change. It's all coded. The code changes every month. I have to write it down on my hand.'

They even had new mugs. But the tea bags were the same dust-off-the-floor variety. I sat on a new chair, dunking a crisp Rich Tea. Five out of five.

'So what do you know about Holly Brou-ghton, recently discovered in the wooden beach garden?'

'A milkman found her this morning. Quite put him off his round. She'd been dead for some time.'

'Was she fully clothed?'

'Yes. But no shoes. She'd lost those on the way. No signs of injury, apart from those inflicted by the stake and I won't go into those. You wouldn't want to hear about them, Jordan. No GBH, no gunshot wounds, no knife. Not drowned or asphyxiated.'

'Autopsy?' She was probably drugged beforehand, like me.

'Too soon for that. And I won't have access to it, you know that. CID stuff. I could lose my job telling you all this.' He eased himself into a chair. He was stiff all right. His joints were creaking and the pain was etched on his face.

'I've just offered you another job.'

'With a pension?'

'Don't be greedy. You'll get a police pension.'

'I've got expensive tastes.'

He grinned at me. He lived in a thirties semi-detached at the back end of Latching. He had a bit of garden, an old car and a saucy grandson on whom he doted. His idea of an expensive meal would be a Thai take-away and a pint of Guinness.

I finished my tea and took the mugs to wash them up. He nodded his thanks. 'I can see you'll be a good boss.'

'Don't bank on it. I can be a tartar. But thanks for the tea. By the way, here's a photo of the bus hoodie, taken in the bus. Look at the tattoo, quite unusual.'

'You're a star, Jordan. I'll give it to the officer in charge of the case. The young lad won't give his name or address. Says its mistaken identity.'

There were things to do. But I had acquired the door code for the month. I'd read it upside down on the back of his hand. Might come in handy.

I ought to pay a fast visit to Faunstone Hall before the police tramped all over the place with their size elevens. Richard Broughton was unlikely to speak to me, if he was there, but Mrs Malee might. It was worth a try.

It would have to be the ladybird and the hope that Mrs Malee would not make a link. Perhaps she would think it a British idiosyncrasy to paint spots on a car.

Spring was knocking on nature's door today and I threw my anorak into the back of the car. I could almost smell the promise of summer's flowers. Shopping list: six bunches of unopened daffodils for £3, two for Doris, two for Mavis, two for me. Yesterday they had been growing in Cornwall. I had an old lacquered blue vase which would be perfect for them.

It was a solemn drive but I could still appreciate the countryside bursting to life. I ought to be immune to violent death by now but I wasn't. In a couple of days the whole scene had changed, young shoots and buds emerging, trees and hedges turning green, birds building nests and nipping off the heads of banks of crocuses. Yellow and mauve petals danced away on the sly breeze like exhausted butterflies.

The sun was warming my hands through the windscreen. No sun for Holly. No expensive tan shown off with white jeans. The electronic gates to Faunstone Hall were open, which was strange. I drove in and parked to the side nearest the stables and kitchen area at the back, well away from the front door.

The police were already there, patrol cars parked skew-whiff, any old how, as if they had jammed on their brakes after a breakneck chase. At least they had turned off the flashing lights. It was odd not to see DI James in charge. I wandered in, hoping to look as if I worked there. There was no one in the kitchen although the kettle had been recently boiled. A constable stopped me in the hallway.

'Sorry, miss. You're not allowed in here,' he said.

'But I work here,' I said.

'Oh yes. What do you do?'

Pity I hadn't dressed for the part. Florist? Masseur? Manicurist? Charwoman from the village? Flash of inspiration.

'I'm Mrs Broughton's diary secretary. I arrange all her appointments and invitations. She's a very busy lady. I keep track of everything for her.'

'No longer quite so busy, miss. I think you've been made redundant,' said the officer, unable to resist giving me bad news. I blinked innocently.

'I don't understand.'

'Didn't you see all the police cars outside?'

'Why, yes, I saw them but I thought it was something to do with the recent burglary. Loose ends to tie up or something.'

'A very loose end, miss.' Quite the station gossip, this one. I wondered if I ought to report him. But not yet.

'I don't understand.' Limited vocabulary for a secretary. They are usually articulate and sharp.

'Haven't you heard? Don't you listen to your radio? Mrs Broughton has been found dead, impaled on a stake on the beach, one of those fancy tree things. Very nasty.'

I went into minor shock, neatly, without falling over and hurting myself. The constable guided me to a chair and fanned the air in a useless manner. I wondered how he had passed his first-aid course.

'Poor Mrs Broughton,' I sobbed. 'How dreadful. How did it happen? I know she was depressed by the court case, but she had won it. There was no need to kill herself.'

'You'd hardly call being impaled on a stake committing suicide, now would you, miss? It looks like it was murder, and a very nasty one at that.'

'Murder? Oh my God, oh no, how awful. How was she murdered?' It was half acting, half genuine.

'I don't exactly know, miss. Post-mortem report and all that. But I should imagine it was an overdose of some drug. Then someone got rid of the body by leaving it on the beach.' He was very forthcoming, which was unusual for uniformed.

'Surely if someone wanted to get rid of a body they would tip it into the sea to be washed over to the Isle of Wight or the coast of France, depending on the tides? Seems odd to leave it on the beach, waiting to be found.'

'You're right there, miss. Very odd.'

'Is Mr Broughton at home?'

'I believe he was at his London flat when he was informed. He's driving down now.'

I faked a bit of a recovery. 'I'd better cancel all her appointments. It's the least I can do for her. Can I go through to the study, er … my office?' Neat touch.

'I should think so. It's not part of the area being finger-printed.'

The whole house would be finger-printed in a murder case. But it suited me to give him a tremulous smile and walk unsteadily to the study, which I remembered was at the far end of this hall. I was every inch a secretary in shock, taking the three steps down carefully. Sorry, Holly, but I am still working for you. Trust me.

I switched on the flat-screen computer and went into My Computer. A huge list of files came up. It would take me hours to go through this lot, even if I knew what I was looking for. But I had better make a start before the officer was relieved from duty and someone more keyed up spotted me.

It was all fairly ordinary. Builders, antique dealers, auctions, holiday reservations, beauty treatments, garages and car-hire firms. I went back to the auction files. Holly had bought a tapestry two months ago. She'd bid £8,000 for it. I know nothing about tapestries but apparently this was a nineteenth-century Beauvais tapestry so finely woven that it could be mistaken for an oil painting. The elaborate border was a copy of picture frames of that period. The catalogue description said the design was based on a rural painting by the eighteenth-century artist, François Boucher. Never heard of him.

So where was this valuable tapestry now? Perhaps she had sold it. I could do with a tapestry on my north wall. Sometimes my bedroom was like an ice box. The wind at its worst. Bed socks at the ready.

The auction file was an eye-opener. A year back she had bought a genuine antique suit of armour from the English Civil War (1642–9). I went cold. She'd paid £9,500 for it as it was in fine condition and had the original buckles. It even had the armourer's marks and a series of five small dents in the breastplate made by a pistol fired to test the strength of the armour.

I didn't have to ask where this armour was now. I knew. It was in the boiler room of the pub, or had been a few days ago. I had fingered those dents. I was starting to feel sick, either from what I was discovering or from lack of food.

Then she'd sold the suit of armour for £11,000. Perhaps Richard didn't like it at Faunstone Hall. Not a bad profit. She'd sold it to someone called Pointer.

I was about to go into a file marked 'Court Case', when two men came into the study. It was my friendly constable with someone in civilian clothes.

'And this is Mrs Broughton's diary secretary,' the PC said. 'You may want to ask her a few questions. She's a bit upset.'

'I'm sure she must be upset,' said the big man following behind. 'And I'm sure I'd like to ask her a few questions.' He glanced down at me, not quite glaring, but near. I recognized the six foot three.

'Hello,' I said, shrinking. He'd seen me. He knew me.

'Hello, Miss Lacey. Perhaps we ought to talk? You can go, constable.'

DS Duke Morton continued to tower over me. 'Diary secretary now, eh? So tell me what you have found out, secretarial-wise.'

He was not quite so nasty as DI James

would have been in the same circumstances. The attitude was obviously catching. I took a good look at him for the first time. He had a gentle giant look, but the eyes behind the glasses were non-committal. He had a cleft chin and a shadow already. Two shaves a day man.

'Hi, there,' I said, reminding him. 'My trusty driver.'

'Not today,' he said. 'CID in charge of this murder investigation.'

'So it is murder. Then I can help you and you can help me.'

'That's pretty optimistic. Firstly, what are you doing here? Did you lie your way in?'

'Not exactly. I was working for Holly Broughton, and still am as she paid me in advance. I am happy to share what I have found out, if you are equally generous.'

'I'm not a generous man.'

'I don't believe it. You have nice eyes.' I do lie outrageously sometimes, but he was not easily taken in.

'What have you got for me? It had better be good,' he said, looking as if he was about to order me out.

'Holly was into buying antiques, real antiques, not my kind of small junk. One of her purchases was a full set of armour from the English Civil War which she recently sold on. It sounds a lot like one I've seen recently in the boiler room of the pub called the

Medieval Hall, which DI James and I have personal interest in. It could be the same one that has put DI James out of action.'

'That's interesting.' Duke Morton was not committing himself. 'But you have no proof. And I can't see any connection.'

'I'm going to find a connection,' I said grimly.

'Come back to me when you have.'

'So how did Mrs Broughton die?'

'Not yet known. Anything else?'

'There's pages of expensive antiques that she has bought. But I'm wondering where they are now.'

'I suggest that since you have finished what you call "cancelling her engagements", you should switch off and leave our experts to unravel the rest of her computer files.'

'Very well, officer,' I said demurely, going through the logging-off procedure. He seemed satisfied and walked away, dipping his head to go under the low doorway.

I'd already downloaded a copy of this personal file on a CD. I always think in advance.

Eleven

Find a connection, he'd said. And I was determined to do it. I'd come to a spectacularly dead end with the rabbits. None of them matched Arthur Spiddock's descriptions, but maybe the unscrupulous would paint a white ear black. He was coming in to see the photographs that afternoon. I wondered if he would bring Nutty.

He brought Nutty.

I had a bag of dog biscuits from the Easy Weigh shop and Nutty was delighted and grateful. He was my slave for life, slobbering all over my ankles.

'He likes you,' said Arthur.

'What I've always wanted, a genuine canine friend,' I said. 'Please sit down. Would you like to look at these photos of rabbits currently for sale in the Latching area?'

He put on his glasses. The lenses were so smeared with sweat and dirt it was a wonder he could see the chair to sit on.

'Ah ... rhum,' he said, turning them over. 'Nope, nope, nope. None of them rabbits are mine. How much are they asking for them?'

'Sorry, I didn't make a note. You see, I wasn't actually buying them so the price was immaterial.'

'Right. Understand. Well done, missy. You are really trying, aren't you? I'm impressed. How about the hens?'

'Rather more difficult,' I said. 'I don't wish to upset you but they are probably in someone's deep freeze by now or in the pot.'

He looked downcast for a few moments and then perked up. 'Well, I'm supposing that were their fate anyways. Only it should have been my pot and not some other bugger. Except the bantams. I'd still like to catch who stole them.'

'So would I.'

'How much do I owe you so far?' he asked, patting his back pocket.

'I'll send you an invoice when the case is finished,' I said. 'I noticed that you didn't put an address when you filled in my contract form. Only a phone number.'

'I'm between addresses at the moment,' he said.

I knew the answer instantly. He was living on the allotment. There was a shed at the back with a curtained window. It was against the law but I wasn't going to tell anyone. I gave Nutty some more biscuits and made a mug of instant for Arthur. I was full of goodwill. One of the photos had unexpectedly turned into pure gold. A spotty-faced youth of about sixteen was holding a couple of the rabbits. Nothing remarkable ... but on his arm was a tattoo of a serpent entwined round a dagger. His address could be confirmed.

When Arthur and Nutty eventually left after more coffee and more biscuits, I went straight to the police station and handed the bunny photograph to Sergeant Rawlings. He was impressed again.

'So you're not just a pretty face,' he said. 'He won't give us his name. Got the name?'

'Not a name, but I do have the address.' I checked my notes and wrote it down for him. 'I went there to buy a rabbit.'

'There's no accounting for tastes,' he said. 'Or were you going to make a pie?'

'I see your sense of humour has returned intact.'

'It's a gift. Thanks for the address. I think the officer in charge will be making a house call.'

I wondered if I had a gift. If I did, it had not materialized into a recognizable form. Then I thought of the dozens of different roles I had played in various surveillance scenarios. Perhaps that was my gift, being able to hide myself behind different characters.

A sort of plan was forming in my mind. I felt sure it was the same suit of armour as Holly Broughton had bought that I had seen hurtling towards me, lethal toes pointing at my throat. It was those five small dents, finger-width apart. But what was her connection with the Medieval Hall pub? I doubted if she would have given the time of any day to the surly owner.

Yet DI James thought the accident had not been an accident. His professional thought process would not rule out foul play. Maybe it would help with his recovery if I could put his agitated mind at rest.

I sat in Maeve's Café having an early lunch, or was it a late breakfast? She was cooking me grilled plaice and chips. Mavis knew how to cook fish, not a minute too long. And her chips were golden perfection, the best in Sussex. She always served a side salad of iceberg lettuce, rocket, red onion and bits of tomato.

She sat me at my usual table. 'Don't look so glum,' she said. 'The dishy DI will soon be back. Not long now from what I hear.'

'Dishy DI? I can't think who you can mean,' I said, straight-faced.

'OK, play dumb. Read the paper,' she said. 'Get yourself a proper job.' She put the *Argus* in front of me. I leafed through the pages reading all the local news. Latching was bursting with news. I doubted if the BBC or ITV could cope with such an onslaught of high-profile news items, and all far more interesting than the Commons or people walking in and out of number 10.

I moved on to Situations Vacant, more out of a sense of duty than anything else. If Mavis had served up my plaice and chips then, I would never have seen the ad.

BARMAID WANTED
Evenings only
Medieval Hall pub
temporary position
no experience necessary
01997 518437

No experience necessary, temporary position. So they were still planning to move the Hall. But it was business as usual till the day it closed. Time to give thanks to whoever invented mobile phones. I don't think it was Bill Gates.

'I'd like to apply for the job of barmaid,' I said, adopting a lovely Sussex accent. 'I don't mind temporary. I'm a student, between universities.'

'Can you come for an interview?' said the man who was answering the phone. The accent didn't sound like the owner's. It was someone much younger and slightly foreign.

'Sure.'

'Two o'clock today?'

'Sure.'

'Do you know where we are?'

'I'll find you.'

'And what's your name?'

Quick think. New name required. 'Polly Baker,' I said, taking the lead name from the Gershwin show *Crazy for You*, which I love. She's a feisty cowgirl from Deadrock, Nevada, who sings show-stopping songs.

Mavis arrived with my succulent plaice and chips on an oval plate. I couldn't get up and leave now – too cruel to the cook. Another twenty minutes wouldn't hurt.

'Smashing,' I said, spearing a chip.

As I ate, I was mentally going through my box of tricks. This was going to be IUC; don't try to pronounce that: investigator under cover. There wasn't time to dye my hair and it would be a sin to cut it off. But it had to change. I didn't stop to think if this was a sensible move. DI James would be annoyed, but then he wasn't going to know, if I could help it.

Car or bike? Car today but parked at a discreet distance, like half a mile away. I rushed back to my shop and hung up the 'CLOSED' sign immediately. I didn't want any customers. Tight hipster jeans, skinny pink top scattered with sequins, bare belly. Short anorak with fur-edged hood. All very current modish girly look. I added long earrings and bangles galore till I tinkled like a cash machine. The hair was still a problem. It would have to be my own baker-boy cap, but that was back at the flat and I was

165

already cutting it fine. Those damned speed cameras would catch me if I put my foot down.

Then I found a gaudy scarf in Persian blues and reds. I wound it round and round my head like a 1930s turban and tucked the ends in, fixing it all securely with pins, and set a cheap necklace tiara-style on it. Not a scrap of hair showed. Perhaps he would think it was some religious thing.

I really like the Medieval Hall pub. I'd liked it the moment I walked in with James, all those months ago, the strains of jazz greeting my ears, the ancient bricks vibrating with the sound. Of course, being with James might have coloured the moment. It could have been a McDonalds and I'd have fallen for the golden arches. As long as the man by my side was James.

Nothing much had changed except it looked different in the daylight. Empty and dusty and faded. No casual drinkers. No soft lighting. No music. A pub in the glaring mean light of day was not an inviting place. It smelt of stale beer and sweat, not just from last night but from centuries back.

My eyes went to the canopy over the bar. No suit of armour on his perch above the drinkers. The bar was in good shape, optics sparkling, clean glasses in neat rows, mats freshly laundered, taps gleaming. No sign of sawdust these days.

A slight, olive-skinned young man came through a door behind the bar carrying a cardboard box full of packets of crisps. He was in his thirties, neat in black trousers, white shirt and red bow tie, spikey black hair on top. He nodded towards me.

'Come for the job?' he said.

'Right. Polly Baker. I phoned earlier.'

'Sit down. I'll bring over some coffee. Sugar?'

'No sugar, thank you.'

He must be some sort of assistant manager, a level down from the owner that I had met the other day. At least he was reasonably pleasant. He came over with two cups of filter coffee which looked good.

'Thanks,' I said. 'It smells nice coffee.'

'I'm Carlo, undermanager,' he said, sitting down.

'Hi.'

'Worked in a bar before, have you?' he asked.

'No, only student bars at uni. We served beer, lager, fizzy drinks and a few tons of crisps.'

'We serve coffee as well at the bar. Could you learn how to use the machine? It's fairly simple.'

'Just show me how and I'll learn it.'

'The till is easy. It's all computerized these days. You feed code numbers and how many and it does the sums. Tells you how much change to give, just like a supermarket till.'

I grinned. 'Piece of cake.'

'Then you've got to collect dirty glasses, ashtrays, wipe tables, fill the dishwasher. It's an endless circle of work.'

'Sounds all right to me. But the advert said it was only temporary.'

'*Si*, we don't know how long the Med will still be here. There's much talk of us closing down. It could be any time, a week, a month...'

'Suits me,' I said. 'I've got to earn some money. Can't go on with my studies until I can pay my way. I'm studying astrophysics.' I thought celestial bodies was sufficiently vague to protect me from scrutiny. Carlo did not ask me what it was.

'It's only the minimum,' he coughed, saying the dreaded words. The minimum was the lowest hourly rate any employer could get away with paying. 'But you get free bar gear to wear and coffee. No alcohol unless a customer pays for it.'

That would save a lot of worry. 'What gear?'

'White shirt and tie. Provide your own black trousers. No jeans. Boss doesn't like them. But your hair is all right, tied up like that. Looks hygienic. Could you find a black scarf?'

'Yes. When shall I start?'

'Six o'clock tonight till half an hour after

we've closed.'

'And when's that?'

'About half eleven.'

It would have to be the ladybird all right, parked at a prudent distance. I was not cycling home in a sea mist at that time of night. Too much activity from the younger generation at a loose end.

'*Ciao*, see you this evening, Pollee.' Carlo pronounced it with a long vowel sound at the end. I liked it.

'*Ciao*,' I said cheerfully. It would not be difficult to work alongside Carlo. I realized that not once had the accident come into my mind in the last twenty minutes. Perhaps it was because I was being Polly, not Jordan. And Polly was a dreamy astrophysics student ... Why did I chose that subject?

Carlo picked up the cups and saucers and disappeared behind the bar. 'See yourself out, Pollee.'

Funny how I lost my way, but only for ten vital seconds. The suit of armour was still in the boiler room, sprawled on the floor. I wanted to check those five finger-width dents in the armour. No one saw me slide in and slide out. The five dents fitted the fingers of my left hand. It was Holly's suit of armour. Individual sounds separated themselves as I glided through the old hall, suddenly reminding me of those moments of terror. The dripping of a tap, distant voices, creaking of a stair tread, a door swinging on a rusty hinge. I had to get out fast. I needed air and space. The day was changing from grey to charcoal. Shopping: batteries for torch, black scarf, disposable camera, paracetamol.

The ladybird was parked behind some shops, several of which were shuttered and locked up, forced out of business by the supermarkets. It was an ideal place to hide her and was only a five-minute walk from the pub. Once in the car, I pulled on a dark fur hat and tipped it down over my eyes. Not a full disguise but looking different from Polly, the new barmaid.

I still wasn't sure if this was a good move or if James would fully approve, but I couldn't hang around hoping someone else would find out the truth. Holly Broughton's death was not for me to solve, but as I had been working for her, her case was still on file.

The scene-of-crime area on the beach was deserted but the yellow tape still fluttered in the wind. The tent had been dismantled; so had the stake on which Holly had been found. It had gone to the forensic laboratory to be examined closely. But it was possible to walk round the rest of the beach. I changed into old trainers and tramped over the slippery pebbles.

This wooden beach garden was the inspiration of some modern artist. He'd got a generous grant from the Arts Council. Lumps of wood and rocks and palm trees making some sort of exotic experience for people who were bored by the expanse of sand and sea. There were twisting paths and groups of visual shapes, rocks or sculptured tree trunks, to distract the jaded eye if the changing shapes of the sky and moving sea were not enough.

The wood was smooth to the touch, the patina a rich mellow shine with the rings of time. My feet scuffled the dust and gravel. Something glinted and I bent down to pick it up. It was cold in my hand but I knew instantly what it was and to whom it belonged. Something that the police officers had missed, bless their squad-issue thermal socks.

Twelve

The turn-round time was tight. Carlos wanted me back by six o'clock and I had things to buy, clothes to find, people to phone.

The phoning bit was tricky. DI James had to know what I was doing, just in case. I did not like to think about the just-in-case aspect, just in case.

I rang his number.

'DI James,' he answered.

I could not tell from his voice if he was still prone or into the next stage of his recovery. I had lost track of time.

'Jordan,' I said.

'I know who it is.'

'Wow, what it is to have instantly recognizable breathing. What's it like? Breathy, voluptuous, fearful, timid?' There was no answer. 'How are you?'

'The same. Slight delay in treatment but I am not going into that. What have you found out?'

'The Hall is still going to be moved, apparently. They are only taking on temporary staff. What did forensic say about the broken support?'

'They said it had been sawn through at a crucial point, but they thought the suit could have been held in place by strong nylon fishing line. Then someone had only to slash the line to make the suit topple.'

'Nasty. Any clues?'

'You can buy the line at any anglers' store. A saw is a saw, although these technical wizards can match up teeth marks. It has probably been disposed of long ago.'

'What about the slashing?'

'Find me a man to go up a ladder, check the canopy for shreds. However carefully disposed of, there's always bits left behind.'

'Bit of a blank there. But I'll make discreet enquiries. It should be a lot easier now I've got a job at the Medieval Hall.'

'You've got what? A job at the pub? Jordan, you must be raving mad.' James's voice rose.

'It's the one way that I can find out what really happened and what's going on.'

'It's too dangerous. I forbid you to go.'

'Forbid? Do I recognize that word? Excuse me, but when did I last work for you? Never, buster. This is Jordan Lacey, Private Investigator speaking, self-employed and I can do what I like.'

'They tried to kill me, have you forgotten that?'

'And I got in the way. That's no reason to try and kill me again. I'm not a threat.'

'They won't look at it like that when they find out who you are. They will link you to me and then you're in trouble.'

No one had ever linked me to him – James. It was a heady thought, like I might be a real person at last. Someone that he would look at, decide to have as a friend, perhaps as more than a friend. Like a dream, a fantasy, some woman who drifted in and out of his sleep in diaphanous robes. Surely James had dreams?

'Do you ever dream?' I asked him curiously.

'Are you feeling all right? Have you got a fever?'

'I was wondering what your mind did when you were asleep, whether you ever dreamed of women in flowing white robes.'

'With wings? All the time. Angels frequent my dreams with regularity. We are on first-name terms. Patsy, Gina, Sharon.'

He was laughing at me. I was not sure if this was a good sign or a bad sign. I hoped he wouldn't tell me to relax. It was the tension that was holding me together.

'I have to go now,' I said stiffly. 'I'm on duty at six.'

'If you must. Give a full measure and draw the Guinness slowly. Too much head can spoil the first mouthful,' he said with what was almost a regretful sigh. He missed having a drink with his mates. A beer in a feeder was not the same.

'Shall I give you a ring when I come off duty?' I sounded like a wife. 'So you'll know I'm all right?'

James paused, summing up the implications. 'That's very thoughtful of you, Jordan,' he said. 'But they pump me full of nighty-night pills around eight o'clock so that they can play poker at the nurses' station. I'll be asleep, brushing up on my two-step with Sharon,' he added.

'By the way, the suit of armour is very similar to one that Holly Broughton bought way back last year. English Civil War, around 1642–9. She paid a lot of money for it. What do you make of that?'

'Some women have a funny taste in men.'

I was exactly one minute late and the day barmaid was already fuming. She came over to me in the staff locker room, yanking off her white shirt and flinging it into a laundry basket. She was blonde and florid. Her 42DD white extra support bra was grey and the strap needed mending. I'd seen her somewhere before. But my ragbag memory couldn't place her.

'What time do you call this?' she said. 'I'm not paid to work overtime.'

'Sorry,' I said. 'You can go a minute early tomorrow.'

She threw me a spiteful glare and struggled

into a shrunken pea-green T-shirt. 'And I want to find everything spick and span when I come in tomorrow morning. If you leave a single ashtray unwiped, I'll report you. I'm not paid to do your work.'

She was sure putting out the welcome mat. She didn't like me. Jealous? But of what? 36B wired cups?

'Naturally,' I said. 'Same as you won't be leaving me trays of dirty glasses left over from the lunch trade.' I could see them out of the corner of my eye, hidden under the bar counter. I fastened the white shirt buttons and put on the elasticated bow tie. The shirt almost fitted. There were three sizes, small, medium and large. My hair had disappeared under a black turban. It looked a bit as if I'd had a dose of chemotherapy, but that was not my intention.

Carlo waved to me from the bar. 'Hi, Pollee...'

'Hi, Carlo. Sorry I'm late.'

'*Prego*. Did you meet Lorraine?'

'I did. She gave me a lovely welcome. I didn't see her when I came for my interview.'

'She was on her lunch break. You get a coffee break, if and when there's time. We're pretty busy every evening.'

Pretty busy was putting it mildly. It was three deep at the bar and no music apart from the endless tape of wallpaper guitar and bass beat. Carlo had me wiping tables, collecting and washing glasses and making and serving coffee. Learning the till could wait. It was an endless round. I barely had time to gulp down a cup of cold coffee. But I did learn how to stack the industrial dishwasher. It only took three minutes to wash a load. Magic. And they came out sparkling.

'Where's the owner?' I asked in a ten-second lull. I was putting clean glasses on shelves in rows. 'Have I seen him yet?'

'No, he's moving to Spain. Having a villa built. Gone out to check on his property. Yes, sir? Two ginger-beer shandies coming up. Pollee, put on a fresh filter. See the couple coming through the doorway? They always have coffee and appreciate if it's almost ready to serve them, piping hot.'

I got a tip. A whole fifty-pence piece for serving two large coffees. I didn't know what to do with it. There might be a tipping box that was shared out. I wondered if the luscious Lorraine put her tips in it.

A property in Spain. So he was moving and so was the Medieval Hall, if the owner got his own way.

'What's going to happen to the rest of the pub?' I asked as I went past him to collect more dirty glasses. 'Has it been sold?'

'Don't ask me,' said Carlo. 'I only work here.' I detected a disconsolate note in his voice. Either he didn't know what was going on or he did know and didn't like it. This wasn't the time to probe. I had to earn his confidence first.

'Is there another owner?' I asked. 'Or another barman? A round, jovial man, in a white apron. I thought I saw someone else.'

Carlo shook his head. 'There's only me. We don't wear aprons.'

The best sound of the evening was when Carlo rang a ship's bell and called out, 'Last orders, please.' No one moved or even appeared to listen. It took another call, ten minutes later before anyone started to leave. I was so tired. I'd run my legs ragged. I ached everywhere and I still had the taps on the pumps to clean. My bed called loudly. I wondered what time I would get home. There was still the clearing-up to do or I'd have to answer to the luscious Lorraine.

Carlo paid me out of the till. 'I'll pay you cash for tonight,' he said. 'We'll do the paperwork when the boss comes back. You done good, Pollee ... See you tomorrow, pleeze?' He sounded hopeful. Perhaps temporary bar staff never came back.

'Sure. Six o'clock. I got a tip from the coffee couple. Where do I put it?'

'*Si, signorina*, in your pocket,' he grinned.

It was not a fast walk back to my car. I dragged my legs along. They were wobbling. I hadn't worked that hard for years. My appreciation of barmaids and barmen soared. I pulled off the turban and found my

178

hair was drenched with sweat and stuck to my head in knotted lanks. I was not a pretty sight. And I was still wearing the white shirt and necktie. The roads were dark and empty with fearsome shadows.

The ladybird started up like the gem she is and took me home, almost without me driving her. I parked her behind my shop and had to walk to my bedsits. This last midnight walk was agony, although the air was cool and the sky bright with stars. All my joints had seized up. The drunks had passed out in various doorways although I heard voices shouting and laughing along the front. I hurried indoors and closed the door, putting down the catch.

It was too late to phone James. He'd be off in the land of Nod now with Sharon and Gina and Patsy. I had to laugh. He wouldn't know an angel if it handed him a gold-engraved business card.

But I would, if I ever saw one. He could be wearing jeans and a navy duffle coat, not your flapping-white-wings category. I might not recognize him at first, but he would be tall with a gentle smile and eventually I would know.

I rolled into bed and slept deeply, the aches warming and easing with every minute. If I dreamed in the night-time wastes, then the dreams were light and flimsy and wafted through my thoughts like feathers. Sometimes I flew and became a bird, nearing the sun or round the moon, swift and graceful. I woke in drifts, surfacing then falling back into the warm pillow, pulling the duvet up to shoulder height for a few more precious minutes.

The strong sunshine filtering in refused to let my eyes close again. It was time to get up to a beautiful morning. The cold spring had fled at last and an early summer was knocking at the door and this time it would not be denied. Every leaf was dancing with light. The sea would be a carpet of gold dust.

I scrambled into clean clothes and ran down to the shore. The morning was washed with dew, every pebble a gem, the sea the most perfect sparkling blue. The coming summer filled my veins with strength and healing in my bones.

The moment of elation passed and I hurried to Maeve's Café, longing for caffeine. Mavis was sweeping the floor. I took a damp J-cloth and spray-cleaner and began wiping the table tops. Mavis raised her eyebrows.

'What's this? Work experience?'

'I've been practising,' I said.

'I can see that. Nice action.'

'Shall I fill the cruets?'

Mavis nodded. 'Why this enthusiasm for menial tasks?'

'I've had a brief look behind the scenes in

a pub. How we take all the work for granted.'

'You're right there. Would you like to take another brief look behind the scenes here and put the coffee on?'

We sat together having the first coffee of the morning. Mavis could sense a busy day ahead. The sun would bring coachloads of pensioners not straying too far from the pier. I could sense customers for my shop: hopefully there would be day-trippers wanting a modest souvenir of Latching, something which was not factory-churned. I needed to dress the windows of First Class Junk, with an emphasis on souvenirs.

I was hurrying back to my shop, going inland along Amos Street, when I felt a sharp pain to the side of my eye. I had no idea what had happened. It was a sudden sharp pain. I put up my hand to my face and there was blood.

It must have been a stone, kicked up. Perhaps I'd kicked it up myself, but there was nothing on the pavement, nor was there anyone around who might have kicked it up. Tissues to the rescue. Blood trickling down my face was not going to soothe the customers.

A police helicopter zoomed overhead, glinting in the sun, but I could not look up. My eye was squeezed shut. I tried not to think what would have happened if it had been even closer to the eye. I still thought it was a stone.

Doris was cleaning her shop windows. She took one look at the soaked tissue. The blood was running between my fingers and down my arm.

'For goodness sake, what have you done now? Been in a scrap? Come in and I'll clean you up,' she said.

'I've done nothing. It happened, suddenly. A sharp pain and then all this blood. I can hardly see.'

'I'm not surprised. Sit down and hold this pad against your eye. Do as you are told. Don't move. Somebody ought to take a look at this.'

'I'm not going to hospital. I've got a job to do.'

'You do argue, Jordan. I've never met anyone so awkward. What did you say did this?'

'I think it was a stone. I don't know. It was so sudden. This sharp pain, then all the blood.'

I sat down. I was beginning to feel faint. Doris changed the pad. The blood was beginning to congeal. She put the kettle on.

'Shock,' she said.

'Double honey,' I said.

'I'm not opening a new jar for you. I sell the stuff, I don't eat it. It'll be two spoonfuls of sugar.'

The tea was welcome, sweetened her way. I was thirsty, but I was also anxious to get back to my shop. I'd be all right once the bleeding stopped. Heck, it was only a stone.

'It's stopping,' I said.

'Yeah, you'll live. But you ought to let the hospital have a look at it.'

I shook my head. 'I can see fine. There's no damage to my eye. It's back to work. Thanks for the tea and TLC.'

Carlo was pleased to see me that evening. Perhaps the bar staff didn't last long. Maybe the luscious Lorraine scared them off. He didn't remark on the bit of plaster by my eye. I'd rinsed and ironed the shirt so it looked good. And the black bandeau-turban was faultless. Polly was in place.

'You can clean the optics this evening,' he said.

'Sure.'

'I'll show you how. You quick learner, Pollee.'

'*Grazie.*'

'Ah, you speak Italian! *Magnifico.*'

I learned fast. The optics sparkled. I discovered I was a dab hand at cleaning. And I remembered what the customers ordered. I remembered the two coffee drinkers. They tipped me fifty pence again and gave me a smile.

The evening was carried away on a tide of trade. I needed some time to find out things. I asked for a break and fled to the ladies' loos then slunk round a corner and headed for the boiler room. I nipped down the stairs in the half-light and found the suit of armour propped drunkenly against a wall. I put my disposable camera on flash and waited till the red light came on and took photos of the medieval knight, especially the finger-width dents. I dusted all the surfaces with a small paintbrush and put the debris into a specimen bag.

Carlo nodded as I returned. '*Scusi*, more glasses, pleeze,' he said. 'We are running out.'

People got through so many glasses. It was as if they used two glasses per drink, pouring it over for a clean rim. The Zanussi worked overtime, tray after tray of steaming glass. I was getting clammy dishwasher's hands.

The legs were giving up again, aching. I leaned against the bar to take off the weight. Did barmaids get varicose veins? Ten to one on the nose, they did. But I'd refuse to wear those khaki support stockings before I was fifty.

It was a long evening. I was never sure when it was closing time. It seemed a movable feast these days. The government had made the drinking laws flexible and the Medieval Hall seemed to have different times every century.

But it did end and Carlo was paying me out of the till again. He said to keep the tip.

'*Grazie*. When is the boss due back?' I asked, wondering which aching bone to think about.

'Tomorrow, I think.'

'Shall I meet him?'

'I doubt it. He doesn't mix. We don't see a lot of him, paperwork and that. He's got a lot of rich friends.'

Like millionaire Russians? I pulled off the shirt, now damp and stained, and put it in the laundry box. Head first into my own plain navy T-shirt, careful of the bandeau.

'You've ripped the plaster off your face,' said Carlo, peering . '*Mama mia*, let me look at that. It's nasty and bleeding. Ouch. How did you do this?'

'It was a stone. It hit me as I was walking home.'

'That ain't no stone,' said Carlo with some authority. 'That air-gun-pellet wound. I seen hit like that before. Kids playing. You've been shot at by someone with an air gun.'

'A sniper?'

'Sniper, kids? Some lunatic was trying to blind you. You'd better get to a hospital, *pronto*, Pollee.'

Thirteen

Carlo insisted that I went straight to hospital and I agreed it would be sensible. He didn't offer to take me there as he was running round in circles, clearing up, cashing up, locking up, putting the money in the safe. I said I'd phone for a taxi but didn't. I drove my own car carefully, holding a wodge of tissues to my eye.

A nurse in A & E cleaned the wound and picked out the pellet, dropping it into an aluminium dish. She was careful and efficient. She put a butterfly plaster cross-wise to hold a flap of skin in place.

'Your skin had nearly started to grow over the pellet,' she said. 'You came in time. Who did this?'

'I don't know. I was walking along the street.'

'You ought to report it to the police. Some-one shot at you.'

'A bit late to do that. He'll be halfway to Edinburgh by now and I hope he is.'

'I doubt it. Probably taking pot shots at some other young woman. You should go to the police.'

'Yes, I suppose so. Thank you.'

I continued to drive carefully. It was a sobering thought that someone had taken a shot at me. Latching has a few vodka-fuelled idiots roaming around, so it might not have a sinister meaning. A half-dozen pints and he might have mistaken me for a seagull limping home. Or maybe he was practising for the 2012 Olympics.

It was later than I thought. No time to phone James. A hot drink and bed. I peered into a mirror and saw that my cheek was bruised as well. I seemed to be wearing a perpetual black eye. The latest fashion statement. Extra work with the make-up box tomorrow. A bashed-up barmaid doesn't get tips. The coffee couple would think twice.

My flimsy dreams of pleasure disappeared that night. They were laden with fear as my world cracked into pieces, but none of it emerged from the liquorice dark of sleep. I fell in and out of dreams and still couldn't remember a thing when I woke up.

Breakfast was a nourishing muesli with a sliced banana and chopped apricots. Is it feed a black eye or starve it? This thought kept my mind occupied while I leafed through a book on collectable suits of armour. The more I knew about armoury, the better. The prices were sky-high. A three-quarters cuirassier, made for a horseman riding a horse in 1640, would set you back about £8,000 to £12,000. And that didn't include the horse.

Polish armour with screwed-up balls of newspaper, I read. What a useful tip. Always wanted to know how to polish armour. One of those women's magazines might take it as a household tip.

I found I was scraping an empty bowl. The appetite had returned. Time to go places with a brisk walk.

The allotment was bristling with new plant life. Arthur had planted ragged rows of onions, runner beans, potatoes and leeks. He was not into salad. Not a rocket leaf in sight.

The rabbit hutches and hen runs were empty. Arthur had not replaced his precious brood. The doors still swung open and inside was a wreck of straw and feed. He had trampled over the surrounding ground and the impression was of neglect and abandon.

I trod over the mud. I would never be a gardener or whatever allotment holders were called. A window box was more my style. Pansies and nasturtiums trailing creatively.

There was no sign of life from the garden shed. I stood back, out of view, and waited. Surveillance on an allotment is a doddle, no make-up required. I shrank into my own skin and tried to look like a runner bean on a pole.

There was no way I could watch plants

grow. I pinned my glance on the surrounding allotments, the clusters of sheds, poles, cloches, water barrels, rose arches and tangled raspberry bushes, varying degrees of green-fingered proficiency. It was a ramshackle collection of hopes and wreckage.

A curtain twitched. It wasn't a rat or a bird. More like nervous fingers. My stiff legs almost refused to move. Call me a scarecrow. I might even have straw in my hair.

I went up to the shed and rapped on the wooden door. There was no answer.

'Hello, Mr Spiddock. I know you are in there. It's Jordan Lacey. I'd like to talk to you.'

The air hung with an earthy just-dug smell. Some cherry-blossom petals blew across from the next allotment. They were like snowflakes. The curtain was stilled.

'Hi, there, Mr Spiddock? Open the door, please. I want to talk to you. It doesn't matter to me where you are living...'

The door opened a crack. It was Arthur Spiddock. He peered out, blinking as if daylight was new. He was wearing a threadbare brown cardigan over a shirt, brown cords and slippers on his feet. His seamed face was a mask.

'I was making a cup of tea,' he said. 'That's all. Not breaking any bye-laws.'

'Of course not. Anyone can make a cup of tea in their shed,' I said, pushing the door further open. It was obvious he'd been living in the shed. There was a reclining deckchair with a sleeping bag on it, a bucket in a corner, a small Primus stove, some sliced bread, packets of cornflakes and a carton of milk. Some cans of dogfood and beer. It was so sad. Poor Arthur Spiddock. I had no idea why he had been evicted from his home or what had happened. I didn't even know where he had once lived.

'How long have you been living here?' I asked.

'Only making a cup of tea,' he insisted.

'In a sleeping bag?'

'Some months,' he mumbled.

'Did you lose your home?'

'Yeah. I couldn't pay the rent. The old-age pension is a laugh. Do them toffs in Whitehall really think we can live on it? They're all right, looking after themselves.'

'I understand,' I said. 'But if you are living in the shed, then perhaps you were here when the hens and rabbits were stolen? Where were you that night? Did you hear or see anything?'

He looked confused. 'I didn't see or hear nuffink.'

'But you were here?'

He nodded, rotating his head. 'I was here, but I was asleep. Sound asleep. I didn't hear nuffink. Then I found them all gone in the morning.'

'But there must have been a lot of noise, a van or a cart or something? You couldn't sleep through all that.'

He shook his head. 'I'd had a bit too much to drink, you see. That's the only way I can get to sleep. Have a few pints at the pub, and then another pint or two back here. I passed out, I suppose. Dead to the world. Out on the piss.'

It sounded plausible. He had a florid look, tiny thread veins on his nose and cheeks.

'But what about Nutty? Surely he heard the intruders? He's a very intelligent dog. He would have barked. By the way, where is he?'

Arthur Spiddock stumbled about, putting a battered kettle on the Primus, lighting the stove. His hand was shaking as he found a mug and a carton of milk. He had trouble getting it open, stabbing it with a trowel. I wanted to help, but decided not to go further into his murky, ashy shed.

'I dunno. He went off for a run round, I think.'

'What do you mean, you don't know where he is? Doesn't he live here with you? He's your dog.'

Arthur Spiddock looked close to tears. He spilt sugar over the mug of tea, slopped milk on the counter.

'Course, he's my dog. But I don't know where he is. Gone off somewhere on his own.'

'Do you mean he's run away?' I didn't believe it. Nutty was ridiculously devoted to his owner. There was no way he would run away, even if Arthur was living in a shed. Nutty might actually like it. Rural, and all that.

'So he wasn't here when the rabbits were stolen?'

'That's it, he wasn't here.' Arthur looked relieved that I'd got the message.

'But he was with you when you came to my office to ask me to take on the case,' I added quickly.

'That's right. He'd come back.'

'And now he's gone again?'

'Like I said.' Arthur's face took on a shuttered look; the brackets round his mouth got closer, as if he wasn't going to say any more.

'I don't think you are telling me the truth,' I said.

Arthur was stirring his mug of tea. 'Poor old Nutty. I don't half miss him. He were a good dog. A good friend.'

'Are you telling me that he's dead?' I had to ask him even if it was painful.

He nodded, spilling his tea, dripping it on to the ground. 'Poor old Nutty. Copped it. Road accident.'

'You told me he'd run away.'

'He ran away and then got knocked over.'

'But he was fine when you brought him into my office. And that was after the hens and rabbits were stolen, wasn't it?'

Arthur Spiddock was pretty confused by this time. I could see his brain trying to sort it out. I took pity on him and started to leave. There was no hope of finding substantial clues now it had rained several times.

'I'll have another look round while I'm here. Is there anything you need? My shop has lots of odds and ends that haven't sold yet. I could let you have a few things.'

He shook his head. 'But I wouldn't mind a cushion. My back hurts something rotten.'

First Class Junk didn't sell cushions, but I would find him one. I wondered what else he needed but was too proud to ask for. There were friends I could approach for help, but what kind of support would actually help Mr Spiddock? I could hardly resurrect Nutty.

It was a sea of mud. Even the weeds didn't stand a chance. It was like stepping through sludge. His rhubarb looked healthy, the stalks a rosy pink. No one was picking it. I didn't know how to make crumble but my mother had known. She'd made it crusty golden on top, moist beneath, sugar crystals sparkling.

That had been a depressing visit. Investigation: nil. Clues: nil. Red herrings: dozens. I didn't know what to believe. Poor old Nutty. I took a short cut down to the coast road.

The rain was sweeping along the promenade and a mist was creeping up over the sea. It rolled landwards swallowing anything recognizable. The Latching pier had disappeared as if airbrushed out of the picture. I hoped Jack had battened down the hatches with plenty of coffee. His coffee might survive the mist as it had a head start on murkiness.

My asthma did not like it much – too ticklish. I began to wheeze and as usual had left my inhaler at home. It might be passed its sell-by date but they still worked even when unreadably old. The wheeze turned into a coughing fit and my bottle of water was back at the allotment. It was a long walk to any shop or café or pub. This was bleak, uninhabited seaside. I was surrounded by water and not a drop fit to drink.

I staggered over the pebbles to a group of rocks and sank down on to the flattest top. They were not a natural rock formation but part of the Council's strategy to stop the shore slipping into the sea. I leaned over to catch my breath, trying to slow down the breathing rate. No one would find me here, lost in the mist. And it was damp. A wet asthmatic is not a happy sight.

No phone either. Jordan, you are well prepared for all emergencies. It will be your own fault if you have an asthmatic attack away from all civilization. The NHS don't answer calls in semaphore.

'Are you in trouble? Can I help you?'

It was a nice deep voice. Did I have a guardian angel? Where were the wings? I couldn't hear any flapping.

'It's asthma,' I coughed. 'I need some water.'

'Got your inhaler with you?'

'No. But water helps...'

He was unscrewing a bottle. 'Untouched by human mouth,' he said. 'Here you are, drink.'

I drank and drank. People who don't touch water don't know what they are missing. It is so soothing, slipping down the throat. Delicious, perfect, healing. Half of his bottle had gone before I was able to straighten up. I thought I knew this man but I didn't know where he had come from. He was not a policeman, or jazz player, or junk buyer. Yet I knew his voice.

'Thank you,' I said, starting to breath normally. 'Do I know you?'

'I don't know,' he said. He seemed to have some mysterious private thought. 'Maybe you do.'

'Maybe I do,' I repeated.

'Are you feeling better?'

'Yes, thank you.'

'Would you like me to walk with you back to Latching?'

'How do you know that's where I live?'

'That's the way you were going.'

This was too much for me. I nearly freaked. It was as if I'd taken a great whiff of oxygen. I felt light-hearted. I straightened up to take a look at my Samaritan. He was rather tall, in dark jeans and a dark reefer jacket. His hair was a longish, curly grey but the face was young and unlined. He helped me up.

We talked as we walked but I have no recollection of what we talked about. It was easy talk but everything he said was pleasant and uplifting. He seemed to fill me with hope and determination for the future. Anything could happen. Everything was possible.

The mist began to lift, swirling up on thermals, and the pier loomed into sight, familiar and solid, straddling the waves. A cup of Jack's awful mud coffee seemed very desirable. The clink of the money machines would be music. I could shut my ears to the bangs and explosions of the games boards, however loud. The noise would be tolerable ... to a degree.

Clouds sailed by in ghostly forms, streamers trailing like whispers of smoke, shapes changing as I watched them carried by the wind across the sky. It was fascinating, a landscape laid end to end, bandaging the rents in the atmosphere.

'Isn't it beautiful?' I said. 'All these clouds.'

I expected my companion to agree with

me. But there was no one there. He had gone without my noticing. It was a surprise. I had not been aware of him leaving, so busy looking at the sky and marvelling at the clouds.

He was nowhere in sight, not in either direction. I ran ahead and then back again but the man had disappeared down a twitten or perhaps picked up his car, parked along the front. I felt let down. I'd have liked to thank him again for helping me, asked his name.

Jack was in his usual cubbyhole in the amusement arcade, a booth behind thick glass, door security-coded. I smiled at him through the glass and he punched out the code.

'Com'in, Jordan. Haven't seen you for donkies. Where you been? Wotcha done to yer face?' He was already putting on the kettle jug, searching for two clean mugs or what passed for nearly clean. There were half-a-dozen crusted mugs around. I wanted to wash them all in deep, soapy water.

'Oh, nothing. Got a couple of new cases. I like the blue,' I added, looking around at the newly painted walls. 'Snazzy.'

'Good cases, eh?'

'Except one of them died.'

'Not good news then?'

'Not exactly. I really liked her.'

Jack was stirring instant coffee with instant

creamer into his usual brown gruel. He piled in the sugar. 'Ah, the woman on the stake. I heard about it. Rotten thing to do to a woman. Below the belt. Sorry, not a joke.'

'It's horrible. But we don't know how she died yet. I haven't seen the autopsy report.'

'But will they show it to yer? Now that DI James is out of the picture, so to speak. It won't be so easy for yer, will it?'

'He still trusts me. And I'm working on something for him, a bit personal, so he owes me.'

'Ah, the Medieval Hall. You better watch out there, Jordan. The boss of that place, the guv, Pointer's his name. He's one nasty piece of work. I wouldn't trust him to give me change from twenty pence. You stay away from that place. He'll cut you down sooner than—' He stopped abruptly, remembering the injuries from the lethal suit of armour. His face went stiff. 'Sorry, Jordan. I fergot about wot 'appened.'

'Coffee's lovely,' I said, gulping. 'I needed this. Bad moment on the beach. Couldn't breathe.'

'Your asthma?'

'Worst for months.'

'You need properly looking after, gal.' Jack was as grubbily dressed as ever. Once-white T-shirt, scuffed boots, torn jeans. Ragged hair cut by himself with nail scissors and without a mirror. And when had he last shaved? The stubble was not designer.

'That would be lovely,' I agreed. 'Find me a millionaire.'

'I'm a millionaire,' he said.

I laughed and grinned ridiculously as if it was a joke. He probably was, dammit. But this I did not want to know. I couldn't be bought with a flash Jag and moneybags. The trouble was, Jack had a kind heart under all that tat.

'Can I use your phone, please, Jack? I've left mine at home.'

'Sure. Help yerself.' He passed me his mobile. It was thick with dust and grime. I wiped it carefully with a bit of screwed-up tissue found in the depths of my pocket. I phoned James.

'Jordan,' he almost shouted. 'Where the hell have you been? I've been trying to get to you.'

'I'm on the pier, having coffee with Jack.'

'Where have you been?'

'Busy.'

'I have to see you.'

'OK. Keep your hair on. I have a life, you know, and my own investigations to do. You don't employ me. I can't come this evening as I'm working.'

'No, Jordan. That's not good enough. You come over now. At once. I have to see you now.'

James had rung off, leaving me in mid-sentence. He had a nerve. I looked at Jack. He was grinning with a mocking look.

'You'd better do what DI James says. He's still the boss. Do me a favour before you go?'

'Of course.'

'There's a mad dog rushing about on the pier. He can't find the way off – y'know, the exit. Keeps coming in here and upsetting my customers, jumping up and barking. You're good with animals. Take him to a rescue home. I'll give you the taxi fare.'

'Got any biscuits?'

It was Nutty, without a doubt, fur wet and bedraggled. He was rapturously pleased to see me, gobbled the biscuits and pawed all over me. Then he drank from a puddle of rainwater.

'Sit,' I said. He obeyed, his tongue lolling. A sense of power filled me.

I made a lead out of my scarf and tied it round his collar. The scarf was not one of my favourites. We went to the nearest charity shop and I bought two cushions and an old blanket for Nutty. Then I picked up one of the taxis waiting in the Clock Square.

'Don't take dogs,' said the driver.

'He'll sit quietly on this blanket and I'll pay you extra,' I said. Funny how that always works.

'Sit,' I said again.

'I am sitting,' said the driver.

Fourteen

As Mae West said, I'd like to get out of these wet clothes and into a dry Martini. My jokes are not as sophisticated as hers, but a glass of a dry red would be more than acceptable. I called in at a Threshers on the way to Brighton and bought some decent Australian Shiraz and some mineral water. 'Good with meat and BBQs', it said on the label. I forgot it needed a corkscrew. How many things had I forgotten today? It must have been up to double figures. Clearly early-onset Alzheimer's.

Mr Spiddock had been pathetically grateful for the return of Nutty. They were all over each other like long-lost lovers. I left a fiver pinned to a cushion.

'Buy Nutty a good dinner,' I said. 'He's hungry.' I hoped Arthur wouldn't spend it on beer.

James was sitting in an upright chair, rather stiffly, near a window. He looked furious, not ecstatically happy as he should have looked, having been promoted from bed to chair. It meant all was going well. That nasty sharp piece of bone had not pierced any-thing vital. It was a relief, but I wasn't going to talk about it if he wasn't going to talk about it.

'I can't let you out of my sight for one day and I find you are up to no good.'

That was a great start. I waved the Shiraz at him. It was my happy wave. 'So we're celebrating,' I said. 'Where do you keep the glasses?'

'So what are we celebrating?' he said, his tone of voice simmering down barely one decibel. 'The fact that you are working at the Med, the pub where we were both nearly killed? That you are getting yourself involved in one of the nastiest murders in West Sussex this year? That you got shot at and a pellet lodged near your eye? It could have blinded you.'

'Oh dear,' I said. 'How do you know all this? Oh yes, I forgot: you're a detective.'

'I suppose we should be celebrating that the pellet missed and that Pointer hasn't bumped you off yet. And that the sadistic murderer of Holly Broughton hasn't decided you are a threat too and devised a similar demise.'

'Doesn't sound good,' I said, pretending not to understand a word. 'Do you think the nurses would have a corkscrew?'

'I'm sure they have. They collect weapons of torture.'

I went out to the nurses' station. Yes, they had glasses and a corkscrew. They thought it would cheer up DI James and were all for some alcoholic encouragement. They called him Dishy James, but not to his ears. There was enough wine for us all.

DI James is a beer man but he had the civility to taste the red. He liked it and took a few more sips. I could imagine it slipping down his throat and easing the pain and frustration. I did not want to spoil the mood, but I had to ask.

'So how did Holly Broughton die? Do you know? I presume you have had the path report by now.'

'You'll be surprised. She was poisoned. Digitalis. The leaves of the foxglove to you and me. And where do you find foxgloves growing? In gardens, especially at Faunstone Hall. You said it had lovely gardens and a wild corner. The leaves are the most toxic, containing digitalis and two other compounds, digoxin and digitoxin.'

'How weird. Foxglove?' My conversational talent had almost disappeared. 'She was poisoned?'

'The purple flowers are toxic if eaten. You can be poisoned if you drink the water these flowers have been standing in. It causes headaches, nausea, blurred vision ... Does this ring a bell?'

'It does. But the hospital thought someone

gave me the date-rape drug and I had severe confusion as well, remember?'

'I think it was more likely to be a small dose of digitalis poisoning. You were tested for date-rape because that's what we assumed it was. Have you ever seen the gardener?'

'No.' Note: check Tom, the gardener.

'And in extreme cases, like Holly's, it causes laboured breathing, convulsions and death. Holly Broughton was already dead when she was impaled on the stake. That, at least, was a mercy for the poor woman.'

I didn't want to think about it. But I knew that I would and I was going to have to go back to Faunstone Hall and scout around. Warning: don't drink anything, especially not out of a vase.

'And what about this Pointer person? Why is he a threat? And who is he, anyway?' I asked. 'If he's the manager, he wouldn't know me now. I was being a ghost hunter when he chased me out. And is there a connection? He isn't even around the pub these days. You asked me to find out more about the suit of armour and that's why I'm working there. Here, I've got some debris for forensic.'

'Thanks. Pointer is the owner,' said James, putting the specimen bag on his table. He sipped some more wine, which meant its therapeutic properties were getting to him. 'He has a record and a murky past. He's sold the Medieval Hall to this Russian and stands to make a million, if he can move it. We opposed the move on the grounds of waste of public funds, but it may now be going ahead.'

'I'm only working there temporarily,' I said.

'Very temporarily. I don't want you to go back.'

'Hey, you can't say that. I'm getting paid real money, cash in hand.'

'You're not broke any more, Jordan. You've got the reward money.'

'It's all tied up. I can't touch it till I'm sixty.' I allowed myself a small smirk. Lady of means. DI James didn't rule my life.

'I'm glad to hear that you have bought yourself a pension,' he said. 'I couldn't bear the thought of having to buy chips for a geriatric private eye. Zimmer frames are pretty slow moving.'

I didn't know whether to smile or cry. Was he planning to be around here in thirty years' time? No, it was one of his warped comments, not easy to understand but typical.

'Carlo likes having me work behind the bar,' I said. 'I can't let him down. And he spotted the pellet and made me go to hospital. I'm good at bar work. I even get tips.'

'Let him find someone else.'

'So when will you be out of hospital?' I asked, changing the subject. 'We must have dinner and celebrate.'

'I think there is altogether too much celebrating going on.' He had finished his glass and the wine bottle had disappeared. I could guess where. I could hear glasses clinking outside.

'I was suggesting fish and chips at Maeve's Café. With Mavis and Doris, Jack and Carlo.'

'Now, I'll go for that.'

'Why would someone turn out a dog that they loved?'

'Perhaps it's a crucial witness.'

'A dog could hardly give evidence.'

'I envy you, Jordan, all these complicated cases. You live such a high-powered life. Ask Sergeant Rawlings. He knows everything that goes on in Latching.'

'Like the new look,' I could not resist saying.

He was not amused. 'A spinal waistcoat is hardly high fashion but it beats staying in bed. They say that the fragment of bone will eventually dissolve.'

'If that bit of bone is going to dissolve, then what about your other bones?'

'Ask my doctor. Something about lack of nourishment. Bones have to be fed, you know.'

I phoned Carlo before I left the hospital, mumbling about the eye not being a pretty sight, but he stopped me abruptly.

'I'm sorry, Pollee ... but the pub has closed. They are moving the Medieval Hall. They started to jack it up this morning, inch by inch, on to a big trailer. I was here all night moving everything out.' He sounded tired and upset.

'Oh I'm so sorry,' I said, repeating his words. 'How awful, Carlo. You're out of work now and you are so good.'

'I'll soon get more work.'

'I might be able to help.' I was not sure how. Guilbert's had a rooftop restaurant. I could ask Francis. 'We'll be in touch.'

'*Ciao*, Pollee...'

I obeyed all the road rules driving towards Faunstone Hall, as I did not want to be caught by a camera or breathalysed. My clothes had dried out and my hair looked like a war zone. It had sand and petals in it and smelt of hospitals.

Faunstone Hall looked as if it was in mourning. There was no scene-of-crime tape. Curtains were drawn across some windows, glass panes too scummy to wink back the pale sunlight. Even the garden seemed to have gone fallow, daffodils and tulips faded and finished, wallflowers drooping. Not a foxglove in sight. Surely that wasn't a cobweb hanging off a shrub? Somewhere a bird sang a flat note.

I parked and knocked on the front door.

The brass lion-headed knocker needed a polish and there were crumpled leaves blown into the porch. Where was Mrs Malee and her broom? It was not like her to let things go.

She was not answering the door. No twitchy curtains here. The house was very still, with a growth of grieving. I expected to see a ring of mushrooms sprouting on the front lawn.

I went round the side of the house to the back entrance. It was the same there. No answer to my ringing the bell. I peered into the kitchen area. No welcoming light, counters bare and wiped, the table unlaid. It did not look as if it had been used for days.

'Hello,' I called out, knocking on the window. 'Is anyone at home?'

It was a house voided of feeling. It had lost its soul. Nothing but bricks and cement round an empty shell. But I knew Faunstone Hall would recover. It was an old house with a long history. It could not be the first time it had been branded with tragedy and one day it would recover with new life and a new family.

I am not normally reticent about entering a house if it will help with my investigations. But this was different. It seemed wrong to go into Holly's home without being invited. I fiddled with the handle of the back door. It was a purely reflex action.

And it opened. They had forgotten to lock the back door. People do that when they leave in a hurry.

I slipped in and closed the door behind me. No more calling out hello. I put down my bottle of water and took off my trainers so that I made no noise. As I moved through the kitchen I picked up a mallet, the kind you beat the hell out of sirloin steak with. It settled comfortably in my hand.

Downstairs seemed to be much as I remembered it but curiously forlorn. Holly and Mrs Malee had given character to the house but now they had both gone. There were dead flower arrangements but none of them were foxgloves. The water in the crystal vases had the aura of verdigris. The furniture had not seen a duster in days.

I crept upstairs, slowly and silently. The house might not be empty. I clutched the mallet tightly.

Holly had shown me her bedroom and dressing room, full of expensive clothes. I went along the landing, not counting the other doors. Someone might come flying out with a bigger mallet.

The door to her bedroom was ajar. I noticed that the pile of the carpet was brushed the wrong way as if something had been dragged along. A body. Had the police been here at all? I pushed the door open slowly. The room was silent.

Her king-sized bed was as before, smooth and unslept in. So she had died before she'd slept in it. Or had someone made the bed after her death? The dressing table was a clutter of expensive cosmetics and creams. Her bottles of perfume in orderly rows. She had a wide taste. I looked closer.

The lid to her jar of classic retinol moisturizer had not been replaced, nor the cap to her black extra-length mascara. Was this carelessness or had nobody noticed? I went into the dressing room. Drawers were open and a sliding cupboard door drawn back, some outfits and undies were thrown across an armchair. Had she been in the middle of dressing when this toxic drink had been administered? Yet she had been found fully clothed. Or had she? I needed a list of what she had been wearing.

Something was not right. Something that the police would not have noticed. Nor necessarily me, with my lack of knowledge of the right thing to wear or the current fashions. But I had the feeling that Holly had been disturbed in her dressing routine and that the murderer had finished putting on her clothes. Perhaps he'd enjoyed it.

So who had come into Holly's bedroom, her dressing room? Surely it could only have been her husband? Mrs Malee was far too slight to have removed the body to the beach and put it on a stake. It would have taken two to drag her downstairs and into a car. There had never been any mention of a current lover or a boyfriend. Holly had been in love with her husband, as she said.

Richard Broughton. Maybe he had wanted her out of the way before she did any more damage or tried to have him killed again. She was an expensive wife, even if she'd never meant him any harm.

But why had Richard Broughton decided to kill her? She must have known something else. She had prior knowledge, extra knowledge, something that would have ruined his financial dealings. I starting to get the feeling of a more complex web of relationships.

The room began to swim as all the convolutions of Holly's death began to come to me. She had been poisoned here, in her dressing room. Had Mrs Malee brought her the drink in a cut-glass tumbler, or hot tea in a bone-china cup, to refresh her while she dressed? I wanted to believe that Mrs Malee had not known the contents of the drink and that she also had been removed before Holly was dragged downstairs to the sea front.

I wanted to hear her voice but the room was silent. I was missing something. Holly was trying to tell me but I was too thick to notice. What should I do? Stay or leave? Search through more rooms? Take her bedroom to pieces? If only the walls could talk. I wanted to put my ear to the floor and listen.

I began to make notes. Position of clothes, cosmetics, the state of her bathroom. The bathroom. She had been disturbed at some point, but at which point? The bathroom had been tidied and cleaned but not to Holly's standard. I could see areas that had only had a perfunctory wipe round. The towels were only roughly folded. Then I looked at the lavatory. The seat was up. What does that tell you? A man had relieved himself in her bathroom.

I was beginning to feel what might have happened. Holly had been having a bath and asked Mrs Malee on the internal phone to bring her a drink. She had not yet decided what to wear. But it was her killer who'd brought the drink, and maybe sat around talking while she drank her last cuppa.

Holly had died here. Had the police taken samples from the sides of the bath where she had convulsed and died? It had been wiped clean. The killer had watched her die, then dried and dressed her with the nearest clothes – those from the previous day, probably – and dragged her down the stairs to a car. He had driven to the beach and impaled her on a stake in the wooden garden. His moves had been cold and calculated.

It was time to get out of the house before he came back. Because he might come back. He knew the house was unoccupied. Mrs

Malee had gone. I hoped that she was still alive. If I could find her, she might have some crucial information.

The house was giving me the creeps. I hurried downstairs and got out as fast as I could, struggling into my trainers as I hopped towards my car. I had opened the driver's door when I suddenly remembered what I had left in the kitchen. My bottle of mineral water was on a counter. If the killer came back and spotted something different in the house, he might come looking for me.

I turned to go back and grab my bottle. As I did this, there was a loud explosion and a sudden rush of hot air. I was thrown to the ground. Flames leaped skywards, smoke billowed all around. I struggled up, shocked and horrified, coughing, staring at my car.

I don't normally cry. I'm not a weeping woman. But now I wept as my black-and-red ladybird car burned before my eyes. My sweet companion. My fun car. My unique and wonderful wheels. She was wrecked and burning, flames shooting in all directions, bits flying and cracking, the noise like an inferno, a small inferno. The door had been wired to explode when I got into it. But I had not got in. I had turned back.

My hands were trembling as I keyed James on my mobile. Twice I made a mistake in the number.

'James?'

'Yes. Jordan?'

'Someone has just b-blown up my lady-bird,' I said.

'Get out fast, wherever you are. Move, girl.'

'I'm at Faunstone Hall.'

'I'll send out DS Morton and a team immediately. But you start walking now, Jordan, start running. They thought you would be in it when it blew up. They might still be around.'

'I'm not leaving her. She's burning to bits. It's awful. I'll stay till it's finished. I can't leave her.'

There was a long pause and I suppose he heard my sobs.

'You're quite mad,' he said.

Fifteen

DS Duke Morton arrived in a patrol car at the same time as the fire brigade lumbered up the drive. It was far too late to save anything of the ladybird. The hunky firemen rushed around with fire extinguishers and hoses but they were left with a steaming pile of twisted metal and debris.

I stood watching, not caring if the arsonist/murderer was still around. I felt like going back into the kitchen and bringing out the sharpest knife.

'What happened?' asked a helmeted fire officer.

'Incendiary device,' I said. 'It was timed to go off when I opened the door. You'll no doubt find a few wires or something.'

'Doubt if we'll find anything,' he said. 'It's pretty much burnt out.'

'There'll be something,' said DS Morton. 'There's always a trace of a toxic material, and as you were the target, Jordan, we'll have to regard this as attempted murder.'

'Third time lucky,' I said dryly. 'There was the poisoning, then the pellet, now the car.

I'll make the *Guinness Book of Records* at this rate.'

'If you wouldn't mind coming to the station to make a statement,' said Duke. 'Then I'll drive you home.'

'Story of my life, making statements. I've made more statements than you've had hot dinners. I could write a book on statements that I have made. Good title. "Statements I Have Made". It would be a best-seller. They could make it into a TV series. Amanda Burton could play me.'

'She's a blonde.'

'Hair dye. We could easily find the exact shade. How about Holly Hunter? I like her. A good actress.'

'She's very short and you are tall. DI James said you talk a lot of nonsense. Now I know it.'

'What about my ladybird? We can't leave her here.'

'I'll get the Council to come and clear the wreckage after the forensic squad have looked it over.'

'No way,' I said vehemently. 'She's no ordinary wreckage. I'm not having her taken away and dumped at some breaker's yard as if she was rubbish. The ladybird was special, vintage, my friend, companion, trusted member of the team.'

DS Morton looked at me with suspicion, as if he might have to fetch a straitjacket.

'She was a car, Jordan. Bits of metal. A very old car.'

'An old car with black spots and brand new wheels. I'm not having her carted away by the Council.'

'OK,' he said. 'What do you want? Full-scale funeral, hymn sheets, local vicar, flowers, wake in a pub?'

I tried to simmer down. 'I don't know what I want,' I said. 'Give me time to think about it. It has to be something special, different. The ladybird was no ordinary car. I'm not having her tipped into a dip.' I was still rhyming.

'You'll need a new car now.'

I clamped my mouth. 'I've got a mountain bike.'

'Hope you don't get blown off. We're in for some windy weather. Summer's not here yet, running late this year.'

'I don't mind the weather. I like wind, rain, storms, gales. They don't worry me. Rain is good for the skin. It's a natural moisturizer.'

'Naturally wet,' said Duke with a grin. 'Get in the car, Jordan. The natural moisturizer is about to descend whether your skin needs it or not.'

I liked him. He didn't try to put me down as DI James often did. He was genial without being excessive, kind and straightforward. I got into the passenger seat, without looking at what was left of the ladybird, smouldering in a heap on the ground. I couldn't bear it. I was silvered with sweat. She wasn't just a car. She meant more than that to me.

I remembered when I had fallen in love with her, up in the hills, at a tree nursery where a pond of valuable waterlilies had been stolen. Somehow I'd managed to scrape together the asking money and driven her home, the proudest car owner in Latching. Not exactly the right car for undercover surveillance, all those black spots; but she had never let me down.

No point in looking back. The ladybird had gone. Nothing left for a cosmetic makeover. But she had been wonderful for my morale. The perfect vehicle for someone like me. A scatterbrain, an eccentric, an oddity, brave and foolhardy.

DS Morton noticed my quietness. 'You need a cup of tea,' he said. 'Shock. It's been a shock. We'll stop at the next pub and get some tea.'

Pubs were scarce along this part of the coast. But a red brick row of three cottages appeared, now operating under the collective name of the George. Duke parked well to the back of the car park so that the resident drinkers did not take fright at the sight of a patrol car. I appreciated his tact.

He took me to a quiet corner of the pub. It was a friendly, low-ceilinged place with a small fire burning in a stone grate to take off the chill. A big dog lay stretched out, gathering the heat on his back. Faded brown pictures of the village and the cottages in earlier times hung on the walls. There were also ancient farming implements hung from the ceiling, some still with wisps of straw. I began to relax as a tray of tea appeared, complete with teapot and jug of hot water.

'I'll be mother and pour,' said Duke. The cups were blue-rimmed china, differently patterned, good quality. My 206 bones and twenty-three pairs of chromosomes sank into the soft, upholstered sofa. Duke sat forward so that his weight would not tip the sofa into another less comfortable angle. He was a heavy man.

'Thank you.'

'Sugar?'

'I prefer honey but you wouldn't know that.'

'Sorry, no honey. Sugar?'

I nodded. 'For the shock.'

'Definitely for the shock. One spoonful.'

The detective sergeant was kind, like a big teddy bear. He didn't try anything on. He was quiet, not talking too much, drinking his tea, giving me time to accept what had happened. He made a few calls on his phone. He had brown eyes, intense and lit with golden specks, behind his glasses. A bit like Miguel, but not with a dark Latin look. Duke was very English. I wondered how he'd got his name.

'Were you christened Duke?' I had to ask.

'No.'

'So it's a nickname.'

'Sort of. My parents christened me Windsor.' He suppressed a groan and I didn't blame him. 'The kids called me Duke at school.'

'Parents have funny ideas. I'm named after a river.'

I began to think that it was fitting that the ladybird should have gone in the line of duty. No failing her MOT or humiliatingly rusting away, back of the shop, like a decrepit old pensioner clinging to her last breath. She had gone out in style.

Duke poured out a second cup of tea, adding hot water. How did he know that I preferred weak tea? Perhaps he had a sixth sense, or was it another DI James briefing? Eventually he had to drive me back to Latching. The tea ceremony couldn't be prolonged any further.

Sergeant Rawlings was on duty behind the posh new reception area. He looked up and grinned.

'What they got you in for this time?' he asked.

'Someone blew up my ladybird. My lovely car. She's gone, burnt out.' I couldn't help sounding pathetic. I sniffed and straightened up. 'Obviously another attempt on my life, only their timing was out. I'd turned back for a bottle of water.'

'To put out the fire?'

'To drink.'

'Narrow escape,' he said, offering me a box of tissues. 'I'll put you in interview room B. It's got the best view. Very sorry, Jordan, about your car. Know how you liked it.'

DS Morton was decoding the door to the inner sanctum. They'd changed the digits. I memorized the new ones and when I got a private moment, wrote them in the palm of my hand. Could be handy. DS Morton switched on the tape.

'Detective Sergeant Morton interviewing Miss Jordan Lacey, time—'

'Your watch is slow,' I said.

'Please don't interrupt.'

'Sorry.'

We were five minutes into the statement when Sergeant Rawlings came in with two mugs of tea. It was the usual strong station brew but I tried to look pleased and grateful.

'How kind, thank you. Sergeant Rawlings, can you tell me why someone would throw out a dog they loved? You might have some ideas. It's a dog called Nutty.'

DS Morton switched off the machine with a resigned look. He stirred his tea and studied his notes, silently praying for patience.

'Does he answer to his name?'

'He answers to anything. He's seriously

deranged.'

'Sounds my kind of dog. No, I don't know but I'll give it some thought. Is it a retriever? Brings things back?'

'Could we get on with the statement?' said DS Morton. 'We don't have all day. Jordan, go back to what you were doing in Faunstone Hall.'

'I didn't break in if that's what you are insinuating. The back door was open. I was looking around, trying to find some sort of clue as to why or where Holly Broughton was murdered. Something that the police might have missed.'

'And had the police missed anything?'

I nodded mysteriously. 'As a matter of fact, I believe they did. I need to know what she was wearing when they found her. I need to know exactly, every article of clothing, nothing left out for modesty's sake.'

'I can get you a list,' said DS Morton. 'Though I don't suppose I should. It won't take long. Then what happened?'

I described the rest of my search and the moment when I went outside to my car and opened the door. 'I turned to go back for my bottle of water. As I turned, I heard this explosion and the car burst into flames. My ladybird was on fire.'

'Did you see anyone when you were in the house?'

I shook my head. 'I didn't see or hear

anyone. But someone must have been there. They booby-trapped my car while I was in the house.'

'And that takes a few minutes, even for an expert.'

'I didn't see a soul. The house was deserted.'

'They were outside waiting, or maybe they had followed you to the Hall.'

'Not a happy thought. I didn't notice anyone following me. There was a tractor ahead at one point, pulling a trailer of hay, going at about four miles an hour until I could get past.'

'Whoever it was won't be there now. We had a look round. No tractor or car tracks.'

'A bicycle wouldn't leave any tracks. Motorbike?'

'Not if it was dumped in a ditch.'

I was tiring. I was losing the thread of the statement I was making and wanted to go home. No wheels. I would have to walk. If I went to see DI James now, it would be by the new high-speed, automatic-doors train. Back to train strain again. I remembered once sitting up half the night in a Brighton hotel bar, waiting for the first train back to Latching.

'They sell our laid-off patrol cars, y'know,' said Sergeant Rawlings, as I left. I would have to go back later to sign the typed-out statement. 'They get auctioned off at a depot. Usually only a year old. I can find out for you.'

'I've no wish to drive around in a bright psychedelic yellow-blue-green-and-orange-patterned vehicle.'

'No different from spots.'

'Thank you for the thought,' I said, exhausted by the whole idea of having to find something new. I couldn't bear to think about the hassle. The ladybird had been love at first sight. It couldn't happen twice.

'Here's a print-out of that list of clothing that you asked for,' said DS Morton. 'I want it back.'

'Thanks,' I said. 'I'll bring it back tomorrow.'

I needed to walk the pier and clear my head. And clear the smell of burning from out of my nostrils. The wind had freshened in the last hour. The flags streamed southerly, poles rocking and creaking, and the sea was churning into mud-coloured froth. It was almost too difficult to breathe as I struggled round the far end, deep out at sea. The water was dark and fathomless.

I nipped into the amusement arcade to lean against a wall and catch my breath. Jack strolled over, juggling some tools. He'd been repairing a faulty machine, a high-powered rocket-propelled car-drive game which was apparently refusing to go anywhere.

'So I hear you lost your wheels,' he added.

224

'Is nothing private? How did you hear?'

'Dunno. It was a fireman, I think. Came in off duty to throw away some money. Blown up, was it?'

'I don't want to talk about it.'

'Please yourself. Wanna borrow the Jag? You can if you like – suits me. About time I had a new car. I fancy a Roller,' he said. 'Something flashy.'

His silvery-blue Jaguar was twice the length of the ladybird. I'd never be able to park. I shuddered at the thought of all that power throbbing under the bonnet. It would not take kindly to my careful thirty miles an hour along the leafy lanes.

'That's very kind of you,' I said, struggling to be polite. 'Let me think about it. I need a couple of days to get my head together.'

'Wanna lift anywhere, I'll drive yer.'

'Now that would be helpful,' I said, warmly. 'I may take you up on that.' But I knew he would not care to drive me to Brighton to see DI James. Certain things were beyond his kind heart.

My feet dragged as I walked to Latching station. My clothes smelled of the fire. There'd been no time to wash or change. I needed a hose down. I wanted to look foxy for James but there was no convenient time. He'd have to see the worn-out version.

The countryside flashed by, past the airfield at Shoreham dotted with tiny private planes, then over the river Arun, which was at high tide, water lapping the banks and small boats rocking at anchor. I knew the walk to the hospital on autopilot. Shop windows reflected back the stressed-out me, accentuating every wrinkle, every downward droop. Brighton had great shops. I looked awful. A cat wouldn't even drag me in.

A skinny shop model stared back through her inch-long black lashes, disdainful and emaciated. Her white jeans shimmered with silver leg embroidery and a belt hung round her hips in layers of plaited white fringing. The top was bright poppy-red cotton, a clingy camisole style with a collarless cropped jacket in navy. I had to have it. It went against the grain to pay with plastic but I had no option. I needed that outfit. Red, white and blue. Very patriotic. It even fitted. I walked out of the shop wearing it, security tags carefully removed, my own clothes bundled into a shiny posh designer bag. Call me a shopaholic.

It was only a few hundred yards from the hospital when I went into a corner café, drank two cups of black coffee, then washed my hair with liquid soap under the cold tap in the ladies' loo and dried it under the hot hand dryer. Tricky manoeuvre in a cramped space. No conditioner.

The nurses hovering round the nurses' station nodded to me, not entirely sure if it was the same visitor who'd brought the bottle of good Shiraz. I knocked on the door and went into James's room.

James was standing stiffly by the window, looking down at Brighton's myriad rooftops. He looked like a caged bird of prey. He was longing to get out and test his wings. His dark-green shirt looked bulky as if he was wearing a bullet-proof vest. Ah, the spinal waistcoat.

'Look who's standing?' was all I could think of saying. Prime idiot remark. He turned slowly as if he was afraid he might crack or fall over. I'd forgotten how tall he was. His skin had lost its healthy tan. He needed to get out and about.

'Excuse me?' he said. 'Do I know you?'

'I'm a journalist from *Hello* magazine,' I said breezily. 'We want to do a promotion on the NHS and medical vogues. Would you say that your current Incredible Hulk image is likely to catch on with the inmates – sorry, I mean patients – of the NHS?'

'What have you done to yourself?' James asked, peering as if he was short-sighted. 'Is this you? You don't usually look like a fashion plate.'

'I had to buy some new clothes. I smelt like yesterday's barbecue, not very nice.'

He came over and fingered the jacket. 'It's not finished,' he said. 'They've forgotten to put on a collar.'

'Collarless is a fashion,' I said.

He nodded. 'Sorry about your car, Jordan. Neat little vehicle. Were you insured?'

'Of course, I was. What do you think I am? Driving round like a criminal?'

'You'll need a replacement car pretty quick.'

'I know. The walk from the station nearly killed me. I swear it's got longer.'

'I'll be out of here soon. I'm booked to go to the police convalescent home – very informal, residential for officers and pensioners, at Goring-on-Thames. I'll be there for a couple of weeks.'

'It's all going well then?' Second idiot remark.

'The doctors are very pleased. By the way, my mother has sent you a gift. She's taken a shine to you.' He took a small packet wrapped in lilac tissue paper out of his pocket and handed it to me.

I unwrapped it. A small silver brooch lay in my hand, a silver thistle. 'It's lovely,' I said, delighted. 'What a kind thought. I like your mother very much.'

'She obviously likes you. Let me pin it on your jacket. The clasp might be a little tricky. It's got a safety catch.'

He pinned the brooch on my new jacket. It matched the silver embroidery on the new white jeans.

'Thank you. I'll write her a little note. Can

I visit you at Goring-on-Thames?'

'I shouldn't bother, Jordan. You've got enough on your plate at the moment. Anyway, you should keep a low profile till we've caught whoever is after you.'

'Do you know who you are looking for?'

'How should I know? I'm stuck here. I'm not looking for anyone. It's not my case.'

'That's not the answer I want to hear.'

'That's all the answer you are getting.' He looked at me closely. 'Are you wearing a bra under that skimpy red top you've almost got on?'

I blinked. It was the closest James had ever got to a personal remark. I wished I could have recorded it to play over and over again. And I was wearing a bra.

'By the way, that's what I came to tell you.'

'What?'

'Holly Broughton wasn't wearing a bra when she was found on the beach,' I said. 'She wasn't completely dressed. No one seems to have noticed that.'

'And what do you deduce from that fact?'

'That she was murdered by a man who couldn't put a bra on. Men are pretty deft at taking a bra off, but ask them to put a bra on and they are all fingers and thumbs.'

James's face was without expression. 'I wouldn't know,' he said.

Sixteen

It was difficult to hide the small wave of happiness that took me by surprise. It was almost too much. James was thrown by my remark, too. James was standing, at last. James had noticed my new look. Three bulls-eyes in one go. Hallelujah.

He took on board the information about Holly being bra-less and that a man had been the last person to use the bathroom. He said he would pass it on in case no one had noticed the significance. No jokes. It was not a jokey case. Holly had died. But I could not see or understand why.

'I can't see the motivation,' I said.

'It's complicated. The husband had won his case. He was riding high, safe as houses, or so he thought. What we need to know is who sparked the police investigation which led to the trial? That name, as yet, is unknown. She or he is the mystery person.'

'Why do you say it's a she?' I asked.

'I think there's a woman in the case.'

'Maybe you are right. Men don't usually split on each other, but another woman might.'

'A woman who is interested in Richard Broughton. After all, he is very rich.'

'And also very nasty. She needs her eyes testing. That man is totally unpleasant.' I remembered the look in Richard Broughton's eyes and the way they had threatened me. Then I remembered something else. 'James, I think you're right. It's a woman. A woman with an evil sense of humour. I found one of Holly's earrings in the wooden beach garden. Only a woman would think of dressing a corpse with earrings.'

'But Holly married Richard and apparently loved him.'

'Love is blind.' There was no other answer. I didn't think James would know anything about love being blind. True, he had once been married, but I did not detect any of that magic in his relationship. Whereas I was one of those people walking cloud nine every time I was near him.

I slipped off cloud nine as I went to Brighton station and caught a slow-stopping Class 720 train back to Latching. Food? What was that? Had I had any? I couldn't remember.

There was another long walk from the station in the ebbing hours of the day. Damp air clambered up my ankles like fingers. Summer was still unsure of its welcome. The skimpy vest top was letting in draughts. But drifts of blossom touched me from one of the houses that still had trees. Trees were ruthlessly destroyed to make room for parking cars in front gardens.

Parked cars. It was sitting in the drive of a large, double-fronted white Edwardian house. It looked forlorn. Racy, low two-seaters do not take kindly to cardboard For Sale signs prominently on the windscreen. Humiliating. OK if it was a Ford Fiesta.

It was a 1999 two-seater BMW, so low-slung it would be like sitting on the road. I liked the colour immediately – not navy, not blue, but sort of indigo. The bodywork matched my best pair of jeans.

The number plate was eye-catching. At first glance it was V 1O ILA, numbers and letters, but read it even quicker and it became VIOLA. Viola was a character in Shakespeare's *Twelfth Night* and I had played her at school.

A blank, my lord. She never told her love,
But let concealment, like a worm i' the bud,
Feed on her damask cheek.

I remembered the words so easily. It had been one of the parts that stirred a recumbent, reluctant acting ability which occasionally I use in my work. Viola ... Like the ladybird, she had a name. This was appallingly fickle of me. Surely I ought to mourn a little longer for my ladybird?

A racy two-seater was not exactly top of the charts for comfort. But a new PI image was irresistible to my damaged ego. Dark-leather interior, those classy alloy wheels. The price was £7,500, which was staggering for a PI whose current caseload was stolen hens and rabbits, a case for which she was unlikely to charge a penny. Since the reward money was firmly untouchable in a pension, I would have to get a bank loan.

I knocked on the heavy front door, another brass lion's head. Lions were rampant in Latching.

'Hi,' I said. 'I'm here to make you an offer for your BMW. Are you interested?'

My local fame helped. No Latching house-hold ever forgot the rugby tackle on the two robbers in the amusement arcade, even though it was a couple of years ago now. The owners of the BMW beamed at me. The idea of their son's BMW being used for surveillance was tempting after-dinner talk. And I was still wearing the smart white embroidered jeans and cropped jacket, which was a big plus. I looked successful and one hundred per cent with it.

'So what is he driving now?' I asked.

'A kangaroo killer. He's gone to Australia.'

'Can I make you an offer? Knock it down a bit?'

'Of course. Would you like to take her for a drive?'

They were trusting. She drove like a dream, rather refined like the classy lady she was. We would get to know each other slowly. As long as she did not pine for racing at breakneck speeds through the country lanes at midnight after a wild teenage party.

We exchanged phone numbers and they took the notice off the windscreen. I would be getting in touch.

The bank manager agreed the next morning that it was rather a lot for a second-hand car but also agreed that a high-powered PI needed something fast. He offered me half.

I could scrape up some myself. How many rich friends did I have? Jack, amassing money as swiftly as the punters rolled the coin-slot machines. Miguel, doing well with his posh Mexican restaurant; but since I kept him and his adoration at a distance, it would not be tactful. Francis Guilbert, owner of the best store in town ... He would not even ask what the money was for.

His office at Guilbert's was still on the top floor with a panoramic view of Latching. The view had changed a little but Francis had not. He came straight over to me, arms outstretched.

'Jordan, dear girl, what a wonderful surprise. Where have you been? I've missed our little suppers together.'

'I'm sorry,' I said, hugging him back. 'I've kept away on purpose. I thought you were getting too fond of me.'

He understood. 'You are quite right. I was beginning to have wonderful dreams of us taking a Caribbean cruise together, but I would still like to see you occasionally. So why have you come to see me now? You must want a favour. I sincerely hope so.'

I was ashamed. We had once been close, drawn together by the death of his son, but since then I had neglected him. Francis Guilbert was almost sixty, still handsome, silver-haired, stocky. I couldn't raise his hopes.

'I want to borrow some money.'

'Easily done. How much do you want?'

'Pay you back, of course.'

'I know. I said, how much?'

I could not take it so easily. 'Do you remember my little car?' He nodded. 'The one with the black spots on it? The ladybird. She was blown up. Someone was trying to kill me.'

'How truly awful. You must take more care and you must have another car. Perhaps one that's not so conspicuous. I would hate to have you blown up. It would be too awful to lose two special people in a lifetime.' Francis Guilbert was such a nice man, but a couple of decades too old.

'I've raised half the money with a loan from the bank but I need the other half,' I said. I felt so awful, sinking into Guilbert's best-quality-carpeted floor.

'Consider it done.' He was getting out a cheque book. He dated a cheque and signed it. 'How much?'

'Three thousand pounds.'

'Is that all? I was hoping for a lot more, then I could twist your arm into a supper together.'

He was such a dear. Our suppers had always been at his house, something simple. Cheese and pâté, a good wine. Those evenings had been pleasant and I had needed them. James had been more than distant then and a man's admiration had been such a tonic to my diminishing confidence. We had become good friends. Then I had let the friendship slip. I have a mercurial streak.

'I don't know what to say.'

'Just say yes, and agree you'll come for supper one evening soon. I won't tie you down to when, knowing you must be on some horrid case. Why were they trying to blow you up?' Francis shuddered. 'I do wish you would come and work for me again. Flexible hours, excellent pay, staff discount. Can't I tempt you?'

I had to laugh. It was tempting. He wanted someone to step into his shoes now that he had lost his only son. He wanted to groom me, train me up, adopt me. I wondered if I could fit in a little retail therapy. Could I run a store like Guilbert's? Running First Class

Junk was hardly in the same category. I didn't tell him about the drugging and the air gun.

I took the cheque and kissed him on the cheek. 'Supper, yes, I promise, soon. Job – well, I'll think about it and maybe we could talk some more. But really, I'm not good enough or clever enough. When I did work for you, I made a lot of mistakes.'

'We all make mistakes. It's part of life's learning curve. It's admitting the mistakes that's important.'

'I have a friend, a young Italian, Carlo, who needs a job in a restaurant. He's just been made redundant.'

'Send him along to me.'

He looked so sad when I left that I almost ran back and agreed to do everything that he wanted. But it's not possible to fulfil everyone's dreams. He had to find someone else.

Viola was almost within my grasp, her steering wheel under my hands. But I still felt it was too soon since the ladybird had been blown up. What a way to go. No collapsing with the weight of rust, no major engine failure, no serious brake problems. I wanted a fitting end for her. Crushed and reduced to a small wedge of metal was out of the question.

I phoned Duke Morton. 'Look,' I said, 'you won't have her taken to the knacker's yard and crushed into a small metal block, will you?'

'Are you talking about your car?' He didn't know me very well.

'Yes, you've taken her away for forensic. I know they can still find fingerprints and blood even after a fire. But I want her back, all the bits, for a proper farewell.'

'James said you were mad.'

'And you've said that twice.'

This was beginning to annoy me. He had adopted a patronizing tone which I had not noticed before. DS Morton had seemed nice enough; now he was showing that masculine side which I detested.

'Just give me back the bits in a very large cardboard box,' I said in an icy voice. 'And I will dispose of them. Never you mind how. Nothing illegal.'

'You're not allowed to dump them in the sea,' he snapped.

'As if I would,' I said. He was obviously tired, not enough sleep. 'All that rust.'

That afternoon I laid out the cards on my office floor. The shop was dusty. Every index card had some aspect of the Holly Broughton case on it and everything that had happened. It was an old trick of mine. Moving the cards around into different patterns and arrangements sometimes sparked off a new idea, a new line of enquiry.

But my brain wasn't working properly. I

could only see my car burning and the flames licking at her frame. As well as being sad, I was starting to get very angry at the senseless destruction.

I stormed back to my flat, barely looking where I was going. All this up-and-down of emotions was no good for my stress levels. I might go grey overnight. My mother went grey very early.

Since my body needed some sort of sustenance, I made myself a sandwich from stale granary bread, runny Brie cheese, a shrivelled tomato, limp lettuce, walnuts and dried-up home-made horseradish relish. It was revolting, reminding me that I had not shopped for days. I sat on the floor, watching wallpaper television, chewing gunge.

Notes: Who killed Holly Broughton?

Who stuck her on a stake?

Who fed me hallucinatory digitalis?

Who shot at me with an air gun?

Who blew up the ladybird?

Who stole the hens and rabbits?

What about the Medieval Hall?

In that order. It was quite a list. And I had no answers whatsoever. But I had a gut feeling that the first five questions all had the same answer, the same name. But what name? James might know but then he was not on this case.

I couldn't sleep yet. I was still hungry but Mother Hubbard had nothing, not even a past-sell-by-date yoghurt. I prowled the streets wondering what I could buy from a takeaway that wasn't junk. Maeve's Café was closed. My steps took me back towards my shop in the hope that it had a left-over packet of cashew nuts or digestive biscuits.

'Oh no you don't,' said Miguel, stepping out on to the darkening pavement. 'You don't pass my door without saying hello, or coming inside to taste my latest dish.'

I was ridiculously pleased, liking him a lot. I had missed him, this fortyish, darkish Mexican chef who thought I was special. I followed him in, knowing I would be pampered and fed and escorted home all in one piece. It sounded good.

'Hello,' I said. 'How are you?'

'Feeling better now to see you.'

The restaurant was half empty. This was unusual as it was usually full to the brim with a waiting list for cancellations, particularly divorced women on their own, driving in from a large surrounding area.

'There is international soccer match on television, some final cup,' he wailed as he took me to my usual corner table, two chairs, a single rose in a vase. 'They eat takeaways and watch a ball running round a field. I cannot believe it.'

He poured out a red wine without even asking. The glass was a deep goblet. 'I will choose dish,' he said. 'You have not eaten properly for days, I can see that. No colour. Maybe you are still ill. Please wait, Jordan. Do not fly away. Stay.'

'I had a mouldy sandwich.'

'A sandwich? Is that food?'

No thought of flight when sitting in Miguel's candle-lit restaurant, sipping a full-bodied red wine, nothing out of a box. He was cooking for me. Tossing things about in the kitchen, adding garlic. All I had to do was wait and mellow. Again, another good man, waiting for me to make up my mind.

It was a big oval dish of lobster and other seafood, steaming and aromatic, with rice and a side salad. He called it Langosta Con Arroz. Miguel placed it between us and we ate together, enjoying the tastes and the pleasure of good company. Miguel drank mineral water. He was still cooking, had a restaurant to run. But I had a glass of potent red to finish. It went straight to my head.

'So,' said Miguel, his dark brown eyes full of concern, 'what is happening? Why have you kept away from me?'

I did not know what to say. He had helped me out so many times and cared about me. And I had the softest of spots for him, but he kept disappearing back to his home in the hills outside Acapulco. Maybe he had a family out there with dozens of bambinos. James was the only man in my life. It was complicated enough already.

'I am being targeted by some villain,' I said. 'Dose of drugs first, then shot at with an air gun, now my car has been blown up. My ladybird. There's no way I want any of my friends involved in this kind of mayhem. It's too dangerous.'

He looked shocked, a succulent morsel of langouste perched on his fork. He was poised to whisk me out of the country to his hacienda. I could see him mentally buying air tickets on the Internet, checking his passport, packing a shirt without once leaving my side.

'No,' I said firmly before he could say a word. 'I'm not going away anywhere, so put that right out of your mind. I'm staying here to see it through. I've survived three threatening experiences so nothing more can happen.'

'But it is too dangerous. I not believe this. You are in dangerous place. Please, Jordan, let me take you to safe house. I know where. They will not find you again. You will be invisible to the world.'

'That's not my style. I don't run away. I want to find out who blew up my car. I'm really serious about this, Miguel. They are not going to get away with it.' The wine was making me feel incredibly brave and capable.

'You must let me do something. If you won't let me take you out of the country, at least stay in my flat where I can keep both of my eyes on you. Your little flat could be booby-trapped up to ceiling,' he said. His words were getting pretty mixed up.

Miguel had lost his appetite and pushed the dish away. Some customers came in and he got up immediately to greet them. His smile was warm and genuine as he showed them to a table and brought a dish of complimentary croutes to nibble while they read the menu. He hid his concern like the professional he was. I bet he won prizes cooking in Mexico.

I didn't want to move. I felt safe sitting at this table with Miguel around. Like James, he would take care of me. It seemed sensible to stay at his flat. He would be the perfect gentleman and sleep on the sofa. No, I would sleep on the sofa. There was no way I could go home and collect some stuff. My flat might be wired. Making a sandwich had been safe enough but flushing the loo might set off an explosion. I hoped Miguel had a spare toothbrush.

I was getting the strangest feeling of déjà vu. This had happened before. I was seeing a couple sitting together across the room, talking in low voices, already sipping white wine. The man had his back to me but the immaculate suiting seemed familiar. The woman with him was in her late forties with short-cropped blonde hair curling over her ears. I caught a glimpse of diamond earrings and a gold brooch shaped like a clef of music on her black-silk blouse.

I turned my head away quickly and concentrated on chasing the last grains of rice on my plate, my thoughts racing. They had not seen me. Somehow I had to slip out the back way, through the kitchen. The man had a name but not the woman. And I'd seen that brooch before. Holly had been wearing it. It was too much of a coincidence.

Seventeen

It was strange going home with Miguel when the restaurant closed, to his sea-front flat in a prestigious new Georgian-style block towards East Latching. It was so exclusive each tenant had coded entry through the main entrance, a code for the lift, another code for his own front door. It would take MI5 to get in.

The interior walls were painted a silvery white; all the doors were silvery white, subdued lights were concealed in the ceiling, the floor highly polished. I felt I ought to tip-toe. Miguel was out of place in these cool surroundings but he seemed happy enough, whistling under his breath.

'It is because you are with me,' he said. 'Always my dream to show you my home.'

But once inside his flat all Mexico was let loose. An explosion of colour and warmth met me. Handwoven rugs and wall tapestries and vibrant pictures; comfortable armchairs, rosy lamps and a huge plasma television set in the wall. Exotic plants grew rampant in big terracotta pots; more pots and window boxes full of flowers filled the iron-railed balcony facing the sea. Books and magazines lay strewn on the floor.

He began picking them up, returning them to low bookcases along the side of the big window. He collected glasses and took them through to the kitchen. I caught a glimpse of a tangled rope of garlic hanging from a hook.

'This is absolutely lovely, a beautiful flat,' I said, bemused. 'So big and colourful. Fancy living here.'

'You could live here any time you like, Jordan, if you fancy. I don't have to tell you that.'

He was grinning, obviously unable to believe that he had finally captured me. But I was scared, not of Miguel, but because suddenly I realized I should be looking over my shoulder all the time. Someone was out to get me and a fourth time was not out of the question. I no longer had James looking out for me. Duke did not have the same commitment to my welfare.

'Thank you for letting me come here,' I said. 'You're quite right. My flat isn't safe, nor my shop, I suppose. But I don't have anything with me, only what I'm wearing.'

'I can find you a new toothbrush. And if you don't mind, a clean T-shirt of mine for the sleeping?'

I nodded. 'Sounds good. Thank you.'

There was no need for anyone to take a

pillow to the sofa. Miguel showed me through to a second bedroom. The furniture was all fitted. It was mostly white wood but the fabric touches were yellow and orange. It looked like a sunlit room in Mexico on a hot day. A small bathroom was decorated in the same colours, several thick yellow towels waiting for me to mess up. I was going to be so comfortable. I couldn't wait to roll into that bed and pull up the fluffy butter-yellow duvet. Waves of tiredness rolled over me. It was probably the wine at last, and all that had happened.

'I'm sorry but I can hardly keep my eyes open,' I said.

'I know. I can see. Go to your sleep time. Goodnight, Jordan.' Miguel sounded disappointed and I'm sure he was, but there was nothing I could do about it. I had promised him nothing.

'Goodnight, dear Miguel, dearest friend,' I said, kissing his cheek. The curve of his cheek felt bristly. He was a two-shaves-a-day man. 'And thank you again.'

I don't remember washing or cleaning my teeth or falling asleep. I was a walking zombie, suddenly exhausted by all the trauma of the last few days. The T-shirt was extra-large and brightly coloured. It went round me twice, folding me into his dreams. For once I didn't remember my dreams.

Sun streamed through the window, pooling

sunlight and waking me up. I blinked up at the white ceiling, wondering where I was. This was not my flat. It was too big, too clean. A hotel? The hot colours reminded me of Miguel and I remembered he was in the next room. Fast asleep, I hoped.

I peeked in. And he was, worn out by working long hours in a restaurant. I tiptoed past to the kitchen and made myself a cup of tea. He had lovely blue-striped pottery and copper cooking utensils. I poked around his collection of spices and extra-virgin oils. His chopping board was well grooved with knife scars. Herbs grew in pots on the window sill in cluttered array.

If I took him some tea, it might be mis-construed as an overture. I did not want to orchestrate a situation. I took my tea out on to the balcony despite a light breeze blowing off the sea. I sat well back from the road but still in sunshine. No one could see me. I was not there.

It was bliss. I have always wanted a balcony. An unfulfilled dream. To be able to sit and watch the sea at any time, undisturb-ed, no one falling over you, no kids scream-ing. My idea of heaven. A book and a glass of wine.

Miguel staggered into the kitchen wearing a towelling bathrobe. He was rubbing his eyes and face, rasping his shadowed chin. He took in the table I had laid with fruit and cereal, rolls ready to warm.

'Hi,' I said. 'Do you have breakfast? If so, coffee's on the way.'

'I'll make the coffee,' he insisted. 'Sorry, I only like the way I make it. But the table looks most nice.'

'Up to your usual standard?'

'Roads ahead.'

It was a low-key breakfast. Miguel did not talk much. If I had known him better, I would have told him to go back to bed and get some more sleep. He was a bit grumpy. I began stacking the breakfast things in the dishwasher and said I was going out.

'No way, Jordan.' Miguel wouldn't let me go out, even when I promised not to go far. He refused adamantly, got up and locked the front door.

'You are not going out. That is my finality word.'

'You can't keep me in,' I said, alarmed. I hated being locked in, memories of the hermit's cell. 'I can disguise myself. No one will recognize me. It's my trade mark.' Detective work is an art. It was a case of sorting out the clues into some sort of sense. Everything was attached to something else. It was my job to unwrap the past. And I had more clues now.

'I won't allow it.'

'How can I find out who did all these things if I'm shut up in your flat?'

'Let the police do it. That's their job.'

I shook my head. 'They might be following the wrong track.'

'All the more reason for you to stay here.'

This was interesting. Miguel was grumpy in the mornings and a bit bossy although perhaps it was because I had not shared his bed. That would remain an enigma. I would not put it to the test.

He worked on his accounts at a desk and computer, while I tidied the kitchen and put everything away. I'd done this before – cleared up breakfast at James' folly home, Marchmont Tower. But James had not been there and I'd escaped out of a window.

I felt a gust of sorrow sweep through me like an east wind from Portsmouth. Where was I going? What was going to happen to me? My present life was a mess. Temporarily, I hoped.

'That couple in your restaurant last night,' I said, watering the plants on the balcony. My longing for a balcony near the sea swept over me again. I could see myself again sitting on a cushioned cane sofa, with a good book and a glass of red by my side, warming my skin in the late-evening sunshine. But not today and the price was too high. The sun had disappeared and a chalky sky was already hurrying rain clouds.

'Yes?'

'Do you know them?'

'I don't know them but they come in quite regularly. At least once a month.'

'Do you know their name?'

'Broughton,' he said, turning back to his screen. 'They don't ever book and they pay with a credit card. No problem.'

Richard Broughton had not caught sight of me, so that was a relief. The woman with him seemed familiar, but I could not place her. I'd seen her face somewhere before.

Miguel dressed to go out, casual slacks and a fleece sweater to his neck. He felt the cold. He came over and kissed me, smelling of aftershave.

'I'm sorry I have not talked much but I always do paperwork in the morning. Now I have to go to Brighton, to the fish markets and to buy fresh fruit and vegetables, and then to the bank, for banking the money.'

'Can I come with you? I'd like that. I love markets.'

'No, you stay here.'

'May I use your computer?'

He looked relieved. 'Of course. It is connected to the Internet. You can do what you like, Jordan. Check your emails, do the Google. Play a game of Solitaire cards.'

'I'd like to check my emails.'

'Don't tell anyone you are here. People hack into emails for information.' He looked alarmed, hesitated.

'I'll be careful,' I smiled. I looked a picture

of innocent reliability, not a wrinkle in the blanket. He went out, locking the front door behind him. I immediately went round checking the locks. The windows were double-glazed against the noise of the sea-front traffic, and the flat was on the third floor. No easy way down. There was a rubbish chute in the kitchen to some basement incinerator. Not for the faint-hearted or persons of five foot eight.

I went straight on to Internet Explorer and through to Google. I typed in the name of the Holly Broughton court case for a second time and immediately several columns of items came up. Nothing was sacred these days. There were newspaper reports, reports on reports, comments and four pages of photos in the Sales Point. Who would want to buy photos of a criminal court case? Only a weirdo.

I read everything written about the case this time, and there was a lot of it. Richard Broughton was quoted in a statement after the verdict as saying he was glad the case was all over and that they could get on with their lives again. He thanked detectives and also a family friend, Adrienne Russell, whose concern for him had initiated the original police investigation which had led to today's trial.

Adrienne Russell.

A woman called Adrienne had called Holly

when I was at Faunstone Hall. Perhaps she was not quite such a family friend. I clicked on Photo Sales and up came four pages of newspaper shots from all angles of the main contenders coming down the steps of the Old Bailey. Strong stuff.

I flicked through them. Holly looked wan and distraught despite wearing an elegant trouser suit and silk pashmina across her shoulders. The scarf was fastened with a brooch, a musical clef. Now I was sure where I had seen it before. Holly had been wearing it when I had gone to Faunstone Hall, pinned to the lapel of her shirt.

The same brooch that Richard's female companion was wearing last night. Correction: a similar brooch. He might have given both women the same brooch. Men often did that. It saved time and thought to buy in bulk.

I scanned the crowds in the newspaper photos carefully, though I was not sure why. The scenes were unpleasant. People were throwing tomatoes and eggs at Holly and Richard was trying to shield her, his back to the camera most of the time. But maybe there was a nice, kind, friendly family face lurking somewhere.

It was a bit blurred, but that blonde was in the crowd, the older blonde. She was standing behind several people. It was difficult to see clearly but I thought it was her. Time to find out who she was.

I used Miguel's telephone in his study. I didn't want the call traced back to my mobile. But I didn't have my mobile. I asked one of the new firms of directory enquiries for Broughton Bank. Then I phoned through to the head of the personnel department. It was a wild chance. I had nowhere else to start.

'Hi,' I said, silkily. 'Melissa Jones, Barclays Bank group here, head office, personnel department. I'm checking a reference from a former employee of Broughton Bank. She says she worked for you for several years.'

'What's her name?'

'Adrienne Russell.'

I heard a sort of suppressed giggly gasp. 'Adrienne Russell? Are you sure you've got the name right?'

'Yes,' I said. I spelt it out. 'It's quite clear here on the application form.'

'How extraordinary. I've no idea why she should be looking for a job with another bank. We believe she had a very generous alimony payment.'

'Sorry?' I said. 'I don't quite follow...'

'Adrienne Russell was married to the owner of Broughton Bank, Richard Broughton, some years ago. Then they were divorced and I'm sure Mr Broughton gave her adequate provision. A million or so, which was a lot in those days.'

'There must be some mistake,' I said, continuing in the same smooth voice. 'I'll go back to the applicant. Sorry to have troubled you.'

'No problem. That's really weird. Hope you get it sorted out.'

Wow. Adrienne Russell was the first Mrs Broughton. They'd been divorced either before or after Richard met Holly. Whenever the point of divorce, it didn't mean she had to like Holly. This could be one mean lady. No one liked being the vintage model.

There was no way I could stay any longer in Miguel's flat. I had too much to do. I had to find a way out and I had to find a disguise.

I went into my email server and sent a brief message to James. He had to know where I was and what I was doing without actually spelling it out.

'James,' I typed. 'Cooking up favourite hot dish. No worries. Safe recipe. You can bank on it. The result could please you. JL'

I clicked on to Send and sent the email. I never cease to wonder at this miracle of communication. No licking stamps or walking to a pillar box. No running out of envelopes or a pen that won't work. Of course, a computer is needed on hand, and one that is working.

Miguel's flat was on the third floor and there was no way I could climb down. I searched around in case there was a way up on to the roof directly from his flat. If I could get on to the roof, then surely I could find another route down? There must be some service stairs or lift. But I had no code for any lift.

Meanwhile I had found a few items which might work as alternative clothing. I was loath to leave my classy new outfit behind but needs must. I hung it on hangers in an empty wardrobe. As I was changing, a reply came from James on the screen. It was brief.

'JL. Don't. I mean it, don't do anything.'

I deleted it and logged off. No more emailing until this was all over. James would have to wait and wonder.

I still had my shoulder bag so had a lipstick and a hairbrush. Nothing much else. Miguel's bathroom had deodorant and aftershave. My skin would have to starve and shrivel.

There was a small pot of coins on the kitchen window sill. I helped myself and put in an IOU note. I had reached the depths. I was stealing from my friends now.

I couldn't go down and I couldn't go up but I could go sideways. I went out on to the balcony and straddled the wall, trying not to disturb the plants. The adjacent balcony was exactly the same curve in design and not too far away. I lifted the bamboo sofa and laid it across from Miguel's balcony to the next one. Two of the legs hooked over the wall. It did not look too safe but it was my only chance. No way was I going to walk across or jump any distance, but I might just crawl ... slowly, holding my breath.

There was no one in. The next-door flat was empty. They had gone to work or to walk the sea front or take coffee at Nero's. I guessed they ran a boutique. The decoration was minimilistic, hardly any furniture, a few stark wood pieces, several sofas in white leather. No flowers. No books. No personality.

The front door was locked, of course. But I found a key safe on the kitchen wall and a key that was hanging under the helpful label 'Spare, front door'. I opened the front door, closed it and posted the key back through the letter box. They would certainly be puzzled by that.

I sauntered down the unused stairs, hoping not to meet anyone. The tenants had lift codes and used the lifts. I doubted if anyone would recognize me. My hair had disappeared under one of Miguel's old cotton hats. I was wearing baggy shorts and the T-shirt I'd slept in all night, sunglasses. Not exactly designer wear. More like foreign daytripper. I bought an ice-cream cone from Marconi's.

'Pleeze, an ice crime, the punk,' I said, offering a handful of coins.

'Strawberry mint, miss?'

I walked along licking it. A sneaky sun was trying to pierce the clouds. I could have been on holiday.

Sure, I looked on holiday. I lifted my head and smiled at the sun and anyone walking along the front. Not exactly paddling time, but near. I had a lot to do and I had a feeling time was running short. It was not mortal fear but a sudden shiver of dread encasing me that cooled the sun's rays.

I couldn't go back to my flat or my shop. There might be an incendiary device fixed to the door. I couldn't go anywhere. I couldn't be myself. Also I couldn't do anything without a source of money. I only had a few pounds on me. I dared not use a credit card in case it was traced to the machine.

If I called on Arcade Jack or Francis Guilbert, it might draw bad vibes from whoever was out to harm me. And I wouldn't want anything to happen to either of them, or Miguel.

The Anchorage, of course. All that blue-and-white chinaware adorning her breakfast room. Time to call on Mrs Holborn and hope she would keep her word. They would not find me there. I'd even sleep on a kitchen chair if they were swinging the No Vacancies sign.

And the password was 'ladybird'. Gee, rhyming again.

Eighteen

I needed to see the CCTV footage that had been used in the trial and any documentation of the money withdrawn from Holly's bank. DI James was not the man to ask. DS Duke Morton could hardly have his arm twisted on such slight acquaintance. I must know someone who would help me.

It was a surprising decision. Call me irresponsible.

'Two-ways ticket to Londres, pleeze,' I said at the railway ticket office producing my cheque book and card.

'Two ways? There's only one way to London, via Haywards Heath and East Croydon.'

'The goings ways and the comings-back ways,' I explained.

I sat in the train making a list of the things I wanted to check and anything else that might help. Fields and trees and housing estates rushed by.

I was walking into the lion's den. No weapons, just charm and guile and a lorry-load of luck. Richard Broughton's flat was a ten-minute walk away from Victoria station. I was praying that he was not in.

His flat was on the top floor of a tall brick town house in a side street not far from Buckingham Palace. A desirable district. Brownstone bachelor pad, once an elegant home of a professional, maybe a doctor, a lawyer, theologian. Worn steps led down to a basement flat, windows level with the pavement and people's feet. Not my idea of home, sweet home. But it might present a way in. Some people were slack about windows.

I went down the steps, rehearsing a doleful story about not knowing which was Richard Broughton's flat.

'Pleeze, I am looking for Mr Broughton, the bunker.' But there was no one in. I knocked on the door, rang the bell, peered in the window. Typical lost foreign visitor. But I was doing more than being lost. I was wondering if I could get my hand in the small top window that was ajar and reach down to the catch. The window swung open inwards, which was odd, maybe some sort of ancient bye-law, and I climbed in. No one had seen me so far.

The flat was a mess. Two men living together. A single man couldn't get through so many cans of beer on his own. He'd be legless and armless. I closed the window, hurried through and unlocked the front door, slipped outside and shut the door behind me. They would probably blame each other for not locking up.

The hall and stairway was wide and well decorated and climbed up for ever. Each landing was converted to two flats, numbers and names by the door. Richard Broughton had the whole of the top floor to himself. The views over London must be stunning. I wondered if he had a roof garden.

I didn't know what I was going to say to Richard Broughton. Try to get myself on his side, appeal to his better nature, pretend I knew something that he didn't know? The last option suited me and would be easier to carry off.

'Mr Broughton, I have evidence about Holly's death that incriminates a certain friend of yours,' I practised in a low voice, and rang the bell. There was no answer. Did no one live in this house? Did everyone go out to work? What a hardworking lot. But then the rent must be astronomical.

There was no doormat to look under, no fern pot, no ledge along the top of the door. My fingers crept round the fire extinguisher fixed to the wall. I felt the round end of a key balanced on the black handle mechanism and eased it out of its hiding place. People are so trusting.

I was inside Richard Broughton's flat in seconds, closing the door carefully and silently, locking it from the inside. If he returned unexpectedly it would give me some time to escape or hide.

It was a beautiful flat.

Every inch of decoration and furnishing spelt good taste backed by limitless credit cards. I was careful about breathing on anything. Using tissues from the pristine bathroom (was the man a saint?) I protected handles and knobs from fingerprints. In my baggy tourist gear, I felt like a clown who had walked on to the wrong stage.

The desk and drawers were as tidy inside as outside. His wardrobe and chest of drawers were immaculate. Not even a hair in his hairbrush. And not a single ashtray anywhere. Was there a butler? I went cold at the thought of Jeeves arriving, being confrontational.

No one had had breakfast in the kitchen. The waste bin was empty, so was the refrigerator. Only a tray of ice cubes. Richard was not at home, that was clear. Perhaps he was at Faunstone Hall. I took my first normal breath without sitting down.

I stood in the centre of the sitting room trying to sense if anything was out of place. There had to be something wrong in this perfect setting. I swivelled round slowly on my heels. The TV was switched off but a tiny red light was winking. The video recorder was still on. I pressed the Play button and sat on the floor expecting to see a film, something classic. *The Sound of Music?*

A haze of fuzziness flickered on to the screen then steadied and a picture came into focus.

It was Holly Broughton, alive and lovely, talking to a dark-haired, older woman in a coffee shop. It was a pleasant place with pink-check tablecloths and sprigged carnations on each table, large pink china cups and saucers. A fly was buzzing against a netted window. There was no sound but Holly's face was concerned and anxious. She touched the other woman's hand in consolation or sympathy then handed over a small packet. It looked like money, maybe a wad of fifty-pound notes in an envelope. Then the screen went blank. I thought it was all over and sat back.

After a pause, the video continued to play. It was Holly again sitting in the same coffee shop, same flowers, expression looking concerned and anxious. Same fly trying to get out. But this time her companion was a man, someone I thought I had seen before. She handed him the same packet, a wad of notes. The action looked automatic and false. I replayed both scenes. They were identical in every single aspect except that in the first Holly handed the cash to a woman and in the second it was to a man.

The video had been doctored. They can do

anything these days. They had brushed out the dark woman and superimposed the man and it was the second version that had been shown in court. This was the damning evidence that had been shown to the jury in court. No one except an expert could have seen the joins. But the jury had thrown it out.

I let the video run on. Now there was CCTV footage of Holly inside a bank at a counter drawing out a considerable amount of money. But why shouldn't she, if it was her own money?

Had these scenes also been shown in court? They meant nothing. But a sharp lawyer could imply anything about the amount of money being withdrawn. An even sharper one might have noticed the man standing back in line was reading a copy of the *Daily Mail* that had a front page of disaster. Zoom in and enlarge the date and the newspaper might have been published around the time of the Boxing Day tsunami.

That shot of a crooked and broken armchair askew on a mound of wet rubble had been flashed round the world. The footage was old. I had what I had come for. The court evidence had been doctored.

This could be a motive for murdering Holly, if somehow she had found out about the videos. She could have used it to blackmail her husband, but that seemed unlikely.

She would have been more likely to take him to court for falsifying evidence. A conviction would ruin him. And Broughton Bank. No one would ever trust him again.

I slipped out of Richard Broughton's flat and locked the door behind me. I put the key back on the fire-extinguisher handle. What could I do with this information? Give it to James or Luke Morton? The case was over. Holly was dead. It was only me who wanted to clear her name. It was up to the police to track down who murdered her, but a motive might help.

The coastal train left Victoria Station on time. There was a strong police presence patrolling the crowded station concourse, which was not good, but necessary. My tourist gear, crumpled and sweaty, looked worse than ever. It had been hot in London and car fumes clung to my clothes with obnoxious poison. I huddled into the seat and closed my eyes as the train gathered speed out of London, over the Thames, the vista of scenic new river apartments such a contrast to the high-rise council flats built behind in the sixties.

As I thought about what to do with the video, my WPO training took over: 1. Have a copy made. 2. Put each copy in a secure place. 3. Make a hard-copy transcription.

The day was cooling down as the train drew in to Latching station. I left a message on Miguel's answerphone: 'Cannot involve you in all this, but thanks. It's too dangerous. Will return the T-shirt and hat soon.'

I couldn't think of any way of apologizing for my behaviour. Miguel had a generous heart. He might forgive me.

The Anchorage only had a narrow slip of an attic room vacant, barely space for a single bed and bedside table. 'I don't really let this room,' Mrs Holborn said. She didn't ask for the password. I suppose it had been unnecessary. 'It hasn't got a shower. My son uses it when he comes home. Sorry about the boxes. He leaves his stuff here. No breakfast, you said?'

'Right, no breakfast,' I agreed. I was hungry but I had lifted an apple from Miguel's fruit bowl. Stealing again. It would have to stop.

'You can make a cup of tea. I'll give you a hospitality tray.'

I drank two cups of tea sitting on the edge of the single bed. I wanted to sleep and sleep I did despite the narrow bed, the T-shirt acting as a nightshirt for the second night running.

In the morning I thanked Mrs Holborn for her kindness. She was rushing around making full English breakfasts for her guests.

'I may be back, if that's all right with you? A quick errand to do first.'

She nodded, her mind occupied with

orders of sausages, no baked beans, hash browns, no mushrooms, brown toast, scrambled eggs. My stomach was scrambled before I even closed the front door.

I found a shop willing to copy the video for me without asking questions.

'It's for my sister,' I gushed. 'A surprise.'

'Into surprises, is she?' the assistant asked as he wrote down the name Holly Broughton on the sales ticket. 'Ready in half an hour, Miss Broughton.'

While I was waiting, I phoned DI James from one of the few callboxes that had not been vandalized, using my last few coins. 'I've gone into hiding,' I said. 'No need to worry about me.'

'I never worry about you.'

'I've found somewhere to stay.'

'You were at Miguel's flat the night before last. All night.'

'Are you having me followed?' I said indignantly.

'Sort of shadowed. And now we've lost you. You're not moving. Where are you? I have to know.' DI James sounded so near I could almost touch his voice. And he was annoyed.

'You bugged me, that's what you did,' I raged. 'What a nerve. Fixed a tracking bug on my new clothes. I'm hanging in a wardrobe, that's where I am. How mean can you get? Well, I've changed my clothes again and

I'm staying at that really posh hotel along the coast, the one with a private beach, taking the penthouse suite.'

'Liar. We don't have any hotels with private beaches. And I'm having this call traced right now.'

'Pity, I've run right out of money. By the way, those videos of Holly at the trial were fakes, doctored. And I've got the evidence. It's a clear-cut motive.'

'Jordan—' he began, but I rang off.

I went back to the shop and collected the copy. The assistant looked at me strangely.

'Some surprise,' he said. He'd obviously taken a look, hoping for salacious viewing, sister of sister in compromising situation. Nasty mind. I realized that I was not going to be able to pay the bill. Nasty predicament.

'Will you take a cheque?'

'Don't take cheques.'

'My boyfriend has some cash. He's waiting outside. I'll get it from him.'

'OK.'

I picked up the videos. He'd put them into a plastic carrier bag. I walked casually to the shop door, swinging the bag. He was one dim assistant. I would never let anyone leave my shop with the goods before paying.

'Hey, big guy,' I called to an empty corner of the road. A stray cat looked at me. 'I need some money. Dish it out, buster.'

Once outside the shop, I doubled down

and ran. I know the twittens by heart. I raced down the narrow alleyway, took a sharp left and buckled sideways along another twitten. It led to the rear of a street of terraced houses, tall narrow Georgian houses with damp basements and fronted with bay windows and iron balconies. They were once elegant but now mostly divided into flats.

I ran along the back gates and found one low enough to climb over. I almost fell over and landed awkwardly on a small concrete patio, colliding with two earthenware pots, plants tangled and dried out. I would have to take cover here for a while and hope the occupants didn't come back to water their plants.

I tried to stand up and winced with pain. My ankle was starting to swell. This was not good. Injured private investigators don't stand much chance of getting out of tight corners fast. I didn't have a phone. I didn't have any money and no water. A chill was settling in the air and I didn't fancy staying there all day. I sat down on a hard concrete step and waited for inspiration.

It was a long time coming.

Nineteen

The backyard was a bleak and barren place, strewn with mouldy takeaway boxes and dumped Coke cans. Had it ever been any different? The original owners had promenaded for fresh air, spent their leisure in the small private libraries that abounded around then, drinking coffee and playing cards. Libraries in those days were social centres as well as being shelved with the latest books and magazines.

Here was where the maid hung out the washing and removed the household rubbish for collection. I couldn't stay much longer. It was halfway to nowhere and I wasn't feeling too good. My ankle was hurting.

It needed binding firmly and immediately while I could still put my weight on my foot. Derelict backyards don't normally have first-aid boxes with elastic bandages. I took off the colourful T-shirt and tore the lower half into strips, using my teeth to start it off. Miguel would understand. One day his understanding would run out.

It was not a tidy bandage and Miguel's T-shirt was now a ragged cropped version. Very mod but no navel ring. I'd joined the current craze for a draughty midriff.

It was an awkward climb, trying not to use the twisted ankle. A sort of sprawling, crawling roll over the top, dragging myself, using my weight to tip the body. The gate scratched my stomach and nearly tore the carrier bag. Finally I hopped away, grabbing at the sides of the twitten to help my progress along. A handy stick was protruding from a pile of smelly black bin bags at the end. It became mine instantly, retrieved from oblivion.

As I hobbled out on the main road, head down, a flash of blue metal went by with two cones of yellow light piercing a drizzly rain. The car stopped, and reversed noisily. A window wound down and Jack put his head out.

'Jordan, what's up? Whatcha doing?'

'I'm in disguise. You not supposed to recognize me.'

'The limp looks pretty genuine, but I'd recognize you if you were wearing a rhinoceros skin.'

'That's a terrific compliment, thank you.' I suddenly thought of the irate shopkeeper looking for me and wanting his money. 'Are you going anywhere interesting?'

'That sounds desperate.'

'It is.'

'Hop in,' he said, reaching over to open the passenger door. 'I'm going to watch the moving of history. Right ol' history buff, I am. Didn't yer know?'

Jack threw the gears and sped off, accelerating as fast as he could without breaking the speed limit. He didn't have many points left on his licence. The cameras were always catching him. They were on red alert for his blue Jaguar.

'You look a wreck,' he said, not taking his eyes off the road.

'I am a wreck,' I said, miserably. 'I've twisted my ankle and it hurts. I can't go home or to my shop because it's too dangerous. They might have wired them to blow up. I've no money and I haven't had any breakfast.'

There were weak tears glimmering in my voice. Not like me at all. Private eyes don't cry.

'Who's they?' Jack said.

'We don't know. Nobody knows.'

I swear he was grinning. He was wearing his usual gear, grubby T-shirt and torn jeans. 'There's a Kit-Kat in the glove compartment,' he said. 'Help yourself.'

I ate it as slowly as I could. No four-course meal in the offing. Jack was tired of trying to seduce me and failing. All I deserved was a Kit-Kat. I didn't blame him. Anyway, who takes a lame wreck out to lunch?

'So who the hell's trying to scare the pants

off you this time?'

'I don't know. It's something to do with Holly Broughton's death, I think. I'm not sure how it's all connected. I'm not sure about anything any more. It's all a terrible muddle and I'm in the middle of it.'

'Tissues in the glove compartment. Help yourself.'

'You're very kind.'

'You've said it. I am kind, Jordan. I could be kinder but I've realized that you don't care a hoot for me. So I've gotta get over being this wacky guy crazy for you and find some nice piece of skirt who'll go for good looks and a healthy bank balance. It would be nice to have my breakfast cooked for me.'

The silence could have been cut with a knife. Jack had never spoken to me like this before. I didn't know what to say. His testosterone level was racing high.

'I'm so sorry,' I mumbled, crumpling the silver paper. 'I'm not very good at relationships. The worst in the world. You'd better let me out at the next corner, anywhere that's convenient for stopping. There's nothing I can say to make things better. Thank you for the Kit-Kat.'

Jack leaned over and put his hand on mine. I didn't flinch though the skin was grimed and the nails pitted and black. He bit them to the quick.

'I didn't say nuffin' about us not being

friends,' he said, driving on. 'I know you've still got the hots for your detective inspector but he's way out of line when it comes to the romance stuff. His Scottish blood, I reckon. All that cold weather numbing the vitals. But you and me, we could go a long way, being best pals. Don't turn me down on that, baby.'

I could have cried. I turned and put my arms round him and kissed his stubbly cheek. It was the first time I'd kissed him, I think, not totally sure about the distant past. But he needed kissing to heal some of the hurt I had caused.

He coughed to cover his embarrassment and switched on a CD cassette. 'That's enough mush, gal. This is Rod Stewart,' he said. 'You'll like this one. So why are you limping? Wot you busted now?'

As the gravelly voice of Rod Stewart went to my head like a glass of champagne, I told Jack about my criminal activities of the day. It was an impressive list. Breaking out and breaking in, stealing, shoplifting.

'I don't think I want to be associated with you, gal,' said Jack in his new confident voice. 'You've got a criminal record a yard long.'

'Then I was climbing over this rickety gate. It was a bit high and I fell the other side, twisting my ankle. Masai warriors can walk miles on a broken leg, but I can't.'

'You ain't no warrior, walking nowhere. You're coming with me,' said Jack. 'You might change your mind about me if I'm nice to yer.'

'I might,' I said, with a big sigh of relief. I was beyond arguing with him. I wanted to feel safe and looked-after but without strings. 'So where are we going?'

'I suppose it ain't too clever to remind you of your accident – y'know, where it all happened? But they are moving the Hall today. It's costing mega-bucks. Gonna be a great show, free. Move of the century. In all the papers.'

I was going to have to confront the place again, relive all those memories. So they were going to move the Hall after all, despite the local resistance and police opposition.

'I can cope,' I said. 'I've been there before, worked in the bar, part-time job. James wanted me to go and check out how the suit of armour was fixed on the bar canopy. See if there was any monkey business.'

'You worked in the bar? Stone me.' Jack's voice held admiration. 'You never told me. And was there – signs of funny business?'

'Oh yes, the plinth was partly sawn through and it was fixed up with nylon fishing line. It only had to be slashed and then it would fall. It was meant to fall, to kill one of us. Probably James, because he had been the prime opposition to the move. He was against it from the start. But there are some very powerful people around and it was a lost cause.'

Jack had to park the car some distance from the Medieval Hall pub. The surrounding roads had been closed and there were police everywhere. My blood chilled. It had all been in vain. James had endured these days and nights of suffering for nothing. I could imagine the route that the Hall would take. It was a long way and what about that bridge? Had they pulled it down or had the journey been rerouted?

We went nearer the scene, me hobbling on my stick like an ancient beggar. Jack sauntered ahead, waving back to me. He said he had someone to see about something. One of his mysterious deals.

'Cheers. See ya, Jordan.'

A crowd had gathered, interested in watching the great removal, taking photographs and videoing the scene, but kept well back by a cordon of police in yellow jackets. I remembered I still had the videos but I'd left them in Jack's car. I hoped he'd locked it. Moving the Hall was a monumental project and I could see the engineering brilliance behind the planning.

I wondered if the owner of the Medieval Hall pub, Pointer, was watching or if the Russian millionaire who had bought the Hall for his estate had come along. Money had talked and won. I spotted Carlo over the other side of the crowd looking glum. He was easing his weight from foot to foot, nervously.

I drifted forwards to the edge of the crowd, leaning on the stick. The sides of the wood were rough and I had several splinters in my hand. I could see that the Hall had been stabilized and already jacked up, inch by inch, on to a giant trailer. I counted ten pairs of huge wheels each side of the trailer.

It was a beautiful building, the beams weathered by centuries, the elaborate pattern of reddish bricks replaced and repointed over the years by successive owners. The steepled roof was covered in tarpaulin and securely strapped. The Hall was ready to go, but we still had a long wait while the site manager went around checking.

Even the sky was cloudless, motionless. I was forgetting the time I'd been there before. The whole scene was majestic, the Hall almost echoing and surrounded by its past. Some history society were dressed as medieval peasants, dancing folk dances to a piper. Morris dancers clacked and clapped to a different tune. There was a press photographer filming the event.

It was trying to be a festive occasion. I didn't know whether to be pleased or sad. It was still sunny, but getting cooler. Breeze from the sea was wafting inland, taking away the day's heat. Fingers of sea air were stroking my midriff. It wasn't Jack. He had disappeared. Spotted the pal.

I was paying full attention, trying to remember the fine details. James would be interested when I saw him again. He would want to know exactly what happened, every detail, dissect it and file it away in that methodical mind of his.

The Hall was going to be pulled along by a pair of gigantic diesel Mammoet engines. But it seemed the building had to be rotated a few degrees before beginning the week-long snail-pace journey to its new home.

The inactivity was lingering, prolonged. Even slower than slow motion. My mind was drifting away, going back to that terrifying moment in the Hall when the suit of armour had crashed down towards James and I'd run to deflect its fall. And I remembered the denim sleeve, barely seen, but clearly in my vision for a second.

Somewhere in my brain I sensed a sound. It was tiny but I heard it just the same. I looked round, wondering where the noise had come from. I couldn't identify it.

The Hall was quite a distance away. It was majestic, serene, steeped in its own mysterious history that none of us knew much about. It stood there, surveying us all with benevolence, a crowd of midgets here only on this earth for a second of time.

I caught my breath. Somehow I knew what was going to happen before it happened. I felt the merest shudder like an intake of wind. The Hall began sinking slowly with an air of regretful grace, going down on its knees in billowing clouds of red-and-yellow dust. There was barely a sound. It was dying with dignity. It had no intention of seeing out a few more centuries on a millionaire's estate, miles away from its original site.

The Hall sank before our eyes. One moment it was standing there in all its glory and then it had gone. Dust was settling on a massive pile of rubble, quite tidily. A tide of broken bricks rolled into the roadway. The tarpaulin flailed like the gas going out of a hot-air balloon.

There was a shocked silence. A child began to cry. Hushed voices. The dancers faltered, the Morris men forgot to clap. Everyone stood and stared. There was red dust settling everywhere, on my T-shirt, on my arms, hat. It was probably in my hair. No one knew what to do or say.

I could hear raised voices, irate and shocked. It was probably the pub owner and the Russian millionaire arguing about who was responsible and who was going to pay for the removal of the debris. The site manager was white-faced. He took off his hard hat and scratched his head, shaking it slowly.

I remembered the cleaner who'd said he'd probably have to clean up the dust. He'd got a mountain to clean up now.

I love all things ancient and historic but I couldn't mourn the collapse of the Medieval Hall. In a way, it had committed suicide and had every right to decide when to pull the plug. Or crack its foundation. Or whatever it did.

I turned away, not wanting to watch any more. A man was standing across in the crowds, looking towards me. He was leaning on something, but still tall and commanding. He was wearing a black shirt and trousers, a dusting of rust on his shoulders and cropped hair.

He walked over to me, limping, leaning heavily on a pair of crutches. 'So how did you stage-manage that, Jordan?' he asked. 'Pretty spectacular.'

'Single-handed remote control,' I said.

'I thought so. It has your signature all over it. I think we need a drink to wash down this dust. Fancy the Bear and Bait? There won't be any jazz.'

He took in my baggy shorts, shorn T-shirt, cotton hat and badly bandaged ankle but did not move a muscle.

'Looking like this?' I said.

'Do you want to borrow a crutch?' he added.

Twenty

It was James. My Detective Inspector James. I made an instant decision. I was never going to let him go out of my sight again. He was all I wanted in life, standing there before me, breathing. I might stay on the edge of his life, but he had to be there somewhere.

'It's OK. I'm not a ghost,' he said. 'They've let me out. I've been allowed to go home as long as I don't do anything. The convalescent home is full up. No beds. Stairs will be a bit tricky but I'll get the hang of them.'

He had a spiral staircase in his three-storey folly tower on the outer edge of Latching. It gave me vertigo.

'You can't do those stairs. I'll move a bed down for you,' I said quickly. He was leaning on the crutches, hunched over them, not used to them yet.

He raised his dark eyebrows. 'Down spiral stairs? Don't be daft, girl. The station have lent me a camp bed. I'll do fine.'

'You can't sleep on a camp bed. You're convalescing.'

'Get in my car. At least I can drive.'

'I came with Jack.'

'He's over there, negotiating with the owners of the rubble. Probably offering them down payment for the bricks, then he'll rebuild it somewhere and turn it into a theme park.'

'He'll have some scheme. He's full of ideas,' I said. 'I'd better speak to him. Please wait.'

I wandered over to Jack. He had a don't-interrupt expression on his face, this is serious business being negotiated.

'I've got a lift back,' I began.

'OK, girl,' he nodded. 'I'm busy. See ya some time.'

I knew when to retreat.

As we drove back towards Latching, I told James about the video I had found at Richard Broughton's London flat and the copy I'd had made and not paid for. As usual, I sounded an idiot.

'You're an idiot,' he agreed. 'Didn't you realize how dangerous it was to go to Richard Broughton's flat? Someone is after you and it could well be him. But why did he have this video? It shows that the evidence was faked. This is a very complicated set-up.'

'I know but I had to do something. Someone killed Holly Broughton and this tampered-with video evidence could be the motive. If Holly found out about it and threatened Richard with opening up the case again, it would have ruined him.'

'Holly's murder is not my case,' James said grimly. 'But you can give me the videos and I'll see that they get to the right branch. Where are they?'

'I've left them in Jack's car,' I said.

'This doesn't get any better,' he said, under his breath. He was driving with his usual competence. We were turning into the street where the video shop was. I ducked down below the glove compartment, pulling the hat over my face.

'Don't stop, don't stop,' I wailed. 'This is the shop.'

'I know. I'm going in to pay your bill,' he said. 'I don't like to see local shopkeepers being cheated.'

James came back a few minutes later, stowing his crutches in the back of the car before he got in. He had a video in his hand.

'Interesting. He'd made a third copy for himself, hoping he'd have incriminating porno material of some sort, no doubt. I managed to persuade him to part with it. Well done, Jordan. Now we'd better get you spruced up before we have that drink. I'm not going into the Bear and Bait with you looking like a busker that's seen better days.'

'I could get some clean clothes at my flat or the shop,' I offered meekly.

'No way, not till both premises have been cleared of bombs, bugs, incendiary devices.

I've arranged for that to be done now, while I know exactly where you are. Meanwhile I'll get you some jeans and a shirt. What size are you?'

This was too personal for words. I wasn't telling DI James my size of anything. Our old antagonism was returning fast.

I mumbled something about any size would do.

He parked in the furthest corner of a supermarket car park and got out. 'Keep your head down,' he said. 'Don't panic. I'm locking you in.'

This was too weird. James was buying me Tesco brand clothes, bossing me about as usual, locking me in his car. The accident was becoming dream-like, as if I had imagined it, as if all these months of trauma had never happened. I unwrapped the bandage on my ankle and bound it round again more securely. I leaned over and helped myself to a bottle of water. James always kept a bottle in the driver's-door recess. The water cleared my throat. I could even taste the red dust in my mouth.

James came back with a carrier bag. 'I never knew buying women's clothes was so difficult. I didn't know what sort of leg you wanted. There are so many different kinds. No wonder women spend hours shopping.'

'I don't spend hours,' I said.

'Get into these. I'm dying for that drink.

They wouldn't let me drink in the hospital.'

'I smuggled in a few beers.'

'Could I open them, in my state?'

I didn't ask where I was to do this clothes-changing stunt. In the front seat, I supposed. There was no way I could climb into the back. At least James had his eyes on the road.

He'd bought straight-legged black jeans, belted, size 12. Well done, good detective work. He'd bought a one-size red-striped cotton shirt, and, get this, a long skinny red silk knitted scarf with diamante bobbles sewn on each end, just the sort of thing teenagers tie round their necks. I could have kissed him. I wanted to kiss him. Of course.

'These are super,' I choked, struggling out of the torn T-shirt. I did lots of wriggling and pulling on. 'Thank you. I love the scarf. This year's mega fashion statement. How did you know?'

'Glad you like them. And put this on your ankle.'

He tossed over a packet. It was an elasticated ankle support. Not glamorous. Then he glanced at me. 'You're looking good now.'

The man had feelings. He had changed.

The Bear and Bait was full and noisy. The noise sounded like home even though there was no jazz. The crowd at the bar parted when they saw DI James arriving on crutches. They recognized him and wanted

285

to know how he was. He was surprised at their interest and genuine concern. I saw his face relaxing.

The blonde barmaid's face was familiar, set in a false smile. I went over and leaned close to her.

'Have you mended your bra strap yet?' I asked before I went to sit on an upholstered bench seat. It made me feel a lot better. She didn't recognize Polly.

James hadn't asked what I was drinking but came back with my favourite Australian Shiraz in a big wine glass.

'Red to match the scarf,' he said.

I didn't tell him that I'd had nothing to eat since breakfast except a stolen apple. (Stolen again. I was fast becoming a hardened criminal.) I felt like getting completely pie-eyed. Perhaps James was right, I should stick to shopkeeping.

'Cheers,' he said. He had a cold beer in front of him. He was looking at it with clear anticipation.

'Cheers,' I said, clinking glasses. No sentiment here.

'The move to the North is definitely out,' he said, coming straight to the point. 'They couldn't wait. Someone else has got the job.'

'Does that mean you'll be staying on in Latching?'

'For the time being. I've a month off to get fully mobile, then they said something about a desk job. They can stuff that.'

'You've got to be careful,' I began.

'No lectures, please, Jordan. I've had enough of them. I know how my body feels. I'm not likely to run the marathon again, but then once is enough.'

'You've run the London Marathon?' More surprises.

'I was trying to run out grief. Remember? They say it works. It didn't work.'

'What was your time?'

'Three hours, ten minutes and twenty-three seconds.'

'Not bad. I've never run any further than to the nearest bus stop.'

'Not true, but then I'm taking into consideration your prevalence for understatement.' He smiled right into my eyes, but he was smiling gravely. I blinked. 'Jordan, I've seen the forensic report on your car. If the detonator had worked, you would certainly not be here now.'

For a second all the warmth of the wine disappeared. Even my feet were cold. But I was here, in the Bear and Bait. I had survived.

'What did they say?' I asked, gulping down more wine.

'Detonators are either chemical, mechanical or electrical. This was an electrical device, perhaps a mercury tilt switch, primed to go off when you opened the door.'

'But it didn't.'

'Probably because it was poorly assembled by an amateur. The detonator had vibrated loose from the main charge and gave you those extra seconds to get away. If you had got into the car instead of turning away, then you wouldn't have survived. It was a freak escape. You weren't meant to escape. These things are usually instantaneous.'

He was very matter-of-fact about the whole business. No emotion. No 'lucky you, Jordan'.

'Poor ladybird. It was really terrible and I feel awful about it. Yet I didn't see anybody. Did they find any clues?'

'Nobody left their ID in the wreckage, or handy credit card. No DNA. Pity. DS Morton says what do you want to do with the car? It can't stay in the backyard of Latching police station. It looks like a monument.'

'I want to do something special for her. I can't bear the thought of her being crushed in a breaker's yard and piled on top of loads of other wrecks.'

'I understand,' said James. 'The ladybird was special to you. There must be a fitting end.'

We were actually getting on for once. I could hardly believe it. Perhaps one day he would like me – maybe more than like, but I wouldn't bet on it. I had to store up all these small memories. When I was very, very old, like sixty, enjoying my pension, I would get them out and dust them off. The wine was rich and fruity. It was going straight to an empty stomach. I think James noticed.

He ordered a plate of sandwiches, chicken for him and cheese for me. They came, some time later, with lashings of side salad.

'Like another glass of wine?'

The day was disappearing fast. I could hardly remember the beginning. It had begun in Miguel's flat where I had left my smart new clothes and escaped, going to London, searching Richard Broughton's flat, finding the video. No, I remembered, that was yesterday. Today was getting a copy made, twisting my ankle, being picked up by Jack, then seeing the Medieval Hall sink into oblivion. I was a little bit pickled.

Finding James again. Now I was drinking with him, sharing sandwiches, picking up the last of the cress and slices of red onion. We stayed talking till quite late. James was tiring. I could tell. No midnight hours for the Bear and Bait. We walked along the deserted promenade front to get some fresh air. Or rather, we both limped. A couple of limpers.

The night sky was brilliant with stars, twinkling millions of miles away. James actually knew which star conformation was which. Perhaps he had been a Boy Scout. The sea was far out, a faint line on the horizon, shivering with silver. The sand was cold, wet and glistening. A few fishing-boat lights dotted the sea. A few dogs were taking their owners for a walk.

I stopped outside the cream-stone-faced Boulevard Hotel. It had once been a terrace of big Victorian houses, now connected through and converted into a four-star hotel. A line of European flags was flapping gently outside the main entrance.

'Do you really want to sleep on a camp bed?' I asked. All that red wine had given me Dutch courage. His face was starting to look drawn and tired. And he didn't know what to do with me. He did not want to deliver me to Miguel's flat.

'Let's go and see what they've got,' he said abruptly. 'A twin would do.'

'We've only got a double,' said the receptionist, snooty at having to work late and people coming in without any luggage. She knew what they were up to.

'The crutches are for real,' I told her curtly.

'Sorry,' she said. 'We get all sorts.'

'We'll take it,' said James, producing a credit card. I couldn't believe this. I was going to have to sleep on the floor, for sure. The man was nearly dead on his feet. He was going to fall into bed before his shoes were off.

We went up in the lift to the third floor. Room 301 was not hard to find. We went in and switched on the light. The room was facing the sea and the long cream curtains were blowing gently. A king-sized double bed dominated the room. I barely noticed any other furniture.

I whipped off the quilted bedspread and folded it neatly. I'd need it on the floor. I saw spare pillows stacked at the top of the wardrobe. James sat on the bed wearily, his crutches clattering to the floor. He began to ease off his shoes.

'I'll take the floor,' I said. 'Invalid first and all that.'

'Jordan...'

'I bet it's got a lovely bathroom,' I said going through to the en suite. 'Can I try all the freebies?'

'Sure. Take what you want. It's paid for.'

I poured a glass of water for him and put it on the bedside table. I didn't want him falling over me in the night.

The bathroom was my idea of heaven, pale-blue and cream tiles with gold taps. A basketful of toilet goodies on the vanity unit invited plunder, towels thick and comforting. I undressed and turned on the shower. It was bliss to get clean even though the water had a pinkish tinge as it washed the red dust off me. I washed my hair using their shampoo, towelled it dryish. It took a long time. I've no idea how long. I was in no hurry.

The first thing I noticed was his clothes. They were all over the floor – black shirt, black trousers, black socks, strewn anywhere, crumpled. He was sound asleep, the sheet barely pulled up to his waist, his head on the pillow, dark lashes flickering. I turned off the main light so that he could sleep soundly and folded up his clothes. Even in the pale light from the window I could see his face and the big shoulders, still muscled and firm even after his weeks in hospital.

There was a hospitality tray and silently I made a cup of hot chocolate. I was so tired I could have slept in the armchair but I knew I'd get the cramp. He didn't stir. I pulled the bath towel more firmly round under my armpits and tucked in the end. The floor awaited me.

I laid out all the spare pillows and the quilted bedspread. It would wrap over me nicely. But the floor still looked and was hard. I tried it for a few minutes, staring at the ceiling. It was rock-hard.

The alternative was beckoning. It was a big double bed, plenty of room for two if I clung to the far edge. No modesty bolster to put between us. I climbed in tentatively, carefully easing my weight on to the mattress, hoping I would not wake him; but James was exhausted, dead to the world. It would take an earthquake to wake him.

I slid under the sheet already feeling the

heat from his body. It was temptation beyond belief. At first I lay there in the cool sheets, hair still slightly wet, letting the strange intimacy washed over me. I was with James and he was asleep. I turned slightly and looked at the back of his head on the pillow, so near. No way could I stop myself touching the cropped hair.

By then it was too late. I shifted over until I was tucked into the curve of his back. He still did not move. My head lay against his shoulder and my tongue tasted his skin. He tasted of salt and sweat and probably that red dust. But the taste was sweet and I wanted more of it. My arm folded over his bare waist. I floated to my dreams.

Twenty-One

The waking up was hard to do, far harder than the falling asleep. James was still sound asleep, his breathing light and rhythmical, one of the lighter stages, no snoring. I had to get out of bed before he woke up.

I slid over to the far side and down on to the floor. I crouched on the carpet, waiting for him to stir, but he didn't. I then crawled to the mound of pillows, wrapped myself in the quilt and hoped to dream on for a few more minutes. It had been the most perfect night.

My eyes were closed though I could see the morning light through the lids. I wondered if we would get breakfast. I must have drifted off again into some sort of doze where my thoughts floated like tiny white boats with sails.

'Jordan? Jordan, you slept on the floor? Oh my God, you idiot. Why didn't you sleep in the bed? There was room for two.'

James was leaning over the side of the bed, looking fresh and rested. He was wearing black shorts, but his chest was bare. He was looking concerned, but amused at the same time.

'Is your back aching?' he asked.

'Yes,' I said.

'Shall I rub it for you?'

Do I want a million pounds? 'Yes, please.'

He was kneeling beside me and I rolled over on to my stomach. His fingers were moving along my spine, kneeding and massaging. This was worth being shot at and half-drugged. I let out a sort of groan so that he wouldn't stop.

His fingers were strong but gentle. I could not believe that this was happening. I must still be asleep. All I could see was his knees and the dark hair on his legs. I'd never seen his legs before. He'd never seen my back before. Two firsts. The towel was slipping down.

'Just here, or just here?' he was saying. 'Does that feel better?'

'Mmn.'

I would never tell him.

James stopped and got up with difficulty. 'Like some tea, Jordan?'

My plan for the day included DI James, apparently. He was supposed to be convalescing at home but he was itching to get back to work and no one would be checking up on him. I suggested Brighton instead. A leisurely drive into Brighton would not do him any harm.

'So why do you want to go to Brighton, Jordan? I would have thought you'd seen enough of Brighton to last several years.'

'I'd like to treat you to lunch. There are several very good Thai restaurants I'm told. I can't go back to my shop until you lot have cleared it.'

'True. So is this business or pleasure? We could eat at Maeve's Café.'

I shook my head. 'I really fancy some Thai – you know, all that noodle stuff and seaweed.'

'I can see you know a lot about Thai food,' he said dryly.

It was business but with the bonus of a lot of pleasure. My friendly piece of plastic would pay for it. I doubted if every transaction was being traced. I'd made some enquiries at the Boulevard Hotel reception about Thai restaurants in Brighton and there were several. Then I made some phone calls and put them on James's bill. Was there no end to my duplicity?

We could talk about the Medieval Hall more easily now that it was a pile of rubble. The Hall of that terrible happening no longer existed and with it had gone some of the pain. We tried to link Pointer to the accident, or the Russian millionaire, but without success or motive.

'But Pointer knew you were in opposition to the move.'

'You don't try to kill someone because they oppose closing a few roads.'

'There was a lot of money involved. He probably sold the Hall for a cool million and a lot more for the supermarket site.'

'It still doesn't make sense.'

'Then you have another enemy who wants you out of the way,' I said, suddenly hitting the spot. 'One you have forgotten all about. Someone from the past.'

'Now that's the first sensible thing you've said today,' said James, hunting for the impossibility of a parking space in Brighton. 'It'll have to be a multistorey. Dammit. Hate the places. Can hardly park behind the station when I'm supposed to be convalescing at home.'

He parked on the fourth floor and we took the lift down, neither able to face the stairs. Me hobbling, James on crutches. Brighton streets were packed with holidaymakers and residents shopping, its usual busy, bustling throng of traffic and pedestrians. A lot of gay men. It was the gay capital of the south.

I knew roughly where we were going. The restaurant was called the Lime Grass Thai Restaurant. Such a pretty name. It was painted a pale green outside with hanging baskets of flowers. It was pleasantly rural inside, lots of plants and cane furniture. Real flowers on the table. A smiling Thai girl, in long turquoise skirt and patterned jacket, showed us to a table and handed us long complicated menus. James parked his crutches against the wall.

'I don't understand any of this,' I said after reading it through twice. I felt twice the size of the tiny Thai girl and should not have been eating a single bean sprout. 'Can you order please?'

'I thought you knew all about Thai food.'

'I said I liked it, not that I could read a menu.'

'Would you like to order now, sir?' It was the tiny smiling girl again. I noticed she was wearing trainers beneath her long skirt. It made me feel a bit better.

'Menu A for two people,' he said.

I couldn't help laughing. Then we were both laughing and sunshine streamed through the windows of the restaurant and I almost forgot why I was there.

He ordered a glass of white wine for me and mineral water for himself. 'You had enough to drink last night,' he added. 'Now tell me why we are really here. It's not just for my scintillating company, I realize that.'

'You could be scintillating if you tried a bit harder.'

'You haven't answered my question.'

'It wasn't a question. It was a statement.'

'Jordan' – he was exasperated – 'that's not the correct reply.'

Time to hoist the white flag. 'Holly Broughton had a Thai housekeeper, Mrs Melee.' I got out my notebook and checked. 'Mrs Sanasajja Melee. And her sister has a restaurant in Brighton, this one. I've been wondering what has happened to Mrs Melee since Holly died and whether she could throw any light on Holly's murder. I suppose she was interviewed by the police.'

'I'm sure she would have been, but I'll check for you if you like.' He got on to his mobile and had a brief chat with someone, DS Duke Morton perhaps. 'Yes, Mrs Melee made a statement, but it seems it was her day off and she was not at Faunstone Hall.'

'She was here, visiting her sister then. That's what she always did on her day off.'

'Something for you to check. It's not my case.'

The starters had arrived, an overflowing plate of succulent bits and pieces, and was set between us. It was enough for a whole meal. I poised my fork.

'Do you know what all this is?'

'Satay Gai is chicken in a peanut sauce,' James began. 'Koong Hom Par are prawns in a blanket, that's pastry. Poa Pia Thawt are spring rolls in a chilli sauce – be careful, could be very hot. Seekrong Moo Yang, that's pork spare ribs. And these are my favourite: Khonom Bung Na Koong, which are minced prawn on crusty bread and deep fried.'

'Don't you want some tomato sauce?' I asked. He usually had tomato sauce with everything. I wondered if I had gone too far, again, but there was a glint in his eyes.

'Eat,' he said. 'And don't talk.'

We were drinking coffee when I beckoned over the girl. 'Could I speak to Mrs Melee, please?' It was a shot in the dark, or rather in broad daylight. Mrs Melee might be here, taking refuge. The girl was disturbed and looked over her shoulder towards the kitchen area.

'Please, I will see,' she said.

'Not too happy with that,' said James.

We waited some time; then I saw Mrs Melee peering round the kitchen door. She was wearing a cook's striped tabard over her own plain, dark clothes. She caught my glance and her face went pale. I smiled encouragingly and waved to her. She hovered, hesitating.

'Go and get her. She's about to escape.'

I got up quickly, before she could change her mind, and put my hand on her arm. 'It's Jordan Lacey, remember me? I was working for Holly Broughton and trying to help her. Please come over and talk to us. This is my friend, James.'

I didn't introduce James professionally. I thought she would run a mile, several miles, all the way to Beachy Head.

She sat down, still hesitant. She did look

quite scared, as if expecting someone to jump out of the shadows and lay a heavy hand on her shoulder.

'Miss Lacey. Yes, I remember you.'

I suppose she was remembering dragging me into the car and dumping me on the deserted beach. Not a pretty thought. Our thoughts collided.

'We thought they would kill you, if we left you in the conservatory. They were trying to kill you, Miss Lacey,' she said suddenly. 'That day. That's why we took you away.'

'Kill me?' I was taken aback by her outburst. 'But that's not what Holly told me. She said she'd thought I'd been taken ill, a stroke or something, and didn't want any more publicity after the court case. That's what she told me.'

'Not all true. We thought you were in danger, that they would kill you if they could. Because you were on the right track.'

That was news to me. What right track?

'Who?' said James. 'Who was a danger to Jordan?'

'I don't know. I cannot say.' Mrs Melee was very upset. 'Mrs Broughton did not say. She said it was better if I did not know too much.' Her serene Thai face was screwed up with emotion.

'Would you like a drink, Mrs Melee?' James asked. 'A cup of coffee?'

'Some water, please,' she whispered.

He leaned over and took a clean glass from the next table, poured her some mineral water. 'Here you are. Take your time. You are safe with us. We are not going to hurt you. We only want to ask you some questions about Mrs Broughton's death.'

She seemed reassured by James's kind words and calm voice.

'This is a lovely meal,' I said. 'Do you do the cooking here? It's very good.'

'I work here now,' she said with some dignity. 'Mr Broughton dispensed with my service. He said I was not needed. That Faunstone Hall would be closed up. I left immediately. He called me a taxi.'

'That's sad. I'm sorry to ask you, but can you tell us anything about the day that Mrs Broughton died?'

She shook her head. 'It was my day off. I know nothing. I was staying the night in Brighton as my sister was not well. Mrs Broughton said she could manage without me as Mr Broughton was not there. I did not know what happened till I returned the next morning and everywhere was police.'

'Did Holly seem well when you left Faunstone Hall?'

'Yes, she had her usual breakfast in the conservatory. Fruit and toast and coffee. She ate very little. She said to take some flowers from the garden for my sister. And I did.'

'Did you see anyone or anything unusual?'

'No, nothing. Tom cut some flowers for me and gave me a lift to Latching station. He was getting something repaired at a garage. Mrs Broughton was alone in the house.'

A shiver went through me. Holly had been alone. Totally defenceless and at the mercy of her killers. James knew what I was thinking. I could see it in his eyes.

'Thank you, Mrs Melee,' he said. 'You have been very helpful and we're sorry to have taken you back to those distressing days. It was very good of you to talk to us when you must be so busy in the kitchen. It's an excellent restaurant.'

Mrs Melee stood up, regaining her composure. She smoothed down her tabard and looked straight at me. 'I will always think kindly of Mrs Broughton. If it had not been for her kindness and generosity, Lime Grass Thai Restaurant would not be ours.'

'Sana. Sana.' Mrs Melee was being called from the kitchen. 'Please to come...'

I looked past her and saw another woman peering from the doorway, an older, darker woman, her hair pulled up into a tight knot. She was also a cook, holding a big bowl in her arms, and she was stirring the contents as she called.

She was also the woman I'd seen in the first video. The woman in the coffee shop with Holly. Holly had given her a packet of money across the table. This had been the generosity.

'I must go,' said Mrs Melee, apologizing. 'That is my sister.'

'I know,' I said.

We did not talk much on the drive back to Latching. James checked that my flat and my shop were clean. They were. Life could return to some normality. I could not wait to get working again.

'So now we know where Holly's money was going,' said James.

'Yes, she was loaning money to Mrs Melee's sister, or giving it, or investing it. Whatever or whichever, the cash was going towards the purchase of the restaurant. It sounds just like Holly. The sort of thing she would do, helping out.'

'And they already knew you were in danger.'

'Holly knew, but not Mrs Melee.'

'And we can't ask Holly.'

'No, we can't.' It was almost a whisper.

James dropped me at my shop. He was going back to his folly home to open a mountain of mail. First Class Junk looked like first-class dereliction. The 'CLOSED' sign was still on the door. The two little windows were dusty and strewn with dead flies. I didn't like the thought of the police going through my shop and my bedsits. How could I be sure that the shop was safe?

Mistakes could easily be made, something missed.

If I thought like that, I'd never get back to normality. There was a soft parcel and a box on the doorstep. I unlocked the door and pulled them inside. I could guess what was inside the parcel and I was right. Miguel had returned my new clothes. There was a note in his bold handwriting: 'Jordan, you are so thoughtful thinking of your friends being blown up. My hacienda is outside Acapulco, waiting for you in safety. Miguel.'

I had to smile at the way he had put it. I'd known he would forgive me. He always did.

The box was all odds and ends. Books and old magazines, odd china and rather large chipped ornaments. There was very little I could sell. I wondered who had left it on my doorstep. Then I remembered the down-sizing teddy-bear woman, moving from two rooms to one. Perhaps they were from her. In which case I had to put something of hers on show in the window so that she would see it and be happy.

I washed two ornate figures, a shepherd and shepherdess, and placed them in the window so that the chips would not show. I priced them at £6 for the pair. Couldn't separate them after all these years.

The old magazines were worthless and the books in poor condition. I picked up a stain-ed paperback anthology of poems and flicked through it. *The New Era Poets*, it was called, whenever the new era was.

My glance caught the title of a poem: 'Lady on a Stake'. I found myself compelled to start reading it:

I'll pierce your heart
As you pierced mine.
You did not stop to think.
A flick of golden hair,
A sultry look
From traitor's eyes that did not blink.

I stopped reading. There were several more verses in the same vitriolic tone but I did not want to read them. It was not good poetry but I could feel the emotion, the hurt, the desire to hurt back. That was vivid enough.

It was a funny sort of feeling, scanning down to the end of the poem for the poet's name. I almost knew it before I read it.

It was signed Darrell.

Twenty-Two

I was trudging my bike up to the allotments. It was time to put the hens-and-rabbits case to rest and Arthur Spiddock out of his misery. I'd no doubt that his offer of a £100 reward was a genuine offer, but whether he could meet his word was another matter.

Summer was truly here, time for sleeveless T-shirts, stringy vests and cut-off jeans. I had a birthday coming soon. A big three-0 birthday. It would be great to celebrate with all my friends. A party on the beach, again. I could wear my special new outfit, the one that had dazzled DI James.

Arthur's allotment was looking neglected. There were weeds everywhere and he was not picking anything. The runner beans were straggling up poles, needing water. His beetroot were like small footballs, falling over on the earth. A Primus is hardly a cooking utensil.

I knocked on the shed door and called out in a hearty voice. 'Hi there, Mr Spiddock. It's Jordan Lacey. I've come to take Nutty for a walk.'

Arthur Spiddock might have been slow opening the door but Nutty was fast on the draw. He was out the door in a second, jumping all over me, long-lost friend to lick. He was too big a dog to be kept indoors.

'Ah, Miss Lacey. Have you come with my bill?'

'Not yet,' I said cheerfully. 'I don't present a bill until I've solved a case.' Liar. 'I'm going for a walk and thought Nutty might like to come along, keep me company. Have you got a lead?'

'Well, that would be real nice,' said Arthur Spiddock. 'I'm not getting out too much these days – arthritis you know. Nutty'd like a long walk. Driving me crazy, he is. And I can't let him out on his own, because he'd run away.'

'Can I do any shopping for you? A couple of cans of beer?'

His face broke into what passed for a smile. 'Now, that would be right enough. And some baked beans. I've a passion for baked beans. You can eat them hot or cold, y'know.'

I was feeling buoyant cash-wise after having sold the chipped shepherding couple and the anthology of poems to an intellectual soul who apparently wrote poetry himself and was longing to get published.

'I feel very new-era,' he'd said, pushing up his specs.

I let him have the book cheap. There was one page missing, I told him.

Nutty allowed me to attach the lead to his collar. He was a friendly dog despite his size. I wondered how he had got on with the hens and the rabbits. I needed a long walk, so did Nutty. We crested Topham Hill, down the other side, along a shaded lane to the main road. He didn't much like the traffic, but obeyed me by sitting till it was safe to cross.

'Good boy,' I said.

I went into a small village grocer's and bought the baked beans and some beer. 'Training a guide dog,' I explained. Nutty was tied up outside looking abandoned and forlorn.

Then I hobbled into the pub across the way and bought a large glass of house red wine, any vintage, out of a box. 'You can bring your guide dog in,' they said kindly. Word spreads fast. They gave Nutty a bowl of water and some biscuits. He was ecstatic with gratitude, then fell asleep at my feet.

I needed the wine. It went straight to where it was needed. I was short on courage. Somehow I had to get this all together and present it to DI James. My brain would not function and I was wary of getting head-bitten.

When I could drain no more from the glass, I knew it was time to walk on. Nutty was revitalized and as we crossed a field to the coastal path, I let him off the lead.

'But you must come back when I say so,' I said sternly before letting his collar go. 'Understand that?' He agreed, tongue lolling with anticipation. Then he went mad.

It was wonderful to watch. This big dog racing and charging and leaping about with total careless freedom. He needed space and I had given it to him. He chased anything, bees, butterflies, his own imagination. I sat with my back against a fence, rubbing my ankle, which was still aching.

I didn't need to call him. He came back of his own accord and fell against me, exhausted. I stroked his soft head. I couldn't have a dog in two bedsits.

We walked along the coastal path, more sedately, Nutty sniffing the odd windswept bush. Then it was time to head back to the allotments, coming to them from the other end of the grassland. Nutty began to look quite excited but I kept a firm hold on the lead.

The Council had given over quite a generous acreage of land to the allotment holders. Arthur Spiddock's plot was at the top end, out of sight. But Nutty was tugging on the lead and pulling me over to a single shuttered shed at the lower end.

Sheds are not high on my curiosity list but I allowed myself to be dragged over to this one, just to please the dog. Nutty sniffed at the door then sat down across it, looking even more pleased with himself. Then I remembered: he was a retriever.

Inside the shed were eleven hens and four rabbits. All in good condition, in runs, looking well cared for. Plenty of hay, plenty of fodder. I recognized two pedigree bantams and the lop-eared rabbits. They glared at me in a cross-eyed way.

I closed the door. 'Bingo,' I said to Nutty.

Arthur Spiddock confessed all. He'd been turned out of his house because he couldn't pay the rent. He'd reported his hens and rabbits as stolen in the hope that he could claim on his home insurance. But his home insurance did not include the contents of his allotment. Meanwhile, an absent friend, who knew nothing about the scheme, said Arthur could use the shed at the far side to store stuff. He had employed me to make the theft seem more authentic.

'I ought to be able to claim something,' Arthur wailed. 'Other people do.'

Poor soul. I knew that there were people who claimed and got ridiculously high payments for so-called mental suffering, or were off work for months on full pay. Arthur Spiddock had endured mental suffering but he was not going to get a penny from anyone.

'Are you going to report me?' he asked eventually.

'No, of course not. You didn't steal your own animals. You merely moved them to a different place. Of course, it was wrong to report them as stolen but you could say it was a temporary delusion on your part, due to the trauma of being turned out of your home.'

'Yes, I could say that, couldn't I?' he said brightening. 'It were a trauma.'

'So the case is now closed,' I said, going to leave.

'I suppose I ought to give you the reward money,' he offered. 'For finding 'em.'

'Nutty found them.'

'That's what I was afraid of. That's why I tried to lose him. He kept going off down there. But what do I owe you, miss, for your detective work?'

'Well, I'll have to sort it out,' I said, hours of complicated maths ahead. 'Perhaps you'd let me take Nutty for a walk now and then, work it off like that.'

Or walk it off. I was a fool. But how could I charge this poor old man for doing practically nothing?

'Righto, miss. Any time. Nutty really likes you, I can see that. Would you like a couple of beetroots?'

I got on my bicycle and free-wheeled down the hill, bumping over the ruts. It was a great feeling. I had got myself a part-time dog.

I was also one muddy walker. I'd have to

train Nutty not to jump up on me. Shopping list: book on dog training, washing powder and comfort rinse. I called in at Doris's shop. She was stacking tins on the top shelves.

'So where have you been all this time? I saw your shop was closed. It was a bit of a worry, not seeing you. Mavis didn't know where you were either. You could have been bumped off.'

'You're almost right there, Doris,' I said, passing tins to her. 'I could have been bumped off. One day I'll tell you the whole sordid story. I had to go into hiding for a couple of nights.'

'It was three nights by my count. And there were police swarming all over your shop. I thought they'd found another corpse.'

'They didn't find anything, which was a relief,' I told her. 'And I've solved one of my cases. The hens-and-rabbits case up at Topham Hill.'

'So did you find them labelled on a counter at the farm shop on the main road?'

'No, I found them alive and well and thriving in a new environment.'

Doris looked at me with cautious admiration. 'You having me on? You found them?'

'Yes, truly. The owner is well pleased.'

'So are you buying an extra pot of yoghurt to celebrate?'

'What a brilliant idea. I'll take two.'

I went back to my bedsits to do a load of washing, and phoned DI James. There were several things to tell him. But he was not taking the call. I was rerouted to an answering service.

'James,' I said, 'I've got a lot to tell you. I've found a poem that I want to read to you. Could we meet this evening? About seven? We could go for a drink or a hobble along the front. 'Bye now.'

The day's aches and pains were soaked away in the bath and I washed my hair again, towelling it dry. I'd said nothing about a meal so I ate one of the yoghurts. The creases had hung out of my new white jeans and the red top was wearable again. I was still sporting the elastic ankle support but the jeans were long and covered most of it. I plaited my hair and fixed the end with a red flower. Tonight was the Spanish look. But no castanets.

Someone was ringing the front doorbell. It was time I got an intercom so that I could speak to whoever was there. I peered out of the window and saw a large maroon Daimler parked alongside the pavement. It was Richard Broughton's car. I shrank back. No way was I answering the doorbell. It could ring till the entire neighbourhood went deaf.

I spun-dried the washing and began hanging it around the bathroom. Not having a garden was a drawback. The bell was still ringing. I flung up the window.

'Go away,' I shouted. 'I'm not coming down. If you don't go away, I shall call the police.'

The chauffeur was standing on the pavement, leaning back and looking up. He did not look particularly threatening. He was holding a big bunch of mixed flowers wrapped in cellophane.

'Mr Broughton wants to apologize. He's sent you these flowers from the garden. He said he'd like to talk to you.'

'No way. I don't want to talk to him. They don't look like garden flowers, they look like garage-forecourt flowers.'

'It's very important. He wants to explain everything. Please come, Miss Lacey.'

'I have no intention of ever talking to Mr Broughton, not after what I've been through, and you can tell him that.'

'But your detective friend is coming, Detective Inspector James. He's interested to hear what Mr Broughton has to say. He should be at Faunstone Hall by now.' The chauffeur placed the flowers on my doorstep. They looked like mourning flowers. It was creepy.

I wavered. I remembered the threatening way Richard Broughton had behaved in my shop, the way he'd taken Holly to court after the knifing, the way someone had tried to get rid of me, not once but three times. Was he going to explain all that?

'OK, I'll come. But one nasty word from Mr Broughton and I'll be on my phone to the police faster than you can blink. I'll sit in the front with you so that I can see what you are up to.'

'It'll be a pleasure,' he said.

The Daimler was such a comfortable vehicle. No wonder rich people buy Rolls-Royce cars and Bentleys and Daimlers. It's like being transported on a big cushion with no noise, only a gentle purr in the background.

'Smashing car,' I said.

'You should see the back. It's got a let-down desk for Mr Broughton's laptop, a cocktail cabinet, phone links, stereo system and a small DVD and television screen. It does everything but fly.'

'And what about speeds?'

'She's merely cruising at ninety. I don't often take her over a hundred unless Mr Broughton is in a real hurry.'

'Wow.' I was impressed. Then I thought of my ladybird and hardened my heart. 'That's breaking the law.'

'So I understand,' he agreed. 'Sometimes it's necessary.'

We were soon approaching Faunstone Hall. The security gates swung open, recognizing the car or some code. I looked around for James's car but the drive was empty. I felt a slight pang of apprehension but pushed it away. Perhaps he'd taken a taxi to save him driving. Bearing in mind the crutches...

The hall was bleak and untouched by anything except dust. I saw a black briefcase on a Dutch wheelback chair. It was probably Richard Broughton's. It looked bulging and bankish.

'Would you go through to the study? You know the way.'

I did. It was in the oldest part of the house. I went along the hallway, down the three steps into the study, expecting to see Richard Broughton and James already there. The room was empty.

'Where is everybody?' I asked, alarmed.

The chauffeur was behind me. I could feel his breath fanning my neck. I felt both my hands suddenly yanked behind my back and my shoulder bag fell to the floor.

'You are very naive, Miss Lacey. There isn't anyone here that you know.'

He was holding my wrists in an iron grip, wrapping adhesive tape round them. He knew how to do it and fast. He'd been in the army, hadn't he?

Twenty-Three

I didn't go on a police self-defence course for nothing. Although I was disadvantaged by having my hands tied behind my back, I still had my head and elbows, knees and feet.

Wilkes didn't know what had hit him. I swung round on my heel, brought my knee up into his groin and head-butted him at the same time. As he staggered back, I kicked him hard on the softest part of the ankle, which really hurts. He went reeling.

But he was back in seconds, the pain hardening in his eyes like diamonds, and his mouth clenched. He grabbed my hair and jerked hard. My neck was nearly dislocated. He threw me to the floor, kneed me in the back and pinned my feet with one hand while he wrapped adhesive tape round my ankles. I was still struggling.

'You'll be sorry you did that, Miss Lacey,' he said, fighting to gain his breath. A head-butt knocks the breath out of you. 'You're not going to like where you're going.'

'Oh, but they're c-coming,' I gasped. 'I ph-phoned before I left h—' He cut off my words with a nasty piece of wide parcel tape over my mouth. Dammit. He had me trussed up like a Christmas turkey. As he leaned over me, I managed to wrench off one of the buttons on his blazer, closing my fingers round it and cupping it from his sight. I had no idea what I could do with it.

I watched as he shifted a four-drawer filing cabinet away from a wall. All the study walls were panelled in oak, polished and with a patina of age. He seemed to know what he was doing. His fingers moved over the panelling to a corner spot. He'd made a mistake in not putting a blindfold on me. I could watch what he was doing. And I was watching.

It was not a simple press action, but a movement up and then abruptly sideways. Those seventeenth-century carpenters were wonderful. They didn't need computers to work it out for them. A panel of the wainscoted wall slid sideways with barely a sound, revealing a dark space behind.

It was the priest's hole.

The bastard's intentions were clear now. He was going to put me in the priest's hole and probably leave me there. Not a nice way to go, though there would be air. There was usually some sort of small hole where food could be passed to the hidden priest, whenever they remembered.

Wilkes turned to me, kicking my shoulder bag out of the way. 'You won't be needing your lipstick where you're going,' he said. 'I hope you'll like your new accommodation.'

I closed my eyes as if in mortal terror and made terrified noises through the tape over my mouth.

'You started to know too much, Miss Lacey, too much for your own good,' he went on. 'Sorry, and all that. But this time, it's definitely goodbye to the nosy Miss Lacey.'

But this time ... Had he put the incendiary device in the ladybird, the drug in my coffee? Was he the sniper who'd almost hit my eye? My brain fast-forwarded each situation. Wilkes had had the opportunity. But what was the motive? Richard Broughton had all the motives. Wilkes had done it for money.

He started dragging me over the floor by my feet. My hands tried to grasp at anything around that would be useful but found nothing. Then he turned me over and pushed me head first into the priest's hole. I turned my head so that my nose could still breathe. The darkness was all-absorbing, like a tunnel, like sliding into a nightmare. I was thinking, *This'll ruin my new white jeans.*

In those first moments I worked out the size of the priest's hole. The three steps down into the study gave me an idea of the height of the hole. You could sit up but not stand up. It was the length of a man's body, bearing in mind that people were shorter in those days. Width-wise, I didn't know. I was about to find out. I guessed it was going to be extremely cramped.

The panel slid shut behind me. I could see nothing. It was completely black, an all-encompassing darkness. Like being down a mine when they turn off all the lights. But I had the strangest feeling I was not alone.

My hearing is good. I could hear breathing, then I felt a movement against my side. I nearly jumped, if I could have jumped. There was someone else alongside me, generating heat, brushing against me. Then I felt another movement, the other side, and heard a groan. It was horrendous. There were three of us in the priest's hole, lying side by side like sardines. Surely not my James? No, I was sure it wasn't James. I would have known, have sensed his skin, his presence, known it was him. He wouldn't groan.

We were a sandwich and I was the filling. Pass on the mayonnaise.

They were both trussed up, like me. Movement restricted, no possibility of speech. I was not blindfolded so I could see, was beginning to see in the darkness. At the far end was a small access hole in the roof of the hideaway, where possibly food and water had been passed down. No such luck now. But air was filtering through and there was the faintest glimmer of light.

Whoever had made this hole was a master

craftsman. Carpenters were really carpenters then, shaping the wood by hand and knowing what to do with notches, pegs, tongues and grooves. The sides were smooth panels, no rough earth. I wondered if I would find grooves where priests had scratched out their days in hiding. I wondered how long it had been lost to memory, before this lot discovered it again. It had probably been rediscovered when the modern central heating system was put in Faunstone Hall.

There was a pitiful, high-pitched weeping sound coming from the body on my left. And I could smell perfume, a heady penetrating perfume. Very expensive. Nothing light or flowery. From the shape against me, I guessed this was an older woman, well built, beautifully dressed, clothes rustling, in a state of total shock.

From the other side came the grunts and groans of someone straining against the strapping. Waste of time. Struggling only makes the tape tighter. This was a man, trying to do something, but hopelessly ill equipped for the situation. I caught a whiff of expensive aftershave and the smell of fear, which no deodorant can disguise.

This was time for quick thinking and action. Action ... That was a slight overstatement, when the only parts of me that could move were my fingers and my toes. I wondered if the woman knew Hoagy Carmichael's song 'The Nearness of You'. I wondered if I could hum it with tape over my mouth.

I began to hum quite softly, tapping out the tune on her bare arm, trying firstly to calm her panic. We couldn't work together if she was in a state of panic. She froze, probably thinking I was a sex maniac and about to attack her.

The sounds in the study told me that Wilkes was moving the filing cabinet back against the panelled wall. I had not heard the panel close. I could hum a little louder. I hoped she knew the words: '...it isn't your sweet conversation / ... oh no, it's / ... just the nearness of you...'

She was calming down. The tapping on her arm had soothed her breathing and her brain was working in a bizarre way, remembering the words. Every time we got to the words 'nearness of you', I pulled on her arm till she was lying on her side and we were back to back. I was banking on her wrists being tied behind her back, the same as mine. They were.

My fingers found the sticky tape and tried to find the end. It's hard enough to find it on a roll of new Sellotape. I always put a paper-clip or hairpin under the end. The woman kept very still. She knew what I was doing and was making tiny encouraging noises. My nails found the end and prised it up. I started to pull it off, round and round, my own fingers getting caught up in the stuff till I could hardly move.

The woman pulled off the last bit herself, then ripped the tape off her mouth with a gasp. It had hurt. She was heaving and shaking, breath coming in gulps.

'Thank you, thank you,' she choked.

'Shsh,' I hissed against my mouth tape. 'Shsh.'

She understood. 'Thank you, thank you,' she whispered close, somewhere near my ear. Then she whipped the tape off my mouth. It was like having a full facial dilapidation. Very painful. It took all the fine baby hairs off my top lip.

'Erck … phew,' I groaned, moving my mouth out of stiffness. I wanted a drink desperately.

'Thank you, thank you. Who are you? Are you going to get us out of here?'

'Shsh, please. Wilkes may not have gone yet. Keep very quiet. Undo my wrists now, the same way as I did yours. Then do your ankles. Take it very slowly.'

It was hopeless. My wrists and fingers were balled up in two lots of twisted sticky tape, hers and mine. She began to cry with frustration.

'Calm down, take it slowly. Find the end.'

'I can't, I can't. I don't know where it is … I'm so sorry,' she sobbed, lowering her head on to my shoulder.

'Has lover-boy here got a penknife in his pocket, do you think?'

She leaned over me, her heavy breasts almost squashing the breath out of me. There was hardly any headroom. She fumbled in his trouser pockets and came up with a penknife on a chain. This was becoming suffocatingly cosy.

Her fingers were shaking as she tried to open it, not something she had ever done before. People could go their whole lives without opening a penknife. I was beginning to guess who she was, and suspected her next move. She was going to take the strapping off the man's mouth.

'No, don't do that, not yet. He was once very unpleasant to me, very nasty. I'd rather he suffered for a few more minutes. Women and children first, the rule of survival.'

'OK,' she breathed. 'Anything you say. You're the boss, whoever you are. He'll only make a noise.'

She got the blade out and started to saw through the sticky tape. I wondered if I would have any fingers left. It was like an amputation. She was attacking the balled-up tape with enthusiasm. I prayed. 'Steady now,' I whispered. 'I need my fingers for tomorrow.'

She slowed down, taking it off a bit at a time. We both had sticky tape sticking to everything – clothes, face, hair, everywhere. I couldn't see her but I liked her. She was a gutsy woman.

'Hi,' I said. 'I'm Jordan.'

'Hi,' she said. 'I'm Adrienne.'

'I know,' I said. 'You're Adrienne Russell, Richard Broughton's first wife. I know a little about you. It was an amicable divorce, wasn't it? And you're still friends with Richard Broughton? And this grunting body beside me, I take it, *is* Richard?'

'Yes, it's Richard. He seemed to need me even more after the attempt on his life. It really shook him. I'm sorry if he was nasty to you. It doesn't sound like him. He's a very pleasant man. What are we going to do to get out of here?'

'As soon as I'm free, I have a master plan,' I assured her, not all that sure myself. It wasn't all that masterly.

'I like the sound of that,' she whispered, still sawing vigorously. 'I've always liked Hoagy Carmichael too, even more now. That was very clever of you. I got the message.'

The priest's hole was becoming overbearingly warm with all the activity. I wanted to shed my jacket but I dared not. It was our lifeline.

I licked my lips, praying for a shower of rain to come through the air hole. But the hole was probably inside the house, not outside.

'I'm so d-dry.'

'Richard has a flask in his pocket. But it's brandy, not water.'

'Anything...'

More heaving and gasping as Adrienne leaned over me and removed the flask from Richard's pocket. She unscrewed the top and held it to my mouth. I took only a single mouthful. It was a mature brandy, one to savour, but I wanted only the liquid. I let it swill round my mouth before swallowing it.

That was a mistake. I nearly choked as it set my oesophagus on fire. Wow. I nodded my thanks. A very good brandy indeed.

My wrists were almost free. Then they were free and I rubbed my sore skin. We were both sitting up, heads against the roof of the hole. We bent and began to unwind the tape off our ankles. This was easier than the wrists. A lot had stuck to my elastic ankle support so I unrolled it off and the tape came with it. I'd sort it out later, much later. I rubbed my ankles. We gripped hands in the dark.

'What do we do now, Jordan?' Adrienne whispered.

'I have to keep moving,' I said. 'Up and down the priest's hole on my knees, lengthways. Trust me, it's the only thing that might possibly save us.'

'Can I free Richard now?'

'Only his mouth, so he can breathe a bit

327

better, and tell him to keep quiet. Keep him out of the way so that I've room to move. I don't want him lumbering all over the place, getting in my way.'

Funny how eyes can see in the dark eventually. I couldn't really see anything, but I sensed how Adrienne looked, and Richard. He was heavier than I remembered. Adrienne was quite motherly, about fifty, much nicer than I had thought. Funny how we get ideas about people. Ideas are not reliable.

'Jordan?' he said, gruffly. 'Don't I know you?'

'You certainly do,' I said grimly.

I began to crawl up and down the priest's hole. It was all I could think of doing. I had to keep moving, or rather keep my jacket moving. It was no fun.

Richard was still trying to speak. 'Shhh, Richard,' Adrienne was saying. 'Keep your voice down. They might still be around. Jordan is wonderful, she's marvellous. She's trying to get us out of here. How could you be rude to her?'

'I don't remember being rude to her. Was it on the phone or something?'

His voice was croaky. I didn't recognize it. And he seemed older than I remembered. Had he aged in the last few weeks? This was possible.

I was crawling backwards and forwards.

No room to turn round. I had to crawl backwards. It was like a sadistic assault course. My knees hurt. They felt raw. It was agony but I had to keep going. Move, move, move ... I was getting dry again but dare I risk another swig of brandy?

'Shall I do this crawling about for a bit?' Adrienne asked, bewildered.

'No, it has to be me.'

'Why?'

'I'll explain later, I promise. When it works. If it works.'

I was finding it difficult to believe. It wasn't just a straw in the wind. It was a feather in a hurricane.

Twenty-Four

I was exhausted. It was not exactly a marathon but I'd been crawling up and down for what seemed like hours. I'd had a few more sips of brandy and was beginning to feel quite euphoric. There was a sort of cloudy feel to the air. I was beginning not to care any more. So I could die in a priest's hole. You had to die somewhere.

It didn't matter any more.

'Please keep going, Jordan,' Adrienne was saying. 'You have to save us. We don't deserve to die like this.'

'Can you hear anything?' I said.

'No, nothing.'

We'd both forgotten about Richard. He did not seem to be moving so much. He might have dozed off. Adrienne was determined to keep me going. I was on autopilot. I was barely speaking. I was dragging myself along.

'Can you hear anything yet?'

'No, nothing.'

'There must be something soon...'

We were exhausted beyond belief. Adrienne and I both lay down, gasping for breath, the walls closing in on us. I couldn't think coherently. I'd almost forgotten why I was there. Space has a strange effect on the mind. It empties rational thought. It removes the shreds of time. I was a shell.

'There's a sound.' It was Adrienne, sitting up. 'I think I can hear something. Yes, I can definitely hear something.'

'What sort of sound?'

'I don't know. Yes, it's cars. There are cars coming up the drive.'

'Listen. How many cars? What can you hear?'

'I'm trying.'

I dragged myself upright and listened up to the air hole. Cars? Yes, they sounded like cars, but there were no sirens. Not necessarily police cars. We still had to be careful. It could be Wilkes coming back.

I took pity on Richard and we removed the tape from his wrists and ankles. He barely stirred, seemed unwell. Adrienne was rubbing his hands, whispering to him.

Footsteps came into the hallway. I froze. They sounded very close. That meant the air hole might be somewhere in the main hall. But where? I heard voices but couldn't recognize them. It could have been anyone.

Then I heard a voice clearly.

'Jordan?' It was loud. Very loud. He was shouting. 'Are you here? Where the hell are you?'

It was James.

I shouted. 'James, we're here. In the priest's hole.'

He didn't hear me. Couldn't hear me because he was still shouting. He might go upstairs or outside if he didn't hear anything. I panicked.

'Give me something, anything,' I croaked to Adrienne. 'What can I put up the air hole?'

'How about my shoe?'

It was a slim, high-heeled, strappy thing and went through the hole like a dream. My trainers would have stuck halfway. I pushed it into the glimmer of light, waggled it about in a demented fashion. I was desperate that James should not leave.

'James, James,' I shrieked.

Suddenly the heel of the shoe was grasped tight. I couldn't move it. The shoe was gripped in a vice.

'Jordan, are you there? Is that you? It's James. Tell me where you are.'

I nearly folded up with relief. For a moment I couldn't speak. My voice was unrecognizable. It was a croak, disappeared somewhere. Adrienne spoke for me, high-pitched and trembling.

'We're in the priest's hole. Water, please. We all need water. Water, water. Whoever you are.'

The shoe was released and I heard hurried

orders and activity.

'Bottle coming down now,' said another voice. 'Catch it.'

I caught the bottle, wrenched off the cap. I had drunk half the bottle before I thought of sharing it with Adrienne and Richard.

'More water,' said Adrienne. 'We need more.'

'Tell me where you are.' This was James again.

I dragged myself up to the air hole. 'We're in the priest's hole,' I croaked. 'It's in the study. Go to the end of the hall, then down three steps. Move the big filing cabinet that's against the wall. We're behind it.'

'Are you all right, Jordan?'

'A bit squashed. There's three of us.'

It was easier said than done. More bottles of mineral water were passed down the hole. We heard the filing cabinet being moved away but no one knew how to open the panel.

James came back to me. I could feel the concern in his voice, hear his breathing. Adrienne was sniffing weakly.

'We can't open it, Jordan. What did you see? Did you see how it was opened?'

'It was the chauffeur, Wilkes. He pressed on the top left-hand corner of the panel, went further upwards and then sideways. That's all I could see.'

Now I needed a bathroom. How stupid

could one get? No hanging bravely on when nature is pressing on one's bladder. I wondered how long I could last. Both Adrienne and Richard were in a bad way. They were breathing erratically, not talking, lying against each other in a sort of heap of despair.

'You've got to hurry,' I shouted. 'There are two sick people here. We can't last out much longer.'

They couldn't make the mechanism work. I began patting Adrienne and talking to her. 'Hold on, try to relax. They're getting through. It won't be long now. We're safe, nearly safe. It's the police. The police are here, trying to get us out.'

I didn't know how much longer I could hang on. Adrienne and Richard had drifted into a semiconscious state. There was only me now to guide the voices. And even I was losing the will.

Then I heard the sound of an electric saw and drew my knees up to my chin. It was sacrilege, destroying priceless panelling. The medieval mechanism was irreplaceable. But it had to go. It was the only way out.

The sawdust flying in was making me choke. I couldn't stop coughing. The air was full of it. I kept sipping water but it didn't help. Then suddenly the panel was wrenched away and there seemed like crowds of people trying to pull me out, none too gently. I couldn't stand up. My knees did not belong to me. I was coughing and choking, red crab-like claws clutching at my airways.

'Ambulance,' I gasped weakly. 'Two people in there...'

'It's on its way,' said James. 'Someone take Jordan outside,' he shouted. 'She needs air. I'll get the others out.'

Some burly uniformed policeman practically carried me outside. The icy night air rushed to greet me. The twinkling sky had never looked so good or the garden smelt so sweet. It had been raining and leaves were shedding droplets on to my face.

'Will you be all right now, if I leave you, miss?'

I nodded.

I crawled behind a bush. It was already wet, but I didn't much care.

When I went back into the study, both Adrienne and Richard were on the floor, wrapped in blankets, being attended by women paramedics in green uniforms. One was fixing a saline drip into Richard's arm. Adrienne and Richard both had oxygen masks over their faces.

Adrienne was the woman I had seen in Miguel's restaurant, but not looking quite so smart now. She was dishevelled and dirty, her make-up distorted with tears and anguish. She struggled to sit up when she saw me and wrenched off the oxygen mask.

'Jordan, Jordan. You did it. You did it. I don't know how but you did. How can we ever thank you ... I thought we were going to die.'

I knelt down awkwardly beside her and she flung her arms round me. I was smothered in her perfume. Was it Joy?

'So did I, several times,' I said. 'I didn't know if it was going to work.'

'What was going to work?'

'There was a tracking bug somewhere on my jacket. I was hoping that someone would notice that it was moving in a regular pattern after three days on a hanger.'

'Ah, a bug.' She understood that part, but not the hanger bit.

'James put it on my jacket without me noticing, then he told me, which was lucky. So I hoped it was still working. But I daren't take the jacket off in case I dislodged it.'

I knew the explanation was garbled but it was the best I could do. A WPO was coming into the study with a tray laden with mugs of Holly's best Earl Grey and a carton of milk. James brought over two mugs and handed them to us. It tasted good even without honey.

'Who was it, Jordan? Who did this?' he asked.

'Wilkes, the chauffeur. He brought me here, saying you were here too. Otherwise I would never have come. It was all a con. He tied me up and pushed me into the priest's hole. But I've got a button off his blazer if you want proof it was him. Adrienne and Richard were already in there, trussed up.'

'We shall need statements from all of you. How long do you think you were in there, Mrs Russell?'

'I don't know. It was Brian Wilkes, the same. Said we had to meet someone special. I didn't understand it. He was so rough and ruthless and Richard has always been so good to him. There was no reason for it. Oh, it seemed like hours. It was some time before Jordan was pushed in. But thank goodness, she saved us.' Adrienne was overcome with emotion again. 'She's wonderful, just wonderful.'

'Yes, sometimes she's wonderful,' said James.

There was the tiniest glimmer of sarcasm in those words. He could not help himself. He heaved himself back on his crutches, not looking at me. He was on his phone. 'Brian Wilkes, chauffeur, ex-army. Have we got anything on him? He'll be driving a red Daimler, don't know the registration number.'

'RCB 1,' I said. 'And it's maroon, not red.'

'Thank you, Miss Lacey,' he said. This time not disguising the sarcasm. 'As observant as always.'

The paramedic came over to James. 'Mr

Broughton needs to be taken to hospital. He's had a blow to the head, nothing serious. He's conscious but it needs looking at.'

They were wheeling in one of those chair-style stretchers and lifting Richard on to it, wrapping him in blankets. I caught sight of what I could see of his face, with the mask on.

'That's not Richard Broughton,' I said.

It was the receding hairline, the heavier body, a face that had once been handsome but was now ageing. The eyebrows were still dark and bushy, but his hair was almost white.

I went over and looked at him. 'No, that's definitely not Richard Broughton.'

He was murmuring something. It sounded like 'Poor Holly, my poor, poor Holly...'

Adrienne was getting on to her feet, none too steady, ready to go with Richard in the ambulance, looking for her handbag, and talking to me at the same time.

'Of course that's Richard,' she said briskly. She was recovering from the ordeal. 'I ought to know. I was married to the man for ten years.'

'Perhaps you should come to the hospital as well,' said the woman paramedic, looking at me sideways. 'Your asthma should be checked out.'

'I'll bring Jordan,' said James. 'She has an aversion to hospitals. We'll follow the ambulance.'

Adrienne had found her handbag and was shakily repairing her face as best she could in a small mirror. She picked up the briefcase that was in the hall.

'This is Richard's,' she explained. She still had the blanket round her shoulders but now it managed to look like an elegant wrap. She gave me another big hug. 'Don't worry, easy mistake to make after all the trauma you've been through, Jordan. Come and see me very soon. I've got a lovely coffee shop in Brighton. It's called the Pink Geranium. We'd love to see you any time.'

'I will,' I said. 'I'll come and see you.' I wanted to ask her about the musical-clef brooch but this was not the time. There must be an explanation. Perhaps Richard had bought two.

She followed Richard into the ambulance and sat on a pull-down seat beside him. She leaned forward and gave me a wave as the doors closed. The ambulance pulled away, driving slowly down the drive.

'The Pink Geranium,' said James. 'That's a coffee shop, mainly for gays and lesbians. Very popular, I hear. Always busy and crowded.'

'And I bet it's got pink-check tablecloths, pink flowers and big pink cups,' I added. 'It was the café in the video.'

'You may well be right,' he said solemnly.

339

Twenty-Five

'So it worked,' I said eventually.

'What worked?'

'The bug. Wherever you put it on my jacket.'

'Of course it worked. It's a highly sophisticated device. I'm sorry, but it was in the brooch that my mother gave you. She really did send you the brooch, but I had a bug inserted at the back of the thistle.'

'That was really mean, using your mother's gift, but I suppose I have to be thankful now,' I said, touching the brooch on my jacket. I didn't take it off. It had saved us. Memo: remember to write that note to his mother.

'But you were stupid to go to Faunstone Hall with Wilkes. You should have known it was dangerous.'

'But he said you were there.'

'Did I say I was there?'

'No.'

'Never believe what anyone tells you,' said James. 'Always check. But at least you are all right now. We tracked the device to Faunstone Hall. And all this is going to come to an end now, be assured. Wilkes has a record. He's ex-army, ex-SAS, served time for violence. Not exactly clean as a whistle. I'm surprised that Richard Broughton employed him, but then references can be whitewashed. And, of course, he does look good in uniform.'

'Did you notice that the bug was moving? I was crawling up and down, hoping you'd notice the movement.'

'Sorry, Jordan. That sort of movement is not easily detected. The signal moves on a map. Streets, places, not rooms or priest's holes.'

I suppressed a sigh. All that effort... 'Not even a wobble?'

'Maybe a wobble.'

We were driving somewhere. I didn't care where. If James was taking me to Latching hospital then I could guarantee we would be out of it pretty quick. No way was I staying in overnight, even if I had to walk out wearing one of their blue-paper nighties.

'I've got a poem for you to read.'

'Sorry, Jordan,' he said again. 'I'm not into poetry and never have been. I don't understand it. All these odd-length lines and bits that rhyme and bits that don't.'

'I'm not saying that it's good poetry.' I was scrabbling around in my shoulder bag, looking for the torn-out page. 'But it's called "Lady on a Stake" and I think you should read it.'

He slowed the car down, stopped and switched on the interior light. '"Lady on a Stake"? OK. I'll read it.'

I tried to look out into the night, seeing silvery trees and the white silhouettes of birds flying as he read the poem. I could not read it again. It was too gruesome, the details too specific.

'And this was published when?'

'About five years ago, a little after Holly married Richard. But Holly gave up this poet boyfriend, this Darrell person, before she even met Richard. Yet it describes exactly how Holly died. Exactly what happened to her quite recently, all in a poem, written some years ago.'

'Darrell who?'

'It's just signed Darrell. But it can't be a coincidence.'

'I don't believe in coincidences. This poem is the blueprint for her murder.'

He started up the car. 'Do you mind if we go to the station first? I need to check on a couple of things.'

I sank back into the seat, putting my hand inside the seat belt. I couldn't stand anything tight across my chest. It was sore. I'd lost the elastic ankle support in the priest's hole and I was filthy again. My beautiful embroidered jeans were ruined. I wanted a long shower, a long drink and a long sleep. In any order. I wasn't fussy.

We parked at the back of Latching police station. I followed James in. He stood at the interior doors, hesitating. I gave him the door code.

'You never cease to surprise me,' he said, keying the numbers. We went upstairs to office areas I had never seen before. He stacked his crutches, sat down at a computer and went to work. It's not all patrolling the streets these days. I closed my eyes. I was beginning to feel very tired. When had I last slept?

'Jordan, wake up.'

I had a crick in my neck. I'd dozed off in an upright chair like an old lady in a care home. I hoped my mouth hadn't fallen open.

'Want to see what I've found?'

I went over to the computer and the words on the screen danced before my eyes, then they settled down.

'I fed in "Brian Wilkes". Thought it would be a good idea to find out more about him. This is the family tree, mother, father, brothers and sisters. There's a younger brother...'

'Darrell Wilkes. They are brothers. Oh my God, Brian and Darrell. The poet and the trained assassin. Now it's coming together. Love, hate and revenge are very strong motives.' I had to sit down on the chair. This was not good. Everything had to be rethought and rejigged.

'So it really wasn't the husband, Richard Broughton, trying to kill her off?'

'I don't think so. I think it was Darrell Wilkes, stoking up years of revenge and hatred, but getting his brother to do the dirty work.'

'And what about me?' I asked.

'Perhaps Wilkes overheard Holly telling Richard that you were on the right track, that you were digging up new evidence, true or not, but she must have said something that alerted him. Something that really alarmed him. You were a danger and had to be got rid of, or warned off.'

'I did see Holly on the phone, talking animatedly to someone, soon after I'd been with her.'

'Wilkes could have been listening.'

'Then it must have been Darrell Wilkes who came to see me in the shop, who threatened me. He had the car, the chauffeur, the suit, the lot. How would I know the difference? I'd never met Richard.'

'Easily done. It wasn't Richard Broughton at all. He's quite a nice guy.'

'And Darrell smokes but Richard doesn't. Not an ashtray in sight anywhere at Richard's flat or Faunstone Hall. Oh dear, I've made a right mess of all this.'

'You have actually done brilliantly. I'm not quite sure how but it is all working out. Brighton CID tell me that the Pink

Geranium had financial problems for a time, subsidence repairs eating up money, so perhaps Adrienne needed a loan to cover the cost of repairs. Richard probably lent her the money. That could explain her present attachment to him. Perhaps they have always been good friends despite the divorce.'

'But how did Adrienne get the video of Holly and Mrs Melee's sister talking in her coffee shop?'

'She had CCTV installed in the coffee shop after some vandals caused a lot of damage. That's when Brighton police gave her advice on the installation. Holly was captured on film having coffee there one day with Mrs Melee's sister. Brian Wilkes must have been able to get hold of the CCTV by using one of his contacts in the security world. He had it doctored before he gave it to Richard. Digital wizardry.'

'But I found the video in Richard's flat with both of the scenes on it.'

'I should imagine this was the start of some nasty blackmail. Wilkes was going to blackmail his employer, knowing that the publicity of faked evidence would ruin him. This may have been how he lured them both to Faunstone Hall, to confront them. But something went wrong.'

'And the knife attack in the street?'

'That was probably Brian Wilkes. The kind of activity he would enjoy. Black gear, hooded, back to the old SAS days. They'll be going through the DNA evidence again to link it to him. There must be something, a fibre, a hair. And he had every opportunity to steal all the oddments that went missing, the shoes, the earrings, the ironing, and plant them elsewhere. The same with the fake burglary. We'll probably find the CDs at Darrell's place along with anything else he took a fancy to.'

'Darrell would have taken the ivory letter-knife. Because it would make him feel like Shelley or Byron.'

'And Brian Wilkes would have pocketed the World War One bullet case as a war memento. Not sure about the Christian Louboutin shoes.'

'Darrell. He probably walked about in them or took them to bed. It all points to *crime passionel*, a crime of passion, doesn't it?' I said.

'Not exactly. A crime of passion is done on the spur of the moment, in a moment of passion. This has been planned over years. Darrell wanted to damage the marriage, hoped Holly would be convicted of attempted murder. That didn't work because she was acquitted. So he had to think of something else and then you arrived on the scene and you got in the way. First they tried to frighten you off and that didn't work. Then they drugged you, although that coffee might have been intended for Holly too.'

'And it was Wilkes who took a pot shot at me?'

'He would be an expert on rooftop warfare. Have you still got the pellet?'

'Yes, I kept it as a souvenir.'

'We'll probably find an armoury at his place and we'll match it up.'

'Then they blew up the ladybird,' I said, remembering the burning car. 'I suppose Wilkes did that too.'

'His SAS training would have included making incendiary devices and their installation. Fortunately he was a bit rusty.'

'I don't want the ladybird to end up in a breaker's yard. She deserves better than that.'

'You know that by law all the toxic fuel et cetera has to be removed.'

'I should think it got burnt up in the fire. There wasn't much left. Can you find out what has happened to her?'

'I'll do that,' James promised. 'But she'll be needed for evidence now. A kind of reprieve.'

'And Darrell Wilkes?'

'DS Morton is on his way now to Darrell Wilkes's address. I talked to him while you were asleep in the chair. Holly's ex-poet boyfriend will be in custody very soon and charged as soon as we have enough evidence. Brian Wilkes is already in custody, caught trying to fly out from Gatwick. The

Daimler was spotted, abandoned at the airport, by an alert security guard.'

I took a deep breath.

'Now we have to find out who tried to assassinate you in the Medieval Hall and nearly succeeded,' I said, suppressing a shiver. 'They could try again.'

'I must have put away dozens and dozens of villains in the last ten years. It could be any of them. I wouldn't know where to start, Jordan.'

'Perhaps Pointer has a brother that you put away.'

'Or Rik Henderson, the site manager, or Sven Rusinsky, the Russian millionaire. Perhaps I deported his brother or sister back to Russia.'

'Heavens,' I exclaimed. 'I've just thought of Carlo, the assistant manager. He's Italian and...'

He patted my hand in a patronizing manner. 'Not every Italian is related to the Mafia. But keep going, Jordan. Sometimes you get a good idea.'

We turned it into a party, one perfect late summer's evening. It was Bruno's suggestion and I thought it was pretty good. We waded through the waves at the water's edge and climbed into Bruno's fishing boat. Mavis and Doris, Francis, Jack, myself and James. The boat was decked out with fairy lights and black and red balloons. But it still smelled of fish.

We drank decent champagne in flower-patterned glasses, generosity of James. There were hot sausage rolls in some clever heat-retaining bag, thanks to Mavis. Doris provided enough crisps and nuts to feed an army. Francis brought along a stack of rain-proof capes from the store, just in case. Jack had made half a dozen Thermos flasks of his dreadful coffee and remembered sugar sachets and polystyrene beakers.

Me? I brought me and a lot of memories.

Bruno motored out from Latching's shelving beach, crossing the tossing waves, his weathered and handsome face implacable. The long line of lights of Latching began to dwindle. Brighton outshone the whole coast in all its glorious vulgarity. Littlehampton and Bognor Regis came into sight, and to the west was the glowering hulk of the Isle of Wight.

'About here, Jordan?' Bruno asked.

I nodded.

James refilled our glasses with champagne, going round solemnly, gravely.

We turned to the twisted remains of the ladybird, lying in the hull of the boat. That was all there was of her. She had at last been released by the police. She had been produced as evidence in court. Her moment of fame.

I thought I could see scorched remains of a black spot on the red.

'To the ladybird,' said James, raising his glass.

'To the ladybird!' said everyone in one voice.

It took all four men to lift her over the side. Me, too – I helped. The boat rocked violently. I was holding her as she slid into the sea. Sweet ladybird; goodbye, dearest friend. Gulls wheeled and squawked overhead, drowning my voice.

She went with barely a splash. Everytime I walk in the sea now, or watch the waves, she will come back to me. She will always be there.

Mavis went round with the champagne again, sniffing and wiping her eyes. Doris was opening the crisps with vigour. 'Come on, everyone, this is supposed to be a party!' she said.

Bruno had a portable CD player on his fishing boat. Now that was a surprise. Who would have associated the dour fisherman with music? He played Jack's current favourite disc. I would have preferred some jazz, to lighten my spirits. Rod Stewart's gravelly voice wafted the old standards over the sea: '...these foolish things remind me of you...'

James came over to me where I was leaning, watching the dark night waves. 'Have I thanked you yet for saving my life?' he asked.

'Well, I suppose you have, in a roundabout way,' I said, wondering what was coming next. It wasn't like James to thank me for anything.

James took my hand and raised it to his lips, smiling. Then he placed my hand on his chest, drew me close, and kissed me gently on the mouth.

When I eventually opened my eyes, moonlight was streaming on the waves in a cascade of silver and he was still smiling.